Mary's Legacy

"find a girl who needs someone like you"

From the author of:

The 'Manor Trilogy':
CONTOUR
TRIG POINT
BENCHMARK

TWELVE GIRLS

WINDBLOW

SEEKING

GREAYS HILL

DEATH of an ESCORT

MELISANDE

BORROWED YEARS

&

an anthology of short stories & poems:
'PEBBLES FROM A BEACH'
(Limited edition)

Jon Beattiey

Mary's Legacy

Tregertha Imprints

Tregertha Imprints

First published by Tregertha Imprints in 2016

Copyright © Jon Beattiey

Tregertha Imprints

Tree Garth, Church End, Ravensden
BEDFORD MK44 2RP

www.tregerthaimprints.co.uk

ISBN 978-0-9931488-2-8

Typeset in 11pt Times New Roman

Printed and bound by Witley Press Ltd, Hunstanton

Spiritus intus alit, totamque infusa per artus
Mens agitat molem et magno se corpore miscet

༄

The spirit within nourishes, and (the) mind instilled throughout
the living parts activates the whole mass and mingles with the
vast frame

Aeneid bk 6.i.726

Remembering Amy Jean . . .

. . . for all those loved
who have gone before . . .

Mary's Legacy 1

'Perhaps it was for the best.' Spoken in sorrowful tones, he'd heard the phrase too often, far too often . . . for the best? The best for who? Mary, succumbing to an undeserved terminal illness, or for him, left alone as a widower? The well-meaning but trite words had come from people he scarce knew, from an almost alien world of random casual acquaintances. Another vicious tug at his emotions and this increasingly familiar and unwelcome twist, a wrench, a tightening up of shoulder muscles; he stretched, took deep breaths, swallowed and leant back in his reserved seat.

Was this the right choice, the right action to take? Three days since the funeral in Wales, back in her childhood home, where she'd said she wanted to be; three blurred days with an indistinct cushion of grey, furred-up edges interspersed with the dark sharp stabbing pangs of grief.

With an almost imperceptible movement, the panorama of the station buildings now started to slip away before the train's acceleration and the characterless mass of city and industrial depths began to glide away behind him. Committed to the decision - and another wince, that word 'committed' accentuating his loss, last voiced by the sombre cassock-clad priest at the graveside.

Mary; twenty-five years they'd had together. Over the next days, weeks, maybe months, there would surely be constant flashback reviews, duplicate takes of scenes of fun, of laughter and togetherness, with the leavening of occasional sadness, the brief spats and odd periods of separation enforced by their respective roles. She'd been brilliant at her job too; the tears of loss from her professional film crew the hardest to bear.

Would he survive? Another deep breath - would it be for Mary's sake, to keep her memory alive? Or more for daughter Sarah's sake, to ensure her support, for she'd been his rock, lovely girl, perhaps far more the realist with a youngster's mental stamina. Saying 'au revoir' last night, she'd tracked back to Paris on Eurostar, gone back to the slick world of fashion.

And now? North-bound initially, to deal with more memories, to shut down the other side of what was now a remnant part of a happy and fulfilled life torn into two by . . . by - no alternative word - death.

The train was up to speed, the rumble and the sway an ironic comfort, *Mary, Mary, Mary*...the stress and battle with essentials vibrating away, his thoughts in a jumbled, indistinct disarray. In two hours, three, would he be able to let go, to maybe and, with another wry thought, even pray for Mary's liberated precious soul?

Odd snippets of recall; crystal moments, openings into the past, paralleling a séance. Recalling the departed, peering into a crystal? A catalogue of questions, even a compilation of intent?

She'd been adamant, in one of the more lucid times that allowed pragmatic discussions. 'Of course you'll re-marry,' her hand warm and surprisingly firm in his. 'You're far too nice a man to be a wasted, grieving widower. Find a girl who needs someone like you. That'll be my bequest to a worthy unknown woman. Bit like a heart transplant,' she'd almost grinned at him, 'for there'll be someone out there.'

She'd slipped silently away, his precious girl, during that night, leaving a body he'd loved, left him, taking her bright still-burning spirit with her; still to be alive in the cosmos somewhere. His faith kept that aspect going, that indefinite belief in the unbelievable.

A jolt over some points, the train slowed. The first two hours had gone, another one and a bit to go. He shifted in his seat, eased a stiffened leg, caught the eye of the woman opposite and had to offer the polite slight smile. Had he actually been asleep, or had his thoughts taken him away from time's reality? Embarrassing at this time of day. Breakfast - if that's what it was - must have happened a long time ago. He'd left the empty, lonely flat in the early hours, slamming the door behind him, leaving a cavern of regret, of infinite sadness.

'Let it go, dad,' Sarah had said, holding him tight, 'for mum's sake. It's what she'd wanted,' and then shared his tears, an upwelling of grief. There'd been no dissent on the decision to keep the small London flat, at least for the time being, a pied-à-terre for either of them, a necessary work-a-day bolt-hole, even though he knew a return would reawaken aspects of their loss unless time did its eroding trick. Who knows?

After more discussion Sarah had agreed to his idea of the sale of the Lake District cottage, surprisingly, given that a huge chunk of her childhood was wrapped up in the place. Holidays, carefree, careless, random, a function of who they were, what they did. As a child there she'd run free, yet never strayed, amazingly aware of how they'd expected her to behave. Would she have been a different girl had she had a sibling? Hypothetical. She'd made easy friendships, yet retained her mother's sense, offered them both pride in her very existence. She'd matured into a lovely girl with a brilliant sense of dress; brought up on a diet of Christian Dior, Yves St. Laurent; eventually an unmissable opportunity took her into the surreal Parisian fashion world; they'd let her go and she'd blossomed there, inflated their pride to bursting - and he knew she'd survive despite their joint drastic loss.

'Tickets please.' The casual images fled away as reality closed in. He fished in his pocket, handed it over, had it scrutinized and handed back; he eased his leg once more and got another smile from the woman - it should have offered the excuse to open up a conversation, an aspect of any chance meeting irrepressible Mary would never have missed. He looked away, at the passing windowed vision of sketchy scraps of woodland, appearing, disappearing; the fascinating variety of farmland. Another quarter of an hour before Carlisle and the need to change trains.

He'd need to call in at the village Spar shop, get enough provisions to see him through; nothing much edible would be left in the cupboards for it'd been two months since the last visit; two months since they'd left Beckside; the fateful return to London for the ultimate appointment with the oncology specialist, the revelation, the numbed acceptance, the demise of any hope. How she'd stood up, shrugged on her coat, smiled at him, taken his arm; they'd walked back to the car in silence

She'd been adamant, totally against intervention, the consequences of a drug regime seen as far too nauseous, too demeaning and for what? Another month, half a year at best? Accepted her fate - he'd been the one to rant and rave, to argue, but she'd seen him through it. Under sentence but stronger, more determined to relish those final days without much pain.

Now the train had stopped, the smiley woman stood up, hefted her case down and left another smile behind. He followed her onto the platform, stood a moment, took another deep breath - and thought he heard Mary's voice, *'leave me on the train, dearest, let me go,'* in the beautiful soft Welsh lilt he'd never forget. She loved her singing too; oft times she'd sung solo in the parish choir at Easter, at Christmas. *'Leave me!'* Was she cross?

The local three carriage unit, still diesel powered, took him onwards into the hills, the familiar route. Why had they nearly always opted for train travel? Because it was less stressful? Often quicker and it also provided the opportunity for the random chats with strangers, something Mary loved to do, building acquaintances into friendships. Part of her, the essential persona with whom he'd fallen deeply in love and never strayed; inseparable as a couple, envied by many.

Just the hour. The landscape familiar, the beloved Cumbrian peaks. Walking country - the miles they'd walked together, the hills they'd climbed, the rivers followed. Days in the sunshine, days in the rain; all the same for Mary, she'd loved every moment. Why, with her supreme stamina, had her body not fought off the illness that seemingly had lurked unseen, why had it not managed to reject whatever it was that had so swiftly taken her away from him?

The phone in his pocket bleated once, twice. A text message from Sarah; she was back in Paris but had guessed his mood; he had to smile despite the nagging pain of loneliness. Irritating, but a sublimely clever instruction: *"Don't mope, I love you! Call me when you're back at Beckside."* How good it would have been had she managed to take more time off, but it was coming up to her busy time, Fashion Week, and she too involved, too close to the top to miss out. Four days off for the funeral was all she'd been allowed. Mary had, in the period before her increasing tiredness precluded too much travel, managed to go and briefly stay with her in Paris, to say her farewells to those romantic places where he and she had walked together as a newly married couple, walked hand in hand in the spring sunshine those years ago; she'd said her farewells to the Tuileries, the Galleries, the Ile de St.Germaine and Notre Dame, before coming back to London for her last days, looking wan and drawn but still cheerful. *"Don't think you have to come,'* she'd said, *"it'd be too morbid. I'll do this with Sarah!"* and they had, the two women in his life, backtracked, done whatever was necessary for Mary's peace of mind and Sarah's edification of how a proper marriage really worked.

Enough. He typed out *"Don't worry, I'll be fine, xx"*, pushed 'send' knowing full well she'd grimace at his reply. They were very close, Sarah and he, always had been, closer still now; was it the only child syndrome? He missed his daughter, the bright vivacious smile and those very sexy legs they joked about, part of her stock-in-trade in the fashion business. He added the stock *'I love you'* phrase and sent that too.

Soon be there. The scenery so familiar in the shape of woods, the houses nestling with their backs to the hill as though sheltering from life's storms. Was that what he was doing, running for cover to the hills? A final screech of brakes, metal on metal, the pulsating mumble of the diesel unit in idle. Bag off the rack, carriage door open with its sibilant hiss, stepping down to the platform, heard the crescendo of the engine's growl as it pulled away, to leave him alone on the concourse. Home ground. Home alone - he'd hardly ever been here on his own, there'd been no reason for solitude. He squared his shoulders, walked out of the station, the feeling he should have Mary at his side, almost an unbearable expectation. *Here in spirit . . .*

A ten minute walk up to the garage. The faithful old Landrover Discovery left with Ted who might be surprised to see him; they normally gave him a ring when they were coming so he could ensure the old girl would spring to life. 'Old girl', another female in his life, an ancient Discovery - foolish maybe but a strange comfort. Ted was in the office; looked up, at first puzzled, his expression turning to a smile, suppressed; he stood up, gripped his hand, shook his head the once, an acknowledgement with no words needed.

They walked to the lock-up sheds at the back of the yard; Ted unlocked and opened the doors wide. 'She'll be fine, Donald. Let me know if there's ought I can do,' and he walked away, a man of few words.

She - not named, just 'she' - fired up after the third turn, with the familiar chugging rattle. His bag went on the passenger seat; no-one to otherwise occupy it. He sat and let the engine warm up; not that it was a cold day but it gave him another breather. *"You won't be lonely,'* he heard her say; shook his head at the irony, put the old girl into gear and started the drive back to Beckside, the final leg of the pilgrimage. Twelve miles, usually a half hour on a good day, fifty minutes at worst;

an hour and ten today, taken at a steady pace, including the diversion through the village and to the Spar for supplies.

The bottom gate was stiff on its hinges, proof of the lengthy gap in time since they had left - Mary's last goodbye to the place she'd loved was the final closure, the pull of the gate to shut it firmly behind her. Too vicious a pull at his mind too; Sarah, perhaps you were right, it'll be best to sell and the thought brought on the strange idea he was trespassing, that he'd be staying in another's home, not his own.

Up the rutted track, over the rise to see the stone slated roof below, the paddock grass badly in need of grazing, the beck curling away into its shallow gentle meanders; beyond, the lift of the opposite hill towards the steeper climb to the long-distance footpath, the mass of the woods on the slopes solid in the trees summer dress, the warmth of the late afternoon shimmering and distorting the otherwise crisp edge to the skyline.

With the Discovery backed up into her accustomed slot alongside the woodpile, silence returned. The key retrieved from its hiding place in the old shed still had the wooden tag with Mary's firm script-engraved 'Beckside'. His only comfort was the thought she'd be here, somewhere, waiting for him . . . her spirit, her . . . virtual being, free, consoling, ever his guide to life, an empty future.

His bag dumped on the kitchen's stone floor, he recovered the box of groceries from the quick trip round the Spar, spent ten minutes assessing the cupboard stocks and made a mental note of what else might possibly be needed if he stayed on. Routine kicked in; the main switch down on the consumer unit, the immersion heater switched on; he rinsed the kettle out, filled it and plugged it in, rewound the wall clock. Simple domestic actions, oft repeated.

Then he dropped into his armchair, the other side of the low slate coffee table he'd had made especially for her, pulled out his mobile and confirmed his arrival: '*Dear Sarah, Beckside, call me when you can*', subsequently he closed his eyes and let the emotions flow . . .

They had been good times, so much matter-of-fact day to day, so like every other decent family where simple actions strengthened unshakeable bonds. Perhaps they should have had another child but somehow it didn't happen and neither he nor Mary got chewed up about the lack. Sarah had fulfilled their unrehearsed expectations, very much the focus that pulled them closer together and she'd become the happiest child as a result.

Days of joy; the schools she'd attended sent glowing reports back at the end of every term, the exam results always in the top bracket, truly a lot to be thankful for. Was Sarah perhaps Mary's legacy, she the only daughter, the most precious girl? But what of Mary's other spoken bequest? Without any doubt she'd left a desperate hole, now he'd no-one other than Sarah - whose competence was without question - to care for, a care freely and diligently offered, given without reserve, honed over two and a half decades of their lives together. Would this gap in his life become an irritation, an irreparable open sore, or would it close up over time?

The phone rang; a jangling, vibrating irritation to chase these introspective ideas away, before comprehension prefaced the pleasurable anticipation of hearing his beloved daughter's voice.

'Dad - everything all right with Beckside? Hope it's not raining,' then a pause. 'You're not brooding? Wish I could be with you!'

A matter of fact tone adopted for his reply. 'The place seems to be as we left it from what I can see so I suppose it's okay; I've yet to check around. Brooding - well, I'm alone with only thoughts and memories for company so yes it would be good if you were here. How's the fashion world?'

'Hectic. One of our top model's gone off in a sulk, stupid woman, just because she wasn't given Johan's finest creation to wear - he'd made it for the taller new girl. And our best costume mistress has a stinking cold so I expect I'll end up dressing tomorrow's show with Alicia and Marcia. When the dust's settled maybe Karl will give me more time off, if we get a good order book. If he does I'll fly up to East Midlands, hire a car and join you for a couple of days. How's that?'

Her suggestion sounded fantastic and he felt some of the pressure ease. 'Be wonderful if you could, but don't you jeopardise your career for me, Sarah my love.'

Her musical laugh came readily enough. 'They can't do without me now, dad. Don't worry, Karl won't let me come unless he knew I'd come back. Now, cook yourself a brilliant meal and get a good night's sleep. Talk to you after the show. Night! Luv you . . .' and she'd gone.

The past settled down around him, a cloyingly quiet silence. The place brooded, a confining quiet, too stifling. He lifted out of the chair, left the cottage, spun his view around the so, so familiar pastoral scene before he made his way down to the beck where the soothing run of clear water rarely diminished. Today it was less full, a placid flow not even disturbing the weeds on the bank, a mere murmur over the stones, as if in sympathy.

Abruptly, he turned away and strode up the path through the mixed woodland they'd set when first they'd bought the property. The saplings then planted with thoughtful care had turned into sizeable trees, another of Mary's legacies. The path with its fronded edging of exuberant grasses and wild flowers twisted its way round the large boulder left from glacial days, and then climbed steeply upwards to bring him to the gate onto the top pasture.

Across the grass, on the opposite side of the hill and below the mass of Skiddaw the long-distance footpath slanted southeast-northwest, a well-trodden route for walkers, and as he scanned the route, was able to see just such a group, a small party making good progress towards the rock clusters near the far wood boundary. With a couple of hours until dusk, he thought they'd be hard pushed to reach the Youth Hostel even at their brisk pace, for twilight would make the path less clear. He leant on the gate top and watched. They had done that walk many times - the first when Mary and he were first married - subsequently they'd decided to look for a local base for holidays - and found Beckside less than six months later.

Sarah had completed the whole length of the path as part of her Duke of Edinburgh Award when just turned seventeen, a challenge easily met by a girl of her calibre. Maybe, if they had the opportunity, she and he could retrace it together for old times' sake before Beckside was sold?

Now the group had travelled closer, he could make out the number - five, and from their bearing, likely youngsters, perhaps another D of E party. Well, good luck to them. He stayed another ten minutes, watched them near the rocks before deciding it was time he thought about eating and to sort himself out for the night. Tomorrow; he'd reluctantly start on the clear-out, to dispose of all the un-necessary less emotive clobber they'd accumulated over the years. A last glance at the travellers - one of them was climbing up the largest rock, which he'd personally done a time or two, for it offered the best view down the valley from the top, but you needed to take care . . . and then as if by coincidence and with a twist of concern, he saw the individual, boy, girl, he couldn't tell, slip, slide and disappear from view into the bracken at the rock's foot. Not good, not at all; were they a capable lot? Should he check?

There were no other demands on his time, other than supper and bed. Perhaps the best thing, to salve his conscience, was to go and see. He swung open the gate, started on the path that would take him across the flat pasture and towards the hill, not appreciating that the concept of Mary's legacy was about to come clear, that his late wife's spirit was watching, opening his mind to the way life's vagaries would test his concerns and his caring and his depth of love for her soul.

Mary's Legacy 2

Paula screamed, an instant if an out of character and foolish reaction. Stuart hadn't listened, had ignored her concern, strong headed egocentric guy that he was. Adam hadn't been much use in holding him back either, despite being the so-called leader, trainee or not. The other two girls stood in open mouthed helplessness. Susan had gone as pale as her wispy blonde hair; Marianne wasn't much different below her shock of straggly auburn.

The day had not gone well, what with a late start, some bickering over tomorrow's target and the threat of weather turning on them - and now, an avoidable accident. Struggling out of her straps, she dumped the rucksack on the nearby rock slab and pushed her way through the bracken. What would she find? A crumpled heap of disaster, or. . ? But, with a tremendous feeling of relief, saw Stuart stirring in an effort to sit up; he must have slid down the last few metres of the rock face to have his impromptu cascade ended in this ungainly sprawl in the taller bracken growing around the foot of the big chunk of rock.

'Idiot,' was all she could think to say, 'you could have killed yourself!' She offered him a hand. 'Can you stand?'

'My foot slipped.' He reached to grasp her outstretched hand and yelped 'Careful!' as she pulled, but still managed to struggle upright. 'Thanks,' he said, let go her hand and bent down to rub at his lower left leg. 'Don't think anything's broke but I've caught a packet on me leg, it don't half sting.'

'You can walk?' she asked as Adam appeared, the other two girls behind him.

'Yeah, reckon,' taking a step forward, then winced. 'Ouch!'

'Serve you right,' Adam's cross comment, 'but if you can't walk you've messed us up, what with four miles to go and not much daylight left.'

Stuart tried another step and Paula could see the twist of pain in his face. 'You've probably pulled a muscle or tendon. Adam, can you maybe support him? We can't stay here and it'd be silly to call out the Mountain Rescue team out for a sprain . . .'

'If we can't get to a hostel before dark, what then? I don't fancy staying out here!' Susan voiced her concern and Marianne agreed. 'Stuart, why did you have to do a bloody silly thing like that?'

'What he's done, he's done,' Adam said curtly as he put his arm round Stuart, 'put your arm round my shoulders; see if that helps.'

The two boys linked arms and Stuart tried another step.

'That's better,' he said, and with some care from Adam negotiating the bracken, they made it back to the path.

'Give us a minute.' Stuart disengaged himself from Adam and sat carefully down on the bank. 'Sorry folks,' he said. 'Enthusiasm got the better of me.'

'And rather messed up the situation too,' Paula responded. 'I suggest one or two of us go ahead to see what we can find, like a B & B or at least to arrange a lift onwards. I agree with Adam about not calling Mountain Rescue. If Stu had broken a leg or something it would have been different. What do you think?'

Adam looked pensive. 'I don't know that I'm keen about splitting the party, Paula, but I can see the merits. I'll stay with Stu, we'll carry on as best we can; you three girls go on ahead. Give us a call on the mobile if you get any joy.'

'Right-oh. Okay with the idea, you two?'

Susan nodded. 'Better than staying put.'

'I wish I'd swopped my phone last week - then we could have checked what was around,' Marianne added, thinking of how new smart phones were a hell of a lot better nowadays.

'Well, you didn't. So we're back to basics - explore and ascertain. We'll be as quick as circumstances allow,' and Paula looked down at Stuart, 'you'll be glad to get home!'

'Yeah,' his only reply as Adam sat down beside him and made the decision. 'Go on then, girls, see what you can do.'

Paula nodded. 'We will,' and started off along the track with the other two girls trailing behind her.

≈

He saw her first, her pace steady, efficient, purposeful, before the sight of the other two registered, trailing behind her. Well kitted out too, with a high-tech jacket and leggings, a smallish rucksack on her back; in all, the appearance of someone who knew what she was about. Her companions didn't look happy, even at this distance; she'd evidently be the boss girl. He waited until she caught sight of him, not wanting to scare her.

'Hello,' he called across the intervening hundred yards. Was it a look of surprise or relief?

She halted. 'Thank goodness!' Closer now, she had an intelligent look about her as she brushed wayward strands of dark brown hair away from her face. 'I wonder if you could help us? We've had a problem with one of our walking party up on the main track and I'm looking to organise a lift for him . . .'

One of the other two girls, maybe younger than this spokesperson, though stockier, interrupted her. 'Stu fell down the rock and did summat stupid to his ankle, he can't flipping walk.'

'Marianne! Let me explain, please!' She turned back to him. 'I'm Paula; we've left our leader guy, Adam, with Stuart who, as Marianne has just said, did a foolish thing and now we've got a timing problem. This is Susan; we're all on a training hike and had hoped to have made the Youth Hostel by now. Are you able to help?'

The steady look from her pleasantly featured face reassured him. She didn't seem like a flighty girl, though her companions perhaps lacked her commonsense approach. 'Your casualty - can he walk at all? Otherwise we might be better off calling in Mountain Rescue.'

A flicker of alarm floated across this girl Paula's face. 'I'd rather not if we can help it - that might make us appear brainless and I don't think it'd go down too well with some parents.' She cast a meaningful glance at the slim young Susan. 'We can probably get Stuart to the farmer's access track where it meets the path, at least I hope so.'

He knew exactly where she meant. 'Okay, Paula. I've a four-wheel drive Discovery and I do know where you mean.' His intuition had broken into the morbidity of the late afternoon contemplations, injected a meaning into the otherwise ephemeral evening hours before a likely sleepless night and given him a concerning worthwhile cause. 'What do you want to do, come with me or go back to your casualty?'

The girl didn't lack authority. 'Marianne, you and Susan go back and find Adam, tell him we'll be up with a vehicle in a little while and to try to get Stu to the farm track. I'll stay with . . .,' and the questioning grin with eyebrows raised gave her a cheeky yet appealing look.

'Donald,' he answered and offered a hand for her to shake, 'I own the cottage down there. Your two youngsters will be all right on their own?' with enough implied criticism to make the elder of the two bristle.

'Of course we will! Come on Susan,' and Marianne turned tail and strode off, the younger - maybe only a sixteen year old - Susan flinging a tentative grin back at Paula before she scurried after her friend.

∽

'This is a lovely place.' Paula's comment accompanied her appreciative glance around the cottage's environs. They'd not wasted any time, Donald's lengthy stride stretching her pace as they'd crossed the meadow and wound their way back down his path through Mary's coppice. 'I'm envious, able to live out here with only the hills and woodland. So beautifully quiet!'

'Thankyou.' Donald replied 'It'll be on the market soon if you've aspirations. We'd best waste no time, hang on here and I'll get the car keys.'

∽

'You're selling this?' In walking trousers she'd slid easily onto the high passenger seat unbidden. 'There'd have to be a very good reason for me to sell if it were mine. I wouldn't want to ever leave such a lovely place.'

He looked across at her, at the untidy mass of dark glossy hair cascading around the lightly tanned oval face, the high cheek bones, the deep smiling eyes, the full mouth, and saw her through Sarah's professional eyes, her appreciation for fine features necessary to support the well proportioned figure if clad in an *haute couture* bespoke dress. Had this interesting girl some Italianate blood in her, for she had a rare and rather appealing beauty?

'My wife has recently died,' and he found he was surprised both at the open admission and the unique lack of an immediate twist of pain. 'So . . .' he paused and his mind ran on; *so why sell? To help deaden the grief he'd built up, or to start the process of a run away from what had been a blissful life and its potentially cloying memories?* The rest of the words hung unsaid.

:Oh. I'm so sorry,' the subtle tone of voice endorsed an expression of genuine concern as she reached out, softly but briefly laid her hand over his on the gearshift as he moved it into reverse. 'Then you're on your own here?'

Now he had the Discovery backed round to face the track, it was time to concentrate. 'I am. I've a daughter, Sarah, but she's in Paris. Let's go find your boys and girls, Paula.'

She took the hint, but the smile denied any idea she'd been offended by his curtailed explanation. The journey round to where the farm track joined the side road barely took ten minutes and she stayed silent, but didn't need a prompt to slide out and open the gate before the bumpy ride took them up the rutted track onto the hill.

'You used to these?' She seemed to be perfectly at home in the vehicle and he felt something appropriate needed to be said to ease the stiffened silence between them.

She nodded. 'My father used to have an old Landrover, when they were proper four-wheel drives. We went everywhere in it when we were youngsters still at school, holidays, camping . . .'

'And now?'

She shrugged. 'He has a company car. We don't meet up all that often now. Times change.'

'Very true.' *What would Mary have made of this girl? She'd always developed an interest in those who impacted on their day-to-day, part of her attitude to life, becoming involved with people.*

They reached the other track that ran back along the contour and he carefully swung the vehicle left, with only another half mile to go towards the edge of the wood and the nearest point to the footpath that they'd be able to reach with the vehicle.

'Where do you live, Paula?'

She gave him a puzzled stare. 'South London. Why?'

'Oh, just wondered. You don't sound like a country girl.' Looking ahead, he thought he saw movement on the wood edge. 'I think they're at the gate.'

She peered through the screen. 'You're right, on both counts. I live in an office during the day and in a bed-sit otherwise. Boring. Which is why I take to the hills when I can. Will we get everyone in here?'

He chuckled. 'I've had more than six aboard before. Cosy if a little cramped,' and concentrated on the next more soggy part of the track, twisting the wheel left and back right to avoid the deeper ruts.

'You know how to drive,' she said, then apologised. 'Sorry, that sounds patronising. Ignore me.'

'Perhaps I should be flattered,' he replied. 'Do you drive? Or is that a silly question if your dad had a Landrover? Youngsters love learning to drive off-road.'

'Another life,' she said, avoiding the question and its implications, and pointed. 'I think they've got Stu to the gate. He can't be all that bad.'

'You're right. There's four people up there. I don't suppose he's very popular or that he'll easily live it down.'

'No, he won't, but maybe a lesson learnt, at least I hope so. Are you able to run us up to the Hostel? Asking a lot, I know, but . . .'

'No problem, of course I can. It'll stop me moping,' then realised what he'd said. 'Sorry, Paula, didn't mean to inflict my state of mind on you.'

'Oh. Then . . .' and she stopped, her unspoken query left heavy in the air.

'Yes. Very recent. Still coming to terms with the situation,' and oddly, felt he could talk to her without restraint. Was a shadow lifting? 'New experience, being alone after twenty-five years.'

She kept her eyes forward, unsure of her inner reaction and not wishing to impose further on this difficult moment. The Discovery rolled to a stop, and Donald sat still for a moment. 'Now for the tricky bit. Hope your guy isn't so badly hurt that he can't climb aboard. And thanks for understanding.' He opened his door and stepped down without further comment.

15

Her own thoughts swirled. How old would he be? Not much below fifty, if he'd been married for that long. Rugged, hardened to life, she guessed and likely very fit. What did he do? No office worker, but no labourer either; he hadn't got rough hands, seen grasping the steering wheel with casual expertise. Crisp curly hair, a smidgeon of grey maybe under the mid-brown. Good clothes too. How sad, losing a long term partner . . . she wondered about the reason, and shook her head. If he'd wanted to say, he'd have done so. None of her business, but he'd been their saving grace - she'd still be trudging down to the village else. He was chatting to Adam, looking at Stu's ankle; Sue and Marianne were just standing there. Then they all looked up at the vehicle and it gave her an oddly proprietorial feeling, as though she belonged to it, had come with this Donald guy from somewhere else and they didn't know who she was. Embarrassed now, she got out and walked across.

'It's not too serious, Paula,' Donald addressed her as if she truly didn't belong to the group. 'We'll get him in the back.'

Adam, standing close, patted her on the shoulder and brought her back to reality. 'Well done Paula. We won't be too late in. Come on, Stu, let's see how it works.'

In the end they got him sitting on the rear floor, then between Adam and Donald, managed to drag him backwards to sit half propped up, his back against a folded-up seat. Adam sat cushioned alongside him with an arm round his shoulders, the two younger girls scrambled in to sit opposite and Paula reclaimed her front seat as Donald checked the doors, climbed in and they exchanged glances. Something jerked within her, a weird sense of companionship, a thin yet solid acceptance of the confidence he'd shared with her. Then he started the engine again and with evident care, reversed around to retrace their journey down to the road.

He knew the best way, took the lower, shorter route alongside the river which his beck fed and reached the Youth Hostel within the half hour. Stuart was unloaded without a problem and the group stood uncertainly around, waiting on his farewells. 'Are you sure you don't want me to run you down to the Cottage Hospital, Stuart?

'Nah, I'll be okay. Night's kip, then mebbe I'll catch the bus back. Thanks mate. Shan't be such an idiot again.'

'No,' Donald gave him a small smile. 'I don't suppose you will. Could have been a whole deal worse. Luckily for you, you had some sensible people around. Here,' and he passed a card to Adam. 'Give me a call and let me know when you're all safe home. Then I shan't worry about you.' He caught Paula's look, the depth of her eyes unsettling, as though they'd said - yet not said - what each other felt. Then he turned back to the Discovery, climbed in and drove away, leaving the group on the Hostel's forecourt. In the rear view mirror he saw them turn and go through the gateway. One figure hesitated, turned to look back, to lift an arm in a wave. Paula.

Mary's Legacy 3

In the middle of the morning, the landline phone rang, unusually. He'd breakfasted late, not too much concerned with eating, given he'd enjoyed cooking a sausage casserole for supper, even though it was close on midnight before he'd finally done the washing up and crawled into bed to, surprising himself, sleep solidly through until seven, then dozed another hour or two before finally becoming vertical.

'Hello?' His tentative answer expressed the doubt in his mind as to who might wish to disturb him on a Sunday morning, certainly it wouldn't be Sarah and most of his socially biased friends didn't even know he'd be here.

'Donald?' and he recognised the voice instantly, the contralto tones of yesterday's dark-haired, dark eyed Paula despite the hollow sound of a mobile phone. 'You okay?'

'Paula! You're a surprise caller, but welcome none the less. Yes, I'm 'okay', thanks. How about you?' and immediately recognised a failing - he should have asked about Stuart first. 'Got the wounded soldier onto his bus?'

He heard her laugh, the first time a girl had shared a laugh with him for months and the pang of loss with the jarred nerve endings sprang back into life. How very much like his Mary's laugh, and that an uncanny phenomenon.

'No,' she replied, sounding very positive. 'He rang his parents last night and they came and fetched him first thing, in a mild state of panic. They also took Sue and Marianne back with them; the poor things had lost all their remaining enthusiasm for another day's hike. Adam's rather cross 'cos he won't get any brownie points for finishing the expedition. He was up for a NVQ on an outdoor leader's course. He's asked me to go on with him solo, but I really don't fancy it, not just him and me. He's a bit of an odd bod. So . . .' and he sensed her uncertainty. 'I wondered - could I come and spend the rest of the day with you? I don't have to get back to work until Tuesday, and it would do me a great favour, giving me an excuse to duck out from under . . .'

He hesitated. Another person around him? Would she detract from the unconscious thought that he needed time to grieve for Mary in what was his wife's principle domain? *Mary?* He could see her now, reading in the comfy armchair or sitting at the table, specs on her nose, sketching out some plots for the next production, or whistling to herself as she prepared home-grown vegetables for supper. *Mary, Mary . . .*

'Donald? If I'm being too pushy, do say. I won't be offended, really, but perhaps . . .'

He guessed at her motives, emotions torn. 'If you could come back to . . .?'

'Yes, I mean, I didn't really see much of your lovely cottage and . . .'

'I might not be good company, Paula. Or I might find you a job to do you didn't like but feel you'll have to do it because . . .' He was sparring, giving way, he knew he was, but what the heck, she might help him return to the real world, give him back the reason to live, break the misted veil of misery. *'Find a girl who needs someone like you,'* Mary had said in her final hours, but was this what she meant? And so soon after . . . or was it? Did this girl Paula *need* him? Was she looking for something he couldn't know about other than a lame excuse to duck away from a walk into the wilderness with an uncertain companion? Last night, she'd needed him - or rather, someone, anyone, to help her - them - out of a difficult spot. That problem had now gone away, no longer any concern for either of them but here she was, clutching at a transient, fleeting interaction - not a relationship but a flimsy, casual, unsought rapport. Or was he reading far too much into this because - because of what? That he needed company?

'Okay Paula,' he gave in. 'Shall I come and fetch you?'

She laughed again and the shivers ran down his back. *Mary's laugh.* 'No, I'm only just down the road; early morning walk away from Adam and his moans. Be with you in ten minutes.'

Cheeky madam! Opportunistic wench; what would Sarah make of her?

He looked at himself in the mirror. Scruffy, unshaven, hair uncombed, yesterday's shirt, heading into an uncaring, lackadaisical anything-will-do mode. Maybe she could be the excuse, maybe the reason, to alter a mind-set; but who cared? He chucked some more logs into the stove, went up the short flight of stairs to the bathroom next to the so-called master bedroom with its untidy heap of bedclothes, stripped off his shirt and cleaned himself up. He'd just managed to shrug into a clean shirt and tuck it into cleaner trousers when he heard her whistle. She hadn't wasted any time and could almost have imagined she'd run. At least she'd remembered the way back from the main road. She spotted him at the window and waved.

They met on the doorstep and there wasn't any hesitation on her part - she stood on tip-toe, leant in and offered him a polite, social cheek on cheek kiss. 'Thanks,' she said, eyes alight. 'You know, I'm beginning to forgive Stu for being an idiot.'

'Paula, you're flirting.'

'Am I?'

'I'm an expert.'

'Ha!'

'You don't know me. I might be a serial rapist.'

She shook her head. 'Not you. I did some psychology at uni, and I'm pretty good at character assessment, especially lone males. And,' her face going serious, 'you've just lost the closest person to you, so . . .' Her eyes searched his look, '. . . I'm not at risk, am I?'

He moved to one side and allowed her access into the cottage. Apart from the one room downstairs, the large lounge they'd created from three smaller rooms when they'd assessed what they needed, there was only the kitchen cum storeroom leading to the small rear cloakroom next to the other outside door they rarely used, and then the bijou bedspace where Sarah slept in colder weather.

'Cosy!' Her quick look swept around.

'Yes.'

'I love it. Surely you don't really want to sell the place, do you?'

Did he? The day before yesterday there'd been no doubt, with too many memories going sour on him, mouldering away. Yet now another person, another woman, a bright young woman in her mid to late twenties, had inspired some doubt - was she only that age? Another *girl* then - and it was if some mysterious light had been switched on, chasing grey shadows away. *'Told you there'd be another woman . . .'* was he *imagining Mary's ethereal ghost, the repetition of some of her last words?*

'Paula . . .,' what was he doing, bringing her into his life?

Her happy smile dimmed, chased by an expression of - of what, fear, uncertainty, or - simply hesitation? 'Oh lor, I'm sorry. Look, this might not be a good idea. Perhaps I'd best clear off,' and she moved back towards the door. 'I guess it's a difficult time.'

Her simple concern affected him. 'No. No, don't. I'll be okay,' a hesitation, then he added, repeating his earlier telephonic comment. 'I may not be good company. You'll have to take me as you find me . . .'

She shook her head. 'For what it's worth, Donald, I've been through bereavement too. We lost my mum a few years ago. That's what I spoke of yesterday when I said 'times change'. My father . . .' and he sensed her emotion building . . . 'struggled to accept it. He had to change jobs; that's why I don't see much of him nowadays. My older sister Celina lives with him - she and her partner. She's otherwise orientated, see?'

'Oh.'

Then the smile came back at him and her true smile was something else. 'Celina's other half is a lovely girl too, but she doesn't like me, I guess I'm too hetero for her. Father - well, he's accepted her foibles so they actually work together quite well and he doesn't have to worry about housekeeping or meals. Me, I'm choosy.'

Her frankness, from a girl he scarcely knew, decided him.

'Paula, we're standing up in what you've already described as a 'cosy' room, so why don't you get rid of that rucksack, take off that coat and sit down. I'll make us a coffee or something. You do drink coffee?'

Another smile from her, another degree or two of warmth beginning to irradiate his all-pervasive numbness; now he didn't feel too bad about the girl being here, sharing the private space - Mary must like her else he'd have felt a chill. *Mary, tell me?*

'I do drink coffee. I also like chocolate biscuits,' and the smile turned into a cheeky grin. 'As I'm sure you do, you strike me as being a chocolate person.' She shrugged off her rucksack and dropped it on the floor, slid out of her Jack Wolfskin coat.

21

She sure knew how to tweak his sensibilities. 'That's something I've never been called before,' and had to grin. 'You're absolutely right, and luckily for you I called into the Spar on the way up. Sit down, girl. Curl up on the settee if you like. But that chair's sacrosanct,' and he pointed at Mary's chair, the cushions still left un-plumped from the last time - *the last time* - she'd sat there; he'd made up his mind it would be kept as 'hers', a constant reminder she had been his life, his *raison d'etre*.

'Can I take my big sweater off too?'

He chuckled, surprising himself. 'Providing . . .' and left the suggestion that she didn't have to remove anything else unsaid. 'Your boots too, if you don't mind, otherwise make yourself at home. And if you need the loo, it's through there.'

She grinned back. 'Ta.' The outer Aran sweater peeled off, a nice light-weight merino shirt became visible, a mid-purple colour with a simple monogram 'P' over her left breast, the soft wool clinging to an enviable shape, the softened outlines of her bra; a rounded neckline just low enough to reveal a simple gold filigree chain. She wasn't wearing earrings despite the red dots of a piercing and there were no rings on her fingers either. Yesterday's walking trousers had been swopped for a more workmanlike pair of worsted jeans; he rather liked the wide leather belt she wore too, with a fascinating buckle of some darkened brass Italianate figuring.

Boots unlaced and slipped off, the outer walking socks went as well and he had to comment on the near fluorescent revelation.

'Pink socks?'

'Pink socks. To remind me I'm a girl. Walking rough country can make you feel far too macho and unfeminine.' She rummaged in her rucksack and produced a simple pair of slip-ons; now she could have been a Sarah.

He took a chance. *Sarah, this is your doing - she was always prattling on about appropriate underwear.* 'Surely a pair of lacey pants and bra to match would do that?'

He got a coy smile. 'Ah, well, yes, but they don't normally show, do they? Pink socks do. Perhaps I should have said 'to remind my companions I'm a girl. And now who's flirting?'

'Touché.' He smiled back at her. 'I mentioned coffee. Won't be a moment,' and he busied himself with kettle, mugs, a dish for the chocolate-chip cookies, grimaced at the little remaining milk. 'I'll have to go shopping again. Have you further plans, Paula? Now the expedition has come to a juddering halt? And don't think I'm pressurising you, stay as long as you like. You can kip in the shepherd's hut if you want - that's where Sarah often sleeps when she's here and it's not too cold, there's a universally used sleeping bag. There is another bed - through there - but it's a tiny space and a smidgeon claustrophobic.' What was he saying? That he had found her company acceptable, a sudden and welcome change to the tenseness he'd felt when the concept of clearing the place out had turned into reality? Odd, very odd, this feeling that she'd become a sort of make-do Sarah, a lively young daughter-like figure?

'A shepherd's hut? What, one of those old cabin things on wheels with an attached staircase and smoky pot-bellied stove? Box bed and loads of quilts?' Her eyes shone. 'Oooh, I'd love it! Can we go and see?'

'Hey, steady on. I've only just boiled the kettle. Sit down!'

She pulled a face. 'Sorry,' and collapsed onto the little two seater settee, pulling long legs under her to curl up against the arm rest. She pushed her hair back and squinted up at him. 'You're not used to stray females?'

'No, not in my home comfort zones. Elsewhere, maybe. Here,' and he crossed over with her mug and proffered the biscuit dish. 'No more than two.'

'Strict, are you?'

'Women should do as they're told.'

'Why?'

'Because. And it might spoil your lunch, assuming you stay that long.'

She patted the seat alongside her. 'Keep me company?'

'Paula, behave.'

'I am.'

He gave up. Her sparky one-liners lifted his spirits, her very presence an antidote to the depressive state which could very easily have been reached on his own; perhaps his lovely wife's ghostly spirit was already at work, demolishing his self-protectionism, but he sat in his own chair opposite and put his mug down on the slate table. If he'd sat alongside there'd have been too much temptation to reach out and touch her.

'So tell me about you, Paula? What do you do for a living that allows you to go on fruitless expeditions? All you've said so far is that you work in an office and live in a south London bed-sit.'

'You remembered! I actually try and sell display advertising space in an up-market country life-style magazine. Can be boring, can be fun, depending on who you talk to. Some guys can get flirty on the phone, women sometimes rather cattish.' She sipped at her mug. 'So you can see how good it is to get into the hills every now and again.' Another sip and a crunch at a cookie. 'How about you?'

'Ah, well, I don't actually have a *job* as such. I freelance.'

'So?' Her eyes caught his over the rim of her mug. 'Sounds intriguing.'

'I'm an art director. I work in the film industry. Mary was a producer and a very good one too. We worked together sometimes - and that's how we met, on a film set.'

. . . Mary, scarce out of her teens, fresh from drama school, short skirted with bare arms, a bob haircut, plimsolls on equally bare but very shapely legs, a truly scatterbrained urchin-like girl with an immense sense of humour and a ready flashing smile who pulled vividly at his imagination. Within three weeks they'd moved in together, loved together, worked on the set of a long-running television soap before she'd got head-hunted by Warner Brothers for a particularly challenging sci-fi film and he'd tagged along. . .

Her eyes were wide; he recognised the symptoms of awe and astonishment, a regular effect on some when told. 'It's not as impressive a job as all that, you know. Long hours, weird places, unruly crew, stuck-up starlets and pushy producers. Except Mary. Her crew loved her; she just had that wonderful knack of getting the best from folk.' Now his emotions began to well up; seeing her in his private mind's eye and wishing the girl on the settee was Mary; *Mary . . . he was missing her, would liked to have chatted to her about Paula, about . . .* He got up, went to the window and looked across the valley at the far hill. Where they'd often walked, found secret places, made beautiful love . . .

'I'm so very very sorry.'

Had she seen his emotions rise, felt his pain? 'Yes. Thanks. Forgive me, Paula. It's still very raw, her going like that. No justice in this world; she'd everything going for her, and she didn't . . .' He couldn't go on, hearing her voice in his head, remembering the warmth of her, all those random and unplanned things they'd done together, here . . . Beckside, their joint dream.

'Do you want me to go?' Her voice was soft and aware.

He turned back to her, knowing she'd see his moist eyes. No, he didn't want her to go, for in a weird way, she represented an actual physical manifestation of Mary's last words - *there'll be another woman* - but was that woman this young Paula? Twenty years between them, thrown at him within hours of arriving back here by sheer happenstance? Appearing from off *their* hill, a parallel from their declared love of walking these hills, and so soon after his return to their once shared world? So was he simply thinking of opportunism and a conceivable outlet for masculine needs? *No*, no way, instead he was correctly responding to another person's care, a valuable human reaction to undeniable emotion.

He shook his head at her, words had become difficult. What could he do? Ease beloved Mary to the back of his mind? Replace her with another? Or try and resume normality? Paula was a guest in his house, a self-invited guest true, but still a guest. He'd offered her a place to sleep too, a presumptuous move on his part when he didn't know very much about her predilections or how she'd use - or misuse - his hospitality. Instinct told him she wasn't a risk, but a nice, normal, easy-to-get-on-with person with a pleasant and understanding disposition and truly, very easy on the eye.

'You're either in a dream world, or you're weighing up my possibilities, Donald. You've stared at me for a whole minute.' Her words might be rather forward and impudent, but instead they were light-hearted, her smile simple and unchallenging.

Her possibilities? The openings into her world were there, in her presence, her being, her clear mindedness, her evident acceptance of what he was, what he, maybe, could be?

'Too soon, Paula,' and immediately regretted the phrase for it hinted of those possibilities not sought, not even considered until she'd brought unspecified suggestions into mind.

He watched her expression fade, the infinitesimal slump of her shoulders and the slight sag of her body into the cushions. Had the girl seen him as a potential conquest then? What did a girl of her years and background, whatever that was, expect of a casual acquaintance? Were men merely notches on a bed post?

'Donald,' she said, and bringing legs from under her, stood up. 'Don't prejudge me. I'm here because I was presumptuous and asked and you were kind and generous in your grief and agreed that I should come and I'm absolutely sure it's right for both of us, so that's where we are. Now, show me where I can sleep tonight.'

Mary's Legacy 4

This was the second night alone in his Beckside double bed - and sleep came but fitfully, a drift from consciousness slow and erratic interrupted by attempts to rationalise how, after such a brief period, he'd allowed this break into the mourning period his subconscious had perhaps anticipated. Sarah had agreed with his idea and would have come with him had her boss allowed. And if she had, would this girl Paula now be sleeping in the shepherd's hut?

They - his daughter and he - would have still assisted in the recovery of the headstrong Stuart had they perchance walked up to the estate boundary at the crucial moment. Paula would still have been the girl who tactfully organised matters, no gainsaying her role there. But it was unlikely she'd have rung to invite herself back here with another woman, and especially a daughter, in the place. Why? Because he'd not have been seen as vulnerable to mood, or that he had a protective shield in place to stop a predatory female from accessing easy meat?

The Paula girl lay not a hundred yards away, holed up in the 'best place' as she'd exclaimed when introduced to it yesterday. Yesterday. A day that felt like a week, his return here that felt like a month ago. Time that extended, stretched to boundless infinite endless hours.

Only yesterday? He'd taken her to the village, they'd shopped for lunch, for an evening meal, she'd taken his arm, acted like - like a daughter? Strange glances from the shop staff, he being well known as a local and who he was, the now deceased Mary's husband, but he couldn't worry, couldn't explain the strange way he'd suddenly appeared with a different woman in tow. Back at Beckside, he'd shown her the rest of the estate, the vegetable plot that Mary had created with loving care, the rambling walk constructed to the top of the garden, the shepherd's hut that had been Sarah's dream and now, this young Paula's delight. He had purposely not shown her the rest of the house. They'd lunched outside in the sunshine, the evening meal he'd prepared eaten more formally yet still in homely style and her contribution the bottle of wine. They'd sat in the late sun by the trio of silver birches on the rustic benches and talked over his film world, the weird and the wonderful projects, and she'd been all ears, all oohs and aahhhs, then she'd said goodnight and climbed the three steps to her night alone in the hut. No contact, no attempt at familiarity, just company, smiling eyes, and a nice person to have around.

So the day's dawn that had slipped silently across the valley, infusing its sun's warmth through the small window, had also brought with it another set of uncertainties. On his own, he may have lain quietly, a tense body from a restless night gradually relaxing into the known consequences of another day, to let time slip until the onset of simple demands which would have brought necessity's movements. Today was Monday. The start of a working week for most, a return to routines, the journey to a work space, another five days towards ultimate retirement, to . . . no, this brooding had to stop. Mary had died, never to reach retirement, never to share in those dreams of a pleasant life of ease and enjoyment they'd talked over when the most relevant topic was 'where' they'd settle. Oddly, Beckside didn't figure, it was always some other little place abroad, tucked away in the sunshine and near the coast, Italy often mentioned, her grandmother's home country and why dark eyes and sleek dark hair had been the trademark genes apparent in daughter Sarah's appearance coupled with the loving attitude . . .

He must get up. He had a guest and hence obligations. Paula - she'd want to be away on the mid-day train back to London, back to a slot in a world he too, would have to resume in due course. Where it'd be, what it would involve always an imponderable until the phone call or the text message, followed by the script, the director's brief, the meetings, the endless meetings, the discussions over budgets, logistics, the negotiations over remuneration, if it would be fixed sum or a percentage of box office. Would it be so different, without Mary's advice, support, her influence? Being under no illusions that the film world revolved around 'who you knew', what buddies you had, what contacts were made, whether you smiled at the right girl, lunched the right guy, he'd survived and had his work respected, admired even. So it wouldn't be

28

too long before he'd be back in the scrum. *Make the most of the peace and quiet, Donald, and enjoy the girl's lively company while you can.*

Paula was sitting on the hut's top step with a small sketch pad; offered him a smile, tucked her pencil behind an ear and stood up as he approached. This morning she'd not resumed yesterday's trousers, instead there were bare legs under a sensible tweedy skirt, though the purple woollen top was still evident.

'Morning, Donald. It looks like it's going to be another reasonable day.' She dropped onto the ground and walked to meet him, stopped shyly three steps away. 'Thank you for the chance to fulfil a childhood dream. I'd always wanted to stay in one of these ever since I was a kid, but don't ask me why.'

'You slept well?'

She nodded. 'Yes thanks. Can I do anything?'

'Breakfast?'

'I can cook.'

He grinned at her. 'So I should hope. You live on your own?' a loaded question and wondered why he should care.

'Yes,' her face clouded, and a pause before she revealed more of who she was, what she was all about. 'I gave up on a casual 'live-in' expenses share arrangement six months ago. He presumed far too much and was a lazy sod. Anyway, I spend most weekends outdoors.' She changed the subject. 'I do a mean scrambled egg.'

He laughed, surprising himself. 'You're on. I'll make the coffee,' and led the way back into the cottage.

Over her admittedly well turned-out eggs and his very particular brewed coffee they sat and talked. Easy, idle chat, about her schooling at 'Roedean; her job at 'Country World' magazine which had its own following, about her childhood home on the East Sussex coast. He asked whether she'd 'any other siblings?' and after the answer that apart from Celina, another younger sister was doing a university business management course, she asked a question of her own.

'*Will* you sell this place?'

He leant back in the chair and clasped his hands at the back of his head, a habitual stance to add weight to a considered answer. 'It holds far too many memories, Paula, and I'm seeing Mary everywhere. I don't know if I should hang on to those memories or let them go. She wanted me to ...' No, he shouldn't tell her, burden her with private things.

'Wanted you to what? Start a new life? Or keep hold of past remnants? Beckside - surely she wouldn't want you to keep it purely as a shrine, would she? Is that why?'

'She was a very practical person but . . .,' and his emotions rose once more to induce a deep breath and a pause, 'also deeply romantic about life, places, people. Always made friends wherever she went.' . . . *She was there, in the kitchen, doing the washing up, turning towards him, her beautiful smile, the flick of her hand to smooth wayward hair from her eyes. . .* he felt tears welling up, got up out of his chair and faced the window . . . *saw her walking across the grass, long skirt swaying, hair blowing in the breeze.* 'Paula, I'm sorry . . .,' and heard the scrape of her chair legs, heard the footsteps across the flagged floor, felt her arms come round him, the comforting softness of her breasts against his back, the drift of hair against his shoulder.

She held him, unmoving, just the gentle sway of a tender hug, an exchange of understanding, of caring. Then released him and resumed her seat.

'She was a very lucky girl.'

He swallowed, took a deep breath, turned back to face her, dabbed at his eyes and offered her a faint smile.

'I was the lucky one, Paula,' and grasped the back of his chair with both hands, looked down at the table and the two empty coffee mugs, the biscuit crumbs. 'I'm sorry, I've let my feelings get the better of me. You shouldn't have to put up with this.' Practicalities would push his vulnerability away. 'What train will you catch?'

'Half past twelve. I'll find a sandwich at Carlisle. If it isn't too forward a thought, though, I'd have stayed on if you wanted me to, just to keep you company, stopped you from brooding.'

Another smile from her, dear girl, so much like the daughter. 'Very kind and thoughtful of you, Paula, and I'm honestly very glad we met, even if it was at young Stuart's expense. I'm expecting Sarah to call anytime, though she'll be sleeping off the hangover after last night's post fashion parade party if I know her. Maybe there's a chance she'll pop over for a few days, hopefully, now the shindig is over.'

'That'll be nice for you.'

'Yes.'

'Will you let me stay in touch?'

'Of course. I'd like that.'

'Thank you - and please let me know what your next project will be so I can remember to watch it.'

'Sure. It might be a while, though; these things often take ages to come to the screen.'

'No matter. I'll be looking at the credits avidly now, looking for an Art Director's name I recognise!'

'There's a few of us out there.'

'Maybe, but I'll look nevertheless. Shall we do the washing up?'

Afterwards, they walked together, up to the top field, just like Mary and he had done times without number, and just like he had, but very alone, only what, two long days ago. Side by side, they leant on the gate and looked across the uncut wild flower meadow towards the public footpath and the far edge of the wood, watched a solemn procession of Nordic pole addicts walking where she had trekked with her party only the two days ago, and grinned at each other. Then she held his eyes, searched his face, saw the loss, the sadness, the hunger for an indefinable solution to an absence, and couldn't help herself.

Her kiss, tentative, soft, expressive of the indefinable need of the moment, deepened, her arms came round him, he felt her lithe young body tight against his, let his hands instinctively hold her face, saw her eyes close, let the wish rise, glow, subside. And felt an incredible inner peace flow down.

'Paula,' he breathed her name, 'Paula,' softly, aware of a faint whisper of an echo, an echo of Mary's voice, *'there'll be another woman out there . . .' Questioned the recall . . . Too soon?*

She didn't pull away; merely let her arms drop down to her side. Again, their eyes caught. 'Remember me,' she said softly, 'cos I'll not forget this place or the nicest guy who owns it.'

They walked back down; hand in hand for some of the way, then she brought her pack out of the hut, slung it into the Discovery, climbed into the passenger seat and he drove down the track, onto the road and twenty minutes later came down to the station.

'You'll be okay?' she asked.

He nodded. 'I'll be okay. Sarah will come, I know she will.'

'Don't sell.'

'We'll see. Keep in touch.'

'I will. Let me know about the next film.'

He nodded. 'Send me a text when you get back to London.'

'Okay.'

Then the single diesel railcar rattled into the station, she climbed in, and with no delay, it pulled away. Gone.

Mary's Legacy 5

'I know it's short notice, Donald dear, but we felt this was one you'd be abso-looot-ley right for. And don't you have a thing about Italy?'

Donald kept an impassive face. This particular guy had an unfortunate habit of mucking up his words to give an impression he was gay. Not so. With that amount of clout, it was an affectation he could afford to sport and others had to ignore, a speciality of his that might be a means to an end when dealing with egocentric starlets. 'Who's . . . ?' he started to ask.

But he didn't get a chance to finish the question. Booth reeled off the guys they'd already hired, an impressive list and amongst them there were two he thoroughly enjoyed working with, Peter and Jon. Peter he could absolutely trust to get the correct camera angles and Jon, well, the best adaptee in the business; if there needed to be some subtle alterations in script to benefit the camera line and the lighting, he was the guy, script writer extraordinaire. What was more; both had a sensitivity to any mood changes required. 'Okay,' he agreed and Booth beamed at him.

'Knew you would,' he said. 'Time you got back to work. I know,' and waved a podgy hand at him to underline the point, 'we all felt for you, losing Mary like that, but there comes a point . . .'

'When life has to carry on. Don't think I haven't known it,' Donald interjected, 'but I had to wait for the right job.' A couple of weeks had slipped silently by, each day an empty gap in his life, a repetitive sequence of domestic chores, desultory periods of reminiscence and painful elimination of the less emotive aspects of a past life. The phone call from Booth had been a life-saver, brought him back into a world he knew and precipitated this visit to the studios, the first since *that day* . . . and felt the inner twist, the agony of loss.

'Yeah. And this is it. Pick up the script from Jemma on your way out. First briefing tomorrow, half eight, if it's possible; and oh, zero one percentage. It'll be good, damn good.' Booth appeared hard-nosed, perhaps dictatorial, but Donald knew it was a front; underneath he cared about the project, the cast and above all, the crew.

He raised metaphorical eyebrows. Nought point nought one percentage of box office take - not bad at all. He'd had less from earlier deals and they still brought home significant amounts even now. Not many picture-goers realised the units put together for these conceptual feature films were hired on a percentage take basis - far better than a fixed few thousand or three outright payment and then having to stand around for weeks without expenses while directors waited for the weather. He wouldn't argue with Booth; they both knew where they stood.

He picked up the bulky package from Booth's p.a., having the usual wry thought it was akin to a Pierce Brosnan collecting an 007 brief from the current Miss Moneypenny, especially as she blew a kiss at him.

Travelling back in a taxi to the Southgate flat, his thoughts drifted, ambled around his loneliness, the absence of good social events, though admittedly he'd turned down a couple because he couldn't stand the thought of being at a party without Mary at his side. He pondered on how the Lakes girl Paula was; they'd had a brief chat on the phone once or twice when the mood took him or she'd phoned when fed up. The last time they'd spoken a few days ago, she'd complained about how routinely boring her job was getting, how she missed the Lakes, and there'd seemed to be a sort of restrained tension between them, a relic of the brief emotive time together at Beckside. How long ago had that been? Only two weeks? Sarah, bless her, had managed those precious few days she'd promised to wangle, they'd efficiently dealt with what needed doing, and he blanked out the significance of those black plastic sacks they'd loaded into the Discovery for delivery to the charity shops. He couldn't keep all Mary's clothes or her shoes, and even the larger proportion of the books she'd loved to read weren't ever likely to be on his own reading pile. So Sarah had worked methodically through the wardrobe, the drawers, the bookshelves and he'd maintained as an un-emotive view as best he could. Two dresses he kept, or more accurately, one dress and a skirt, a couple of pairs of pants, the lacy bra he'd bought her on the last wedding anniversary. They'd be the talismans, the ephemeral link with her body. She'd worn them with pride; he'd viewed her so dressed with the deep love that they'd shared - something tangible to link the past with whatever the future could throw at him.

He remembered he'd promised to tell her - Paula, that is - when he'd picked up a new job. Well, he'd read through the outline plot and the script first. What had Booth said, Italy? Down in the south of the country the worst of the summer heat would be behind them yet the light would still be intense, the Italians still wearing summer clothes and not yet swathed up in drab black or deep blue amorphous anoraks that characterised their attitude to temperatures less than thirty centigrade. The last time he'd been in Italy, Rome, Verona, Lucca, Milan, wherever, most Italian girls seemed to want to hide their artistic beauty in scruffy jeans and ragged tee-shirts. If - and he'd still to read himself into the story line - they needed city backdrops, they'd want the locals to dress - or undress - in keeping with cinema-goers concept of the country.

He was getting back into the mood - such thoughts proved it. Sarah'd be back in the Parisian top floor flat above the Gallerie by now. He pulled out his phone, sent a text, suggesting it was easier for her to phone him. 'Ring in fifteen. Job!!! Xx'

It took another ten minutes to reach what was home, climb the stairs, let himself in, attempt to shrug off the far too prevalent 'I'm alone here' feeling and chuck the script package onto the desk.

She did as she'd been instructed. 'Job, dad? Great! Where? And who's running it?'

He told her. 'Booth pulled me in. Peter as camera, Jon as script. And,' he reeled off what he could remember of the credit list, a couple of sensuous ladies and one of the nicer male leads everyone loved. 'What's more, Booth suggested 'Italy' but I don't know where yet.'

'When?'

'By the time we've ironed out logistics, maybe four, five weeks. It'll be after the heat's levelled off so should be good.'

'You sound excited, dad. Best thing for you. How's Paula?'

He grimaced. Paula, well, okay, he'd told Sarah all about that incident and she'd given him a very old-fashioned look and then no more was said, but it seemed she'd not forgotten the girl. Neither had he . . . despite the determined attempts of Yvette, the slinky blonde continuity girl with a known crush on him from the last production, to intrude on his loneliness. That one was far too superficial.

'Last time I spoke to her she quoted boredom. Not exactly a scintillating role, unlike yours. You'll be seeing some snippets of the autumnal collection now?'

'Snippets!' she laughed down the echoey line. 'How droll! Far more than snippets, dad, full blown dress rehearsals; you'd love Janie in the russet lace. More holes than dress, *so lacey* it's not true. You can see all her assets clear as clear, and the underskirt's sheer chiffon; shows her lovely legs like no other. Drool drool drool.'

'Stop winding me up, Sarah,' for she'd no hang-ups over describing a model's body as a business asset. 'Not good for my blood pressure. Your legs are far better than any other girls I know. Karl should get you onto the catwalk.'

'Huh! Not me. I'm not tall enough, nor skinny.' She changed tack. 'Will your film schedule allow a stop-over in Paris? Be good if you could. I might even wangle a pre-show pass for you then you'll get to see Janie in all her flirty floaty things. She's a darling really, you'd love her.'

'Um. We'll see. I'm going to order a take-away and read my way into this script. Talk at the weekend? Or could you chunnel over?' 'Chunnel' being their private code for Eurostar, and Sarah had the benefit of her Fashion House account, Business Premier and all, lucky girl.

'Maybe. Won't promise, but might. We'll see,' repeating his phrase. 'Love you!' she added and the phone went dead.

Her chat cheered him up; it always did. A live part of what Mary had been all about, his daughter a lovely girl with many aspects akin to her mother.

He phoned the Chinese place for his take-away, opened up the script package, dropped into his armchair and started reading. Before he'd got beyond the well-drafted synopsis he was hooked. He could already see some of the shots in his mind's eye and reached for the cartridge paper pad and his favourite 2B pencil.

The take-away came; he ate one-handedly, adept at multi tasking, pencil furiously moving. Sketch after sketch, cryptic notes alongside in his far neater writing - there wasn't any point in jotting down thoughts you couldn't later interpret - and by midnight had almost become the director of the leading lady, watching her move from one virtual scenario to another. By one o'clock he knew it'd be good, gave in to nature and went to bed not appreciating quite how his night's dreams would affect the way the emotive legacy would lie.

❦

The dream - Italy - the intense blue of sea and sky, the startling white, the pastels, the smiling humour of the locals, the street cafes, the piazzas, the red tiled domed duomo, the little three-wheeled Piaggios pottering through narrow, steep and shaded cobbled passages between old four-storey buildings dating back centuries - the night had been a furious pot-pourri of sketched scenarios, and brought to mind a frighteningly real image of a girl, a girl like Paula but not like her, too young, too - innocent?

Who was she? Long gloss black hair in two distinct woven tresses down her back, the full simple blouse with short sleeves, a rounded semicircle of neckline above a fulsome bust, a neat waist above a knee length skirt in, yes, the usual black, with naked shapely legs bearing a sun-kissed tan, heeled open shoes, she was high cheeked, dimpled, her slanted deep brown eyes ready to smile a shy welcome, a picture of youthful beauty at her daily work in a shore-side café.

The slap-slap of waves on the boat sides, the purr of an engine, the sting of salt spray, the glare of sun on sea and the white cliffs, with their fishing platforms perched high on impossible stilts and heart-stopping access paths . . . he could see it all through a camera lens, the sheer raw beauty of the country, a complex vista of emotions stirred and thrust onto a screen. Awake after the all-too intense visualisation, he rolled over, stared at the blank emptiness of the ceiling. This was what he was all about, turning imagination into reality - as far as reality could be on a cinema screen.

And then another, more familiar girl, an image of the Cumbrian Lakes, a relic of his last visit to Beckside, the vision of Paula stirred and thrust into his thoughts; suddenly he was aware of the phone's muted ring, breaking his early unfocused reflections into unwelcome shards. The bedside handset he nearly knocked onto the floor.

'Yes?' He couldn't be efficient and business-like at half seven in the morning and after the travelogue of a disturbing yet oddly evocative night.

'It's Paula.' Her voice sounded strained, shaky, perhaps even thin. 'I'm sorry, Donald, you don't mind me ringing this early ...?' *the girl was breaking into his day. He had to be pleasant to her. Coincidence?*

Paula... 'Paula! Gracious me - just thinking about you ...Of course I don't mind you ringing, but at this hour? And you sound, well, perhaps a little strained? What's the matter?' and knew his inane query would sound as if she was a worried child and he the parent. 'I was going to phone you later, with some news.'

She didn't rise to the comment; instead a direct question, a question that must be very much uppermost in her mind. 'Can I come over? I need to talk to someone, someone I can trust.'

Her father figure, was that who he was? 'That sounds ominous. But yes, if you feel you need to, then certainly. You know where I am?'

'I'll find you. Half an hour?'

'Give me a buzz when you're near. I'll look out for you.'

'Thanks, thank you so much,' he heard the catch in her voice. 'I'll see you soon,' and the phone went down.

How odd was that? She'd materialised in his jumbled waking thoughts, and hey presto, the phone rang; but why the directly expressed quest for an audience? He'd never expected to have her on the doorstep, not here. It'd probably take her more than the half an hour, especially during the commuter go-to-work time. Maybe she'd like breakfast? The flat was untidy. And he ought to get some of the snatches of overnight hallucinations sketched out - if they appeared sensible to a fully woken-up brain. What to do first? Tidy the flat.

Slightly less than three quarters of an hour later and the mobile bleeped, once, twice. A text: 'In the street.xx.' He looked out of the window - yes, there she was, walking slowly along the pavement a couple of hundred yards away, unmistakeably her, searching the numbers. A half minute for the stairs, the front door open, down the access steps, he'd timed it exactly right. 'Paula! So good to see you!'

She didn't exactly, as the cliché has it, 'fall into his arms' but very nearly. He held her, just held her, as a response to her strange, hungry, quite desperate look, held her as once he'd held her before, way up in the Lakes cottage garden. 'Paula?'

Tight in his arms, the rugged, hardened-to-life features as she'd once mentally described him way back were a welcome familiarity. Peculiarly, she could only think to apologise. 'So sorry, Donald, sorry to inflict myself on you again, but,' the hesitation all-too obvious, 'I hoped you of all people I know, might understand. There's no one else I felt I could talk to, not like you, not within easy reach.' *She yearned for a kiss, to feel a response, to assuage a hollow emptiness.*

'Then come in,' he released her, stood back and let her into the narrow hallway. 'I'm on the top floor, lots of stairs. Follow me?'

Once into the flat, the door shut, she sagged, shoulders down, gave an exhalation of breath. 'Thank you,' she said, and with a brief look around, as if to get her bearings, produced a random comment, perhaps one that would give her time and help to settle a change in mood, 'this is a nice flat.' He didn't latch on, kept his expression neutral.

'Let me have your coat.' He hung her shorty mid-brown coat onto the back of a dining chair. 'Please, do sit down. I'll make us some coffee. Then you can explain whatever has taken you half way across London to say,' though instinctively he knew something wasn't quite right with her. 'It's nice to see you again. Oddly, I was only thinking about you this morning, moments before you rang. Was that telepathy?'

That evinced a small smile from her. 'Maybe.' She chose the small armchair alongside the coffee table and sat, primly crossing her legs under the well-cut if plain dark green knee-length needle-cord skirt. Her cotton sweater top was in much the same style as he'd seen her wear before but in a lighter olive green colour. Simple shoes too, and no jewellery. A girl who currently wasn't too bothered about her presentation, with her colour scheme very country muddy browns and greens, much in accord with what she'd sported amongst the Lakeland hills. However, the light he'd seen out there had gone from her eyes, the sparkle visible during the Beckside association just wasn't there, a worrying aspect to the day that overrode the possible pleasure to be gained by sharing the description of the new film project now uppermost in his mind.

Coffee was easy and welcomed. She sipped, gave a sigh of appreciation. 'Maybe worth the trip across just for this, Donald. You have a knack.'

He chuckled. 'Mary always left the coffee making to me,' but the simple comment brought its own niggle of pain in the reminiscence. 'She'd have loved to have met you, Paula.' He paused, absorbed the Italianate characteristics, the overly quiet refined loveliness. 'You're not a happy girl, are you?'

She shook her head. 'Not really. I wish I was back amongst the hills. Selfishly, I'd love to be living up in your shepherd's hut right now.'

'So what's gone wrong?'

'Before I say, please tell me to go if I'm being too forward, unloading my troubles on you.' Her quick smile came and went. 'But I'd thought we'd found something in common.' *Something?* She placed the coffee cup on the table alongside.

'Then perhaps I better sit down?' Poised to offer her a refill - or even breakfast, seeing as he'd not yet had that chance, he slipped into the opposite chair, watched her, the empathy building.

Now the moment had come, it didn't appear an easy mission for her. She nibbled on her lip, recrossed her legs, clasped hands and then unclasped them to smooth her skirt down along her thighs. It didn't require a student of body language to understand she was nervous and at the same time, stressed.

'I quit my job yesterday. And I want to, have to, find another flat.'

So that led him to ask the inevitable question. 'Why? Why on earth did you do that, quit the job, I mean? Moving to another flat - I assume you rent - surely that's what people do all the time.'

'Let's just say I fell out with the boss woman; she's been rubbing me up the wrong way for ages. She and I had a stack-up last week; I couldn't cope with the hassle. So I left.'

'But there's something else?' Surely she'd not travel across London merely to tell me that, he thought, and she didn't strike him as a person who'd give up a reasonable paid job merely on a whim. 'So where do I fit in? You've not come to ask for advice, because you've taken decisions. And I can't think you merely want to kip on my sofa - not that I'd turn you down if you were desperate, Paula, but I mean ...'

She looked across at him. 'I'm not suggesting anything I shouldn't. But,' and her head went down, her gaze switched to her knees, her voice dropped. 'I wondered if you'd let me go and stay at Beckside for a while, out of the way. I could look after it for you, keep the grass mown, that sort of thing, provided your daughter's agreeable if she's in the frame. I could sleep in the hut.'

Donald blinked. Surprised, but not surprised. In the back of his mind there'd been a smidgeon of an idea she'd find an excuse to go back there - he wished he could too, but there was a living to make.

'Needs some thought, Paula. It's a lonely place; you'd need wheels and an income?'

'I know. I've an idea I might start to paint, I've always been reasonable with my sketches. And I can walk.'

'It's still a fair way to the village, Paula, lugging groceries.'

She offered a slight suggestion of a grin. 'Supermarkets deliver nowadays, Donald, even to out-of-the-way places. And I don't mind my own company, especially now.'

'Oh?'

'You won't scold me?'

'What for? You haven't fully explained, have you? Not yet,' experiencing a growing sense of her awkwardness and the air of vulnerability. 'Come on, Paula, you wouldn't be here if you hadn't some idea I'd listen. I've a daughter only a little younger than you, so I do know something about what goes on in a girl's head,' *though Sarah seemed to be far more level headed than this one.*

Her hesitancy was still there. He got up, crossed over, to reach down, grasp her hands and pull her up, out of her chair, to wrap his arms around her and hug, felt the initial stiffened reaction sag away and then the warmth of her, her softness and acceptance melt into him. *Mary, this is how we used to stand and feel for each other, remember? Am I sharing my love for you with this peculiar stray girl?*

Her voice was muffled, her head on his shoulder. 'I shouldn't be doing this,' and he felt her stiffen again, as though she'd pull away but he held her firm.

'Paula,' he released one hand and stroked the smoothness of her hair with its rare, expensive scent. 'Whatever it is that's troubling you, I'd like to think I can help, though burying yourself in the Lakes may not be an answer.'

She moved her head upwards, sought his look. 'I shouldn't be doing this,' she repeated.

He let her go for sanity's sake, stepped back, and watched as she sagged back into the chair. 'Maybe, maybe not; whatever, you're here, I'm prepared to listen.'

She shook her head; he watched her struggle with whatever emotion held her in check.

41

'What else can I do, Paula?' and Mary's voice echoed in his head; *"my bequest to a worthy unknown woman. Bit like a heart transplant, there'll be someone out there."* Was he destined to become confidante to any stray female with problems? 'You've quit your job - not a sensible idea unless there's another in the offing, is it? On a whim? Or is there a deeper reason?' He thought back, she'd appeared in his life by accident - someone else's accident - she'd been sensible then. 'Have you attempted to climb a rock, Paula, and fallen off?'

That got another small smile from her. 'This isn't the result of a foolish whim, Donald; at least, it may be foolish but wasn't on a whim. I,' and her voice caught, 'made the wrong choice and it's come back to haunt me; my stupid reaction to an emotive moment. So perhaps it was a whim. I thought, hoped, it'd gone away. But it hasn't and I'm afraid perhaps it never will.'

'You're running away?'

She nodded, rubbed at what might be a tear. 'I remember telling you I was a good judge of character that morning, well; in this case I got it badly wrong. Maybe I thought I'd got shot of him but he's been stalking me. Why I need to get clear away and the shepherd's hut was an overnight inspiration.'

'He?'

'A guy I fancied from way back, when I did the clubs.' A hand came up and rubbed her forehead, a characteristic body sign for '*I wish I hadn't'*. 'He had the car, the patter, gave me the offer of a proverbial 'good time' until,' - another lengthy pause and he wondered why - 'foolishly I got pregnant. Then he turned nasty - and I managed to arrange an abortion, not wanting any child of his or a legal parental tie to a waster. Not what a decent girl might have done, but I would have made a lousy mum.'

This didn't sound at all like the Paula he knew; was she being truly honest with him? Some women used virtual pregnancies as a means to an end. 'How long ago?'

'Over a year. I told you I kicked him out six months ago, actually he went of his own accord; p'raps thought he'd found a cosier bed. Then she must have been brighter than me and locked him out so he's tried getting back into *my* bed. I've had the locks changed twice; I take different routes home, and make sure the street's not empty when I get back - the front door's on the pavement - all that sort of thing. Then he began phoning the magazine's classified ads number, sending texts . . .'

'And your boss began to lose patience? So that's why you quit?'

She nodded again. 'And why I have to move.'

'I see,' he said. 'Well, understandable.' Surely this Paula hadn't sadly followed a well-trodden and thus familiar route? But she'd said so. Why? Insufficient parental guidance - she'd said she'd lost her mother - her elder sister had other ideas about men and there might have been that far too common '*he fancies me*' thought which was the trap for so many gullible young girls who believed the man 'of their choice' would never let them down, would always be good and kind and supportive. He sighed. Would that modern mores weren't quite as lackadaisical, and more thought given to the ultimate outcome of casual irredeemable sexual encounters; he mentally blessed the commonsense approach his own daughter possessed. What reaction was Paula expecting? Should he play 'the heavy father' and then show her the door? Or should he be sympathetic and lend the support she obviously craved? *Mary, what should I do?* 'Doesn't - wouldn't - your father offer you support?'

She shook her head vehemently. *'No way!'*

'That bad? I rather thought you'd had a cosy childhood, you know; adventure holidays, that sort of thing?'

'Mum died,' and her voice sounded oddly thin. 'Poor dad, left with three strange girls who pulled in different directions. An odd trio,' she repeated, 'a good-time girl, a potential lesbian and a serious academic. Harriet is the only sane one. Celina's way out; me, I only looked around for the next date.' She sounded defiant now, as she sought his look. 'Do I shock you, Donald? Would you have seen me as a common tart?'

He shook his head slowly, wondering how first impressions weren't always as accurate as he'd thought. In his line of work, casual liaisons were as much the part of the way things happened as drinking endless coffee from plastic beakers on some film set or other; you accepted it - some of the more moody starlets saw it as a way of relieving boredom, like scratching an itch. Thanks to Mary - and his own ethics - he'd never been tempted though many a girl had thrust her shapely front at him. He'd never have put Paula in the easy girl bracket, not after the sensible way she behaved up on the Beckside hill. The male film crew's version of *'www'* came to mind and he had to smother the irreverent chuckle. *Warm, Wet and Willing;* no, not this Paula, surely not.

'Doesn't sound like the woman I first met up in the hills? Is that side of you now past history, Paula? I'll not help you if all you're looking for is a warm bed.'

She stood up. 'Sorry. I shouldn't have come here.' She reached for her coat, her voice suddenly sounded cool, defiant. 'I guess I'll find somewhere.'

Now he was in a quandary. Turf her out, watch her walk away and he may never see her again, so his conscience would continually nag at him; he'd wonder where she was, and if her last partner had taken physical revenge on her? Help her and there'd always be that underlying tension, a covertly sexual, tautly strung connection because she'd told him something of her past - and he, however strong his principles and feelings were for his lost love, would become as susceptible as any man to a woman who exuded charm and available feminity. Yes, Paula did exactly that, for all the essentials were there, shape, smile, sexuality . . . despite her drab if well-fitting outfit.

'No, I can't let you walk away, Paula. I'll not see you waste yourself on rubbish relationships. You want to go to Beckside, then I'll talk to Sarah. But where are you with your flat now?'

She dropped the coat back into the chair and he relaxed. 'You're a very decent man, Donald. Pity there isn't a younger and free version of you out there. I've to hand the keys in on Saturday.'

He thought. Ahead of him, there'd be a week or two of frenetic meetings and drafting schedules; he'd not be here very much other than overnight. Could he trust her? He had before. 'Okay Paula. If you want, you can stay here while you sort out your flat; though don't think you can fill this place with rubbish. The guest room's yours until you go north, assuming Sarah agrees. But you earn your keep - and don't expect me to cook all the time.'

Unexpectedly, she burst into tears, put her head between her hands and sobbed. The mood changed, he felt for her, the way she'd drifted into some poor association. *'Some woman ...'* Mary's words trickled back into his head. Was he to be saddled with this problem child? And in the here and now, and so soon after his loss? He let her cry; allowing it to lessen the inner tension, believing it was the best course. These tears were of relief, an emotive consequence of realising she had someone who cared about her; about who she was rather than a woman who'd suggested she'd spread her legs in return for a masculine consort. He could never understand why some girls thought they *had* to have a man in their life, an obligatory male who'd run his hands over their breasts or otherwise provide the means to satisfy the inner sexual cravings. With Mary, *dear Mary,* everything had fallen into place. Mutual feelings expressed, loving whenever they felt the joint need, living together a constant pleasure in all the little things that made up a proper partnership. Her loss had left a very large gap in his life, the feeling of empty space he'd tried to suppress as best he could, but now, like a sink-hole, it was opening up in front of him.

Tearful eyes looked up at him, windows into her soul. 'Thank you,' she whispered. 'Whatever you want me to do, just say.'

Poor child, he thought, for that's what she was, a needy child. 'Right now, Paula, you can cook breakfast. I need to be at the production offices in no time flat, I need a shower, you need to wash tears away from that lovely face of yours and then we'll see what needs to be done. Okay?'

'Okay.' The wan smile came as she stood up and reached for him, to seek another clasped hug. 'And I'll try and be good.'

That could have a different connotation, he thought. *Good as in impeccable behaviour or good as in responding to expressed needs?*

45

Mary's Legacy 6

He took her with him. It seemed the simplest thing to do, given she'd no job to go to and sending her back to a flat where she'd obviously feel nervous and vulnerable would not be in her best interests. She'd turned out her signature scrambled eggs, they'd sat in comfortable silence while eating; she'd waited while he showered before managing to repair the tear-streaked damage to her face and he'd acknowledged her efforts with another friendly kiss.

࿋

As Donald ushered Paula into the production office Booth raised his eyebrows, his efficient appraisal of the girl very obvious. With a profound yet purely professional interest in the way people presented themselves, he had no reservations about eying up a girl's figure and looks. 'Donald, dear, I assume she's your new assistant? Good choice. You'll need her. Well done. What's your name, girl?'

She'd been diffident about his suggestion, conscious she'd not made any effort to dress to impress; it wasn't, in her view, that her mission to seek support needed any extra assistance from being seen as sexy, but to be taken clad as she was into the film production world where glamour must be high on priorities wasn't good, was it? She'd asked the question and Donald had simply smiled at her. 'Paula, you're fine. You're with me, not a wannabe babe deficient in underwear expecting half an hour on the casting couch. Leave it to me,' and his euphemistic phraseology hadn't offended her anymore than he'd not appeared affronted by her earlier revelations.

So now she had a role to play? 'I'm Paula,' she said, and tried a tentative smile.

Booth extended a pudgy hand across his desk. 'Well, hi Paula. Hope you enjoy working alongside Donald. He'll look after you, no worries there. Now,' and his bulk subsided back into the groaning armchair, 'I guess your imagination's all fired up. Got anything?'

Donald pushed his file across the desk. 'Italy, you said. Paula's got some vague connections out there. How far south? I'd like to get to Puglia; it's dry, still ancient in outlook and plenty of olive groves as well as decent beaches. It'll suit the story line; will give exactly the right light too.'

Booth spread the papers across his desk, scanned the sketches, his expression impassive, and then swept them back together. 'Yep. It fits. Pass them on to the story board guys. We'll need some city time as well. I think Roma, don't you?'

'Or Turin? Less expensive, and we have the river. Easier run down to Lecce as well. Do we have to fly or can we go Trenitalia?'

Booth pulled a face. 'You and your trains! So long as we get the crew and kit out there, people can make their own way. What about you, Paula?' He turned to her and grinned. 'Are you a rail or fly girl?'

She was taken aback, not expecting to take any part in this, yet it appeared she'd been taken at face value, assumed to be part of Donald's team. A mind blowing scenario; last night she'd seriously thought of walking away from all known connections yet now, after one phone call, her horizons were expanding beyond comprehension.

'I, er . . .'

'Oh, she'll travel with me,' Donald's terse reply gave her no option. 'Can't do without my apprentice,' he added and chuckled. 'She's very good with her pencils too.'

'Is that a fact?' Booth gave him a wink, 'then keep 'em sharp, guys. Now, we need a brain-storming session with production. Lunch at twelve thirty prompt; we've got Annette with us.'

'Right. No problem. Paula,' and Donald, fully aware she had no idea of what could lie ahead, gave her some slack. 'Suggest you go walkabout; get to know where everyone lives. You won't get lost. Just ask for Booth's office close to our deadline, we'll meet you back here then.'

Paula nodded faintly, completely knocked off her perch. Though it had been a daydream to link with Donald's world, she'd hardly expected it to come true and now she felt some tugging guilt at her

47

deception. Let loose in the Studios, the place she'd only heard of, accepted it was seen as a mysterious, almost ethereal, dream world where magic could be part of the everyday - and she'd been given free rein? Booth left them in the corridor; Donald edged her towards the double doors leading to the outside. 'Relax, Paula,' he said, sotto voce, 'if Booth's accepted your presence, and I think he likes you, then we're made. You fancy a trip to Italy? Beats the shepherd's hut?'

'You'll take me with you? Just like that?'

'If you want.' He reached for her hands, held them firmly, 'yes, Paula, I'll take you with me. Look after you. Open doors for you. Then you can decide your own future, okay?'

'But . . .'

'No promises. No 'I owe you' comments, no need to talk of repayments, Paula. This is something I feel I need to do. Something of Mary's life, what she'd have done. It'll please her, make her spirit happy.'

'Mary? But . . .'

'Tell you later. I must go to this meeting. You walk around, anyone stops you, tell 'em you work for me. See you back here in an hour and a half. Go!'

She wandered around in a daze. The huge blocks of Studios One and Two, the sprawl of sets erected on the 'back lot', the occasional actor walking by in costume, the industrial units she found labelled 'Special Effects' and 'Mechanics', the disparate workshops - and no-one accosted her, it was as though she belonged here. Time went; before she knew it, she thought she'd be late and almost ran back to the admin block. Going back to the reception area that Donald had taken her through first thing, the girl behind the desk called at her.

'Miss Paula? I've a studio pass ready for you; we just need your surname?'

'A pass?'

'Oh yes, Mr Booth has confirmed it for you. Your surname?'

'Davison,' she said, even more surprised. The girl typed it into her computer, the printer whirred, and moments later she had her pass, a laminated photo i.d. card, and with her picture? Her photo, taken as she'd entered the building this morning, unsmiling, maybe a smidgeon fearful? Security taken seriously.

'Take care of it, Paula. You won't get past the gatehouse guys alone without it. Mr Stevens is waiting for you. Second on the left, remember?' the girl smiled at her. 'My name's Pat. Welcome to Pinewood.'

They were sitting round the circular office table, Donald, Booth, a girl maybe she'd seen somewhere before, much the same age as herself with beautiful glossy jet-black long hair; and another man; grey haired and rather aristocratic looking. She hesitated, unsure, as they all looked up at her entrance; Donald rose from his chair and beckoned her forward.

'Ronald, Annette, may I introduce Paula, my new assistant? Paula, Ronald is our director producer, Annette our leading lady who's just flown in from the States this morning. We're very privileged that she's been able to come over so early.'

So Miss Raven Hair was Annette? Of course, seen on the cinema screen! A very appealing girl too, who offered a charming smile and a welcome. 'Donald, you've a very pretty assistant. I can see I'll have to keep an eye on her! Paula, my dear, pleased to meet you; come, do sit here,' and Annette tapped the back of the empty chair next to her.

Ronald added his comments. 'It'll be good to have her around, Donald, if it means you can delegate. From my memory, the last time we worked together you hardly had time to eat. Paula, welcome to Intrepid productions. Good to have you on board. Booth - what else do we need to agree? Lunch beckons and I'm starving!'

Booth leant back on his chair, tapped a pencil on his teeth. 'So long as you guys like Italy, and we can rustle up a few more good people for the remaining key posts, then we'll aim for two weeks hence. All we need is Stateside agreement. I can get the main kit out by plane to Milan next week; I've a good warehouse guy out there who'll keep tabs on it. Bettina can have the hotels lined up; our agent will organise the wheels and the catering. Annette, darling, just say where you'd like to stay. I'm sure Paula will lend you support should you need it, provided Donald can spare her?'

Donald grinned at her across the table. 'Would my wishes come before Annette's?'

'Oh, I'm sure we'll manage,' the girl said. 'Come over to Claridges tonight, darling Donald, and bring Paula with you. We'll have dinner together.'

Ronald, impassive as always, nodded at her. 'Then perhaps you can hear what our art director will have you wear or not wear on the beach scenes, Annette. I've seen his sketches. Booth, it's lunch time.'

Donald took her gently by the arm as they walked down the corridor towards the studio's restaurant. 'In at the deep end, Paula? Hope this isn't taxing your philosophical side over much? You happy with the idea of dining at Claridges?' He smiled at her stunned expression. 'Not exactly what you had imagined when you quit the desk job? P. A. to a feature film art director?'

'I don't deserve this, Donald, really I don't. I know I asked you for support, but to be swallowed up in your world, along with *her,*' and she nodded at Annette with her sway, gorgeous legs and high heels ahead of them, arm in arm with Roland. 'I can't believe it. And you said I was good with my pencils which sounded rather like a sexy euphemism; I'm not *all that* good. Yes, I can draw, but ....'

'Don't fret, girl. No-one except me will need to study what you sketch, for sketch you will. That's the best part of it, and I'm not merely being charitable when I said you'd be my assistant. I do need someone and you've fallen into the job exactly right. I know you, and better the angel with wings than the devil with horns, I say. And enjoy your lunch; it's where all the names eat - who knows who'll have sat in your chair last - could even have been Pierce Brosnan!'

She fell silent, matching him step for step along the passageway, lined with film posters from past box-office successes. This was a dream, a colossal, unbelievable dream, and what had she done to deserve this? Been the first woman with a problem to fall under his gaze after he'd lost the undeniable love of his life? Under no illusions that his beloved Mary had been his rock, his focus of all that was right and lovely for he'd made that abundantly clear, she knew he wouldn't simply use her and cast her aside, neither would he merely bed her because she was there - though, she ruefully admitted to herself, she'd happily experience his loving, indeed, she was already under a spell. Why would she have otherwise rung him, foolishly using the rubbish scenario she'd dreamt herself into as a reason? He'd said, hadn't he, it was "*something he felt he needed to do. Something of Mary's life to please her, make her spirit happy*". So she'd been in the right place at the right time? She wished she'd known Mary, discovered what it was in a woman that made a man like Donald become so dedicated to her?

Ahead, Ronald, Booth and Annette had gone on, through the plush doors into the restaurant - Donald held the doors for her. 'Paula,' he said, 'thanks. Just be you, it'll be fine. No-one in the film industry pulls rank, unless they're really worried about status. We all love the job we do. . .' he paused, held her arm briefly, 'but don't allow anyone liberties, eh?' He winked at her. 'Not even me.'

Out of sight of the others and as they were alone in this long corridor, she reached up and planted a kiss on his cheek. 'I can try,' she said, 'cos I'm me, you're you and we've come together by sheer coincidence. I'll honour your Mary's memory, Donald, and that's a promise,' then they joined the others and the conversation moved right round to a discussion on equipment and who would be best for continuity and wardrobe and. . . .

Donald, sitting close, found Paula's hand under the table and squeezed. 'Bless you,' he said, softly. 'Mary'd love you,' and that was the nicest thing he could have said. She felt humbled, yet proud. She'd look after him. Be his prop, his confidante, his ... surrogate Mary?

Mary's Legacy

7

The meal at Claridges was something else; the evening passed in a blur, and it was long gone midnight when she and Donald returned to the Southgate flat. She'd clung onto his arm, feeling well beyond sensibilities, vaguely aware she was alone with a man, in a strange flat with no nightwear and there was every chance she'd end up in his bed - wasn't that what usually happened when a gal got taken out to dinner by a guy? Oh my, but she'd felt so woozily happy, decidedly deliriously different. She'd stumbled on the stairs, felt his arm under her, nestled into the maleness and allowed her eyes to close. Then things were happening to her, beyond any ability to protest or struggle or even assist and the consciousness slipped further away.

When she surfaced, whatever time later, she was alone in a strange bed, but warm and from what little remained of immediate memory, happy, so fell asleep once more.

'You slept well?' He was offering her a mug, a steaming mug, and grinning at her, 'after almost a whole bottle of wine and at least two glasses of port?'

'Eh? What?' Suddenly, she was aware that she'd nothing on bar her knickers, that it was daylight and that Donald - ah, yes, she was in Donald's flat - must have put her to bed, because she sure couldn't remember anything lucid from last night. She felt a rising warmth in her cheeks. 'You . . .' and couldn't actually bring herself to suggest what actually had happened.

'Put you to bed? Yes. Don't mind, do you? I'm expected to be quite adept at removing a girl's clothes,' and the grin got broader, 'though I don't - didn't - take advantage. Should I have done? Love the small clothes. Very lacy, very silky. Sorry - but I wasn't going to leave you in a chair or on the floor, which is where you seemed to want to go. Here, this is tea but you can have coffee if you prefer.'

Given that he must have seen most of what there was to be seen, there didn't seem to be any point in protesting, so she eased up, reached out a hand and took the mug. At least she was proud of her breasts.

'Thank you. And thank you. And yes, I think I slept well. What's the time?'

'Half past nine. Quite civilised. Breakfast? Shower's good - help yourself. I'll leave you to it.'

She took a sip. It was hot, so she carefully put the mug down on the bedside table. 'Donald?' she asked before he left the room.

'Hmmm?' he paused at the door.

'What can I say?'

'Not a lot. Perhaps admit I'm a gentleman?'

Softly, coyly: 'I wouldn't have minded,' there, what else could she say?

'No? Well, early days. I'd prefer a girl to know what's happening,' and he was surprised at his unconsidered comment, 'I seem to remember telling you I wasn't a serial rapist.'

'So you did.' She couldn't actually say how she now felt oddly disappointed, but took comfort in his comment about early days. At least he'd seen her, even if she'd been virtually unconscious. Ah well, maybe another time? 'I'd best get up. Can I shower?'

'Yep, sure,' he said. 'Breakfast in ten minutes.'

Whilst cooking her one of his favourite breakfast dishes, an omelette with smoked fish and tomato, it presented moments of consideration, as to whether he was being honest with himself and Mary's memory, allowing this chit of a girl into his life. Would he have been happier if the first candidate for the perceived legacy role had been more mature, at least in age? Initially Paula had appeared to have more about her than many another of her years, but if these revelations about a dubious relationship were accurate, and he couldn't truly believe she was that sort of girl, perhaps her maturity was in question. Or was it? That she'd

53

taken the decision to abandon a familiar if boring role and seek pastures new was something in her favour. Ahead lay challenges; given his almost automatic concept of taking her to the film studio had been without discussion, the way she'd taken to the situation helped enormously. Yes, he *did* need a gopher, his own continuity girl, a sort of girl Friday as some would call her; whilst working with Mary the need for a dedicated assistant never arose, he borrowed one or other of her team whenever necessary.

She'd crept up on him. 'That looks scrrr-umptious,' peering over his shoulder as he flipped it for the last time.

'Practice makes perfect. Go and sit down, unless you want a Weetabix or something. There's home mixed muesli as well. In that cupboard,' and he nodded at the one at the end of the working surface. 'Sarah's own recipe. Not my scene.'

'I could get used to this,' she said and opened the specified cupboard door. 'My my, how organised! Bowls?'

'In there. And while you're at it, two medium plates too.'

They sat in sociable silence and let breakfast take its course. An amiable half hour passed.

Paula laid her knife and fork neatly on her plate. 'I don't know what I've done to deserve this. Never ever thought a walk in the Lakes would lead to such a, well, a *fantastic* experience.'

'Neither did I, Paula.' He grinned at her. 'Though why you're clinging onto me is another thing. I'm not one of your night club conquests.'

She frowned. 'Donald, please don't. Don't spoil it. Let's just be the best of friends, eh? I, er,' she struggled to explain, 'I want rid of my old life. You've given me sight of a new one. I'd like to try, like I said, to help you fill a gap. Or am I being to pushy?''

He shook his head. 'You're being you. I reckon I can cope with that. So long as you do as you're told, don't stretch boundaries; and behave with a reasonable amount of decorum, it'll be fine. If you want to come with me, you'll have to take quite a bit of stick 'cos the crew are a rough tough brigade with a job to do. Having said that, they're usually a close knit bunch and look after their own so it ain't all bad.'

'Do I get paid then?'

With a chuckle, he shook his head. 'Pay? Don't you realise we work for the fun of it, the fame and glory and your name amongst the credits?

No, seriously, Paula, we get a retainer to help pay the bills, then it's how well the film succeeds. Good box office, good pay. You'll be working for me, so I'll be paying you in turn. And no, I can't say how much because I don't know myself whether it'll work. But you get fed and watered, housed, carried about and so on in the meantime. It's not as glamorous as some would have you believe. Do you still want to come?'

'Can I trust you?' Her question sounded hypothetical and with a trace of humour.

He caught her eyes, held her gaze, saw something there that pulled at his past and a small voice in his head said '*yes*'; Mary, dearest Mary. 'What do you think?'

A small nod, 'I'm coming. "Thank you" sounds too simple, Donald.' A thought struck her. 'Do you know, I might even remember to thank Stu when, if, I see him again for being so daft as to climb that rock.' She stood up, pushed her chair back to the table. 'Can I do the washing-up?'

᚛

'So now what?' she asked, smoothing her hair back after drying her hands.

'We go through the script again. And again. And again. Until we could tell the story blindfold and see exactly what the lead roles are doing.'

'Don't reckon much on your metaphors, Donald. Blindfold story telling?'

He grinned at her. 'You know what I mean. You tell me what you think when I show you what's in my mind.'

He got a sideways return grin; the girl didn't need to say what she'd thought. Euphemisms - didn't they just add spice to the conversations? He guided her through to the work room where his desk was surrounded by shelves of reference books, hemmed in by the table with piles of papers, the filing cabinet drawers bulging with past project documents; even the floor space was cluttered. Sarah hated his confusion; Mary had tolerated it though in contrast she'd been so neat and methodical.

'Oh my goodness! You work in *here*?'

'Sometimes. Mostly I sketch with a pad on my knee and the script papers on the chair alongside - why?'

'It's a mess. Sorry Donald, but it is. If your mind . . .' and she broke off, with another of her speciality grins.

'It's served me well over the years. I know what's what, maybe surprisingly, but I do. Let me show you,' and he opened the A3 pad left on the desk. 'Did you see what I left with Booth? What we discussed?'

'Not really. Too bemused by it all, I guess.'

'Understandable. Well, this is the nearest I get to a storyboard. The guys in the office do the donkey work once I've given them the main scene sketch, but you'll be able to have a go yourself. Look,' and he pointed at the biggest sketch in the centre of the page. 'This is the overall backdrop to quite a bit of the action, where Annette has a brawl with her film 'ex'; there are the chairs, the bar in the background, the Mercedes is behind the wall. These smaller sketches give the specific detail where it's part of what goes on. See?' He flipped the page. 'Now we're in the hotel foyer - quite straight forward but we need sloppy sofas so the new boyfriend can tug her down safely. Plants, large ones, swing doors to barge through - you know the sort of thing. Then there's the girl's suite upstairs, again, wardrobes, dressing table, large bed - unused, you'll be pleased to hear - the doorway through to another room.'

'You sound quite excited, Donald. Do you get carried away by the concept?'

'S'pose so. To do the job properly you have to get into the spirit of the thing. Like writing a book, getting inside your characters' heads. Works better that way. I have known some guys who fall out with the cast when they don't use the kit they're given. You have to get on with them, respect what they can do. Then it works.'

'Oh.'

'Think you can do it?'

'I can try.'

'I'll soon tell you if it isn't going to work, but I have an idea it might. Else Mary wouldn't have allowed me to take you on.'

'*Mary?*'

'If it's weird, then it's weird, Paula, but she's keeping an eye on us. I know she is. Just . . .'

56

She raised a finger to his lips. 'Sshhhusss, remember what I said? That I'll honour your Mary's memory? I mean it - she must have been a wonderful person. I'm honoured that you've allowed me into your life the way you have, Donald. Honoured,' and suddenly, unexpectedly, started to cry.

'Paula, don't, you'll start me off too,' and indeed, his eyes were prickling as the image of the woman who'd been his life reappeared in the back of his mind. Smiling, leaning up against the door jamb as she was wont to do, arms folded, waiting for him to finish a sketch so they could eat together . . .

The girl couldn't help it, opened her arms to him; they stood, gently rocking together, aware of how the memory of the woman she'd never known and he'd always loved had pulled them together, not in lustful passion, but in a bewilderingly close and wonderful friendship.

'Do you *really* need me?' she asked as they drew apart and she wiped her eyes with the back of a hand.

Did he? Need her? As a companion, as a confidante, as a helpmate? Or as a woman?' In reality: 'I need someone, Paula. And I can't think of a better candidate at the moment. Can you put up with me?' his return question.

'Then we need each other?'

'Seems like it.'

'Right.'

'Better get on with the job then.'

'Yes. Okay.'

He leant forward and lightly kissed her, a salutation, a seal on the bond. She closed her eyes. 'You don't mind?' he asked.

'Why ever should I? I much prefer your kisses to any others.'

So he kissed her again and heard Mary's whispered 'well done' in his head.

Mary's Legacy 8

During the course of the following few days, Paula began to learn what it was like to be a 'personal assistant' and had alternate moments of panic and euphoria. She took half a day off in order to return to her flat and finalise the clear out; Donald managed to persuade Booth to lend her one of the Studio drivers with a van which meant she had 'protection' and a very efficient extra pair of hands. Now her few possessions were safely in store at the Studio and she could relax. The oddity was living with the guy who was technically her boss - and keeping to her promise not to demean his wife's memory. After that 'day after the night before', they'd managed to keep conversations on an average level and, hour on hour, day by day, she was picking up the strange ways of the film world. Donald was impressed and said so towards the end of the week. 'Care for a break?' he asked during the now regular omelette manufacturing at breakfast time on the Thursday.

'Yeah, why not?' and Paula, with her unthinking reply, wondered at his broadest grin ever. What was he up to, this complex and often irritating guy who, she had to say within herself, she'd begun to really really love like a - what, an uncle, a father or, dangerously, a tad more than the father?

'Two nights at Beckside then? Take to the hills like you said you'd love to do? We'll catch the late afternoon train tomorrow, be there by ten or eleven-ish?'

She couldn't believe it. Donald, taking her back to Beckside? All that way, for only one full day and with two days travelling? Not that she minded train travel, not at all, for not having a car of her own she'd done quite a bit of rail commuting and she could see how far less stressful it was than hacking up the M5 and M6 - and as far as she knew

Donald's only vehicle was the comfortably shabby four-wheel drive Landover vehicle left way up in the Lakes. It must cost him a small fortune in taxi fares to get around London but no doubt cheaper - and quicker - than housing a car in the city.

'I'd love it - but wouldn't Sarah mind?'

'Why should she?'

'Doesn't she have some say in what goes on at the place?'

He gave her an eyebrows-lifted quizzical expression. 'She may be my daughter, but she doesn't own the place. Not yet,' and in that comment was an underlying thought of maybe reneging on the sale concept - brought on by this slip of a girl. 'No, you don't have to worry. You can sleep in the shepherd's hut as before.'

'I might not want to come back,' she said.

'No Italian trip then?'

'Ah. Um. Would you mind?'

'After taking the trouble to ingratiate you with Booth and show you some - most - of my inner secrets? Of course I'd mind. Anyway, I've gotten used to having you about. Helps to fill a void.'

Paula felt the outreach of his barely disguised sadness, a part of his past that would always be there or so she assumed, a situation she'd never want to be in, losing a love so close, so engrained in one's consciousness. How long had it been now? Two months or so? He didn't speak of his past life quite as much now, though she knew Mary was always present in his mind, in the way he acted, the occasional word, the reflective look she'd occasionally see that would change to a small smile, perhaps a lift of eyebrows, whenever he saw her catch a glimpse of this introspection. The problem was, freely admitted within herself, that she'd grown so very close to him it was difficult, nigh impossible, to curb the instinct to offer him more hugs, for when they did hug, she felt stirrings she rightly shouldn't have, feelings, deeper feelings, for an older man and a recently widowed one at that.

She reached for the coffee pot and steadily poured herself another cup. 'More coffee?' she asked. 'And thank you for the compliment. I hope I won't disappoint.'

She got the routine grin back with his comment. 'I hope so too, or else I won't get much return on my investment. And no more coffee, thanks, I'm hyper enough already. Today we get the decision from the

States, it'll be go or no go. If it's go we'll be in Italy this time next week, so let's make the best of the weekend, eh? Walk the footpath again? Dinner in the pub?'

'Sounds good.'

'Right. Time we went to work.'

Once behind the desk she'd been given in Donald's office and continuing to flesh out the drawings he'd given her - her artistic skills seemed to more than satisfy the system - she could sense the atmosphere. Crunch time. Would the parent company's bosses give the assembled crew the go-ahead for the colossal spend on the feature that everyone hoped for? She knew Annette as the 'leading lady' had a tremendous amount of clout and, from the convivial - overly convivial - evening at Claridges, also knew that lady wanted Booth's production company to have the job. The alternative would be to lose it back to the States, and she could understand how that would be a crying shame. The outfit Booth had put together appeared to be highly motivated, well regarded, and Donald's attitude was one of quiet satisfaction. Maybe he'd see it as a tribute to his Mary, for she and her small but highly professional bunch would no doubt have been Booth's definite 'First Unit' choice. Over the mere ten days she'd been allied to the production company she'd met a few from Mary's original team now led by Peter: if the opportunity had arisen, each and every one had acknowledged her skill as Producer and admitted their own feelings of personal loss. A humbling thought, that she was so close to it all and Donald's personal confidante, a realisation she had a special role to play and aware it could go wrong if she didn't perform to his exacting standard. In this situation she wasn't a foolish flounce of a light-headed female, she felt part of the unit, with an obligation to fulfil.

Around mid-morning came the expected summons to the main office conference room where all the important people could gather without crowding. She joined the mix of a dozen or so, accepted by most now she'd been here for a week or more, and watched the exchange of smiles or grimaces, echoes of concern or optimism according to discipline and depth of involvement or personal interest that went swirling around her. Donald, Booth, Peter who she knew as the First Unit producer or the chief camera guy, Jon the script editor, and a few others whose names she'd yet to get off pat stood around at one end of the room; an air of anticipation hung over them like a diasmic cloak. Then the door at the end opened and in walked Annette and Ronald, together with an elderly man she'd not seen before. The room fell silent.

The elderly man known only as JK raised a hand. 'Boys and gals,' he said in an American soft drawl, 'I've just flown in from the States 'specially to greet all you guys and compliment you on the proposition that Booth's sent over. Our project - launched together with this wonderful little lady here,' and he caught Annette's hand to briefly hold it in the air, 'we've agreed,' looking at Ronald and getting his nodded smile, 'will be produced by you all based here in the U.K.' and the assemblage started to clap until he raised his hand once more, 'but largely to be shot on location in Italy as suggested by Donald,' he nodded in his direction, 'our brilliant Art Director. It'll be a fitting tribute too, to the sad loss of his wife, one of most respected unit directors we've ever worked with; we'll make darned sure her name goes on the credit roll. Guys, you have the job.'

The group clapped again, a few whistles from the younger ones, a few pats on backs, but Paula's eyes were on Donald; she felt for him, his loss being brought into the foreground in this way. She saw him blink a time or three, and experienced the same prick of eyes she knew he'd be having. Mary, the woman who, in her undeserved early death had unwittingly given her, an unknown young female, this role of supporter to a widowed husband, a woman who must have felt the greatest depth of love possible, still acknowledged and thought of with respect by this motley crew. Would she, a girl who'd stupidly told silly stories about how she'd squandered her virginity and adolescent passion on a ne're-do-well guy, ever be able to genuinely offer - and experience reciprocation - the profundity of such a bond?

❧

Donald's own professionalism kept him dry eyed, but it had been a struggle. The strength of the unspoken but very real support for his position had been palpable, the added multiple of thoughts from the gathering being something he couldn't have put into words. He'd felt Paula's eyes on him but hadn't dared look back at her. Intuition told him of her reaction and he purposely left her alone while he could.

During the successive buffet lunch already prepared and waiting on the side tables, there were voiced plaudits, some belated sympathetic noises; a nod, a shoulder tap acknowledgement and an expected *sotto voce* instruction from Booth; a smile and a cheek-to-cheek kiss from Annette, a handshake and a brief 'you do a good job now', a typical Americanism from this guy JK, the representative of the parent distribution company in the States; a few random chats with others of the unit and then ultimately he was free. In the seven minutes it took him to escape from the conference room, walk the corridors and return to his office, he managed to recover his equilibrium.

Paula, unremarked, had earlier, taut with emotion, walked slowly back to the same office as soon as she could, in the hope no-one would catch her before the potential tears had a chance to subside. She was already sitting at her desk, head down, cradled in her arms and did not stir when he entered the room.

'Paula?'

She didn't answer, though he thought he heard a sob. Crying? But why? He stood behind her, stroked her hair, put his hands on her shoulders and kneaded her - taut - muscles. 'Paula, why?'

Another sob, a muffled small voice, barely heard. 'I wish I'd known Mary.'

'Ah.' A moment's silence. 'I wish she'd have known you too,' then admitted his belief. 'Perhaps she does, Paula. I'm sure her spirit is watching, listening, keeping an eye.' . . . *her bright still-burning spirit alive in the cosmos somewhere. His solid faith kept that aspect going, that indefinite belief in the unbelievable . . . unexpressed in religious terms but there, nonetheless.* 'Let's go home. We've a film to shoot. Italy calls. I've had my orders. We go on Tuesday.'

That got her roused; she spun the chair round and faced him, eyes wide and reddened. '*Tuesday?*'

'Yep. But just you and I. It's called 'reconnoitring'. So we can be sure we have everything in place for the crews. It's what art directors do all the time, prepare the ground. I normally take a couple of admin guys but,' and he reached to stop her fumbling hands in a scrumpled up skirt, 'you're much better looking and *very* efficient so it'll be cheaper.'

'Whereabouts? And do we fly, then?'

'Nope, Eurostar and, so we can see Sarah, we'll have the promised stopover in Paris as my perk. In the meantime, we'll have a quick trip to Beckside for the quiet pastoral lull before the Mediterranean storm.

Let's go home,' he repeated and pulled her up from her chair. 'What say we have a celebratory high tea? Fish and chips?'

She could find a laugh then, with an inward rush of relief. This man cared for her, treated her as a lady - or perhaps more as a girl friend with no connotations and she loved him. Mary must love *her* too; she was beginning to sense this comforting feel of a spiritual presence around her. And Donald had used the word 'home' in a way that embraced her usage of the place, so were the pangs of the deep physical loss he'd experienced beginning to dullen?

'I'm not sure fish and chips deserve the cachet of 'celebratory', Donald, but I can see some sense. I'm happy,' and what an understatement that was despite her previous tearfulness. 'I think you are too.'

He raised eyebrows in the appealing way he had. 'Why shouldn't I be? The shoot agreed, JK uttering nice words, and I've a lovely lady to keep me company. What more could a man want?'

A light hearted statement, Paula thought but, with her new-found awareness of the way he thought, one still with undertones of submerged sadness.

They asked the taxi-driver about the best fish and chip shop that'd be open at this time of day, duly got him to stop off and finally reached the apartment by a late teatime. Sitting and eating out of the chippie's wrapping paper on the polystyrene platters somehow didn't seem to matter, but gave her an oddly proprietorial sense of being rightly there, not merely a guest or an interloper in another woman's domain. No conversation, just a quiet munching and rustling of paper.

'You're awfully good to me,' she felt she had to say to break the silence now she was down to the last mouthful.

Donald swallowed his last chip and screwed up the paper. 'You're welcome,' he said, in true waiter-like simple style. 'Had enough? Fancy a drink - tea, coffee or something stronger?'

She stood up, collected his debris to add to her own and moved into the kitchen to stuff it into the bin. 'I'll put the kettle on. It's too early for alcohol.'

'Good girl. Is that common sense or a reformed character speaking?'

'Bit of both. I'd like tea. Shall I make a pot?'

'Do. That's fine. Then I'm going to fling a few things together for Tuesday. We'll pop back to office in the morning and round up all we'll need from there, then hightail it to Euston. That okay?'

'What should I pack?'

'Not a lot. Whatever a girl needs, I guess. Silk stockings, lipstick, high heels . . .,' he was laughing at her. 'Common sense will say, and you're exhibiting a fair deal of that.'

'I hope you won't regret taking me.'

'So do I. But provided you do as you're told and exhibit girlish charm whenever it's needed, there shouldn't be a problem.'

Most of the rest of the evening they spent doing as he'd suggested, sorting and packing for two trips, one up north for the weekend, another to start them off for the unspecified time in Italy. There was one holdall between them for Beckside, one each for Italy. There'd been another of those oh-so-special moments when the logistics of what bags they could use was considered and he'd simply said 'put your things in with mine' so her little pile of girly essentials went alongside his stuff. With every small gesture like that she felt the bond between them strengthening, the undoubted rapport tightening, and alongside it produced an ache, a desire to become his in every precious way but it also came with a commonsense realisation that might never happen.

After a bits-and-pieces late supper, using up left-overs from the fridge that wouldn't keep, there came *that* moment when she lifted out of her chair, gave him a soft 'goodnight' kiss on a cheek and went to her room leaving him to check the door locks and switch out the lights, an accustomed routine. It didn't take her a moment to strip, find her nightdress, slip into the comfortable bed and close her eyes. She'd never normally had a problem about sleeping.

Donald picked up his novel. Reading a chapter or two quietened his mind for this was the time of an evening when he most missed Mary, a time they always had together after the pressures of their days. She'd read more slowly than he did and frequently back-tracked. Paula, he'd noticed, didn't seem to read much, which was rather a pity because it allowed the brain to re-boot itself, looking at a different world; maybe he'd be able to encourage her whilst they were away. The story wasn't as gripping as he'd hoped; his attention wandered. Mary would always take a story as it came and read a book diligently end to end. He often skimmed to reach the better bits. The pages turned, the paragraphs speed read, his mind jittered. Why, oh why had Mary succumbed? The pain, the dull ache, swirled back. '*Mary,*' he whispered, '*Mary, I love you still.*'

'*But you have Paula!*' Instantly he heard her voice in his mind, as though she'd been waiting for him.

'*I can't cheat on our love.*'

Did he imagine her soft laugh? '*You can't make love to a spirit girl, Donald, my dearest.*'

'*I miss you.*'

'*I'm always going to be with you in spirit.*'

'*Not the same.*'

Silence, then:

'*Don't stint your ability to make the girl happy, Donald, follow your inclinations. I don't mind. Treat her as you would me.*'

His eyes closed, he saw Mary as he loved her, the ravishment giving her an ethereal glow. How could he ever not hold these precious moments dear, sacrosanct?

'*Remember what I said, Donald. You're too nice a man to be wasted on a spirit. I'll guide you when you need guidance, but you never needed much help when it came to giving a girl what she wanted ...*' he heard her Welsh lilt and the sexy little chuckle.

'*Mary, oh Mary, why did you leave me?*'

Another chuckle. '*So you could provide what another needy girl wants? Go on, Donald, don't be afraid . . .*' and then it was if she'd glided silently away, into a spirit - spirit? - world.

He sat silently for minutes, wondering, getting cold, as though the heating had gone off though of course it wasn't even on. Bedtime; and a brief but deep-felt thought on how much he craved the feel of his wife's warmth alongside, a woman's warmth and the need to share.

For a chance moment he considered what many another opportunist would have seen as the obvious next move. The girl had already - perhaps unconsciously - sent out 'come-hither' signals though he knew they'd been part of her feminine make-up, an instinctive aspect of who she was; he was under no illusions that with the exchange of a simple word or two, a gesture of invitation, and she'd be in his bed. A warm living woman, lovable, very lovable, sharing a natural inclination to enjoy a basic human need. But love? What deeper significance had there been betwixt he and Mary, the *je ne sais quoi* that kept them together and indifferent to all random sexually driven pulls apparent to so many others in the oddly unconcerned incestuous world they moved in? Whatever it was, it was still there, holding him in thrall to her memory, her spirit, despite the ethereal protestation he shouldn't be 'wasted'. Paula? Was he being fair to her, having more or less taken her off the streets and into his world without much of a consideration over the subsequent reaction? True, she had filled a necessary slot in the system at exactly the right time, though there may have been many another aching to fill the role. True, all those weirdly spiritual conversations with his deceased wife's soul had encouraged him but he still couldn't bring himself to the point of commitment for he was, and he pulled a wry grin, too honest about life's requirements.

Tomorrow he'd take her back to where he found her, seek some clarification in his head and possibly allow her, too, to reassess whether this rapport should continue. So far it'd been too easy for him to welcome her into his life when there was an aching void and, apparently, she'd had a hole in her life waiting for the right man to come along and plug the gap. Was he that right man, was she the right girl? Quandary.

Mary's Legacy   9

'It'll be easier to take the bag with us, Paula, rather than come back here. The Italian ones we'll leave until after the Lakes trip.'

She'd cooked breakfast, even made a passable job of the coffee. Donald might well have felt redundant if she'd not exhibited the pleasant way on her that had intuitively attracted him in the first place, that momentous late afternoon up on Beckside's hill. Between them they washed up, put everything away, tidied the flat and then it was time to go.

'All set?'

She nodded. 'All set. Another chapter.'

'Some book.'

She grinned back at him as they went down the stairs. 'Best seller. Let's hope the film gets a nomination.'

'Huh. It's not that type of plot.' He opened the street door. 'Films that reach the dizzy heights of a nomination aren't always nice to watch. Like your "best seller" novel, sold on reputation and cover name, not on content.' He let her slide past him and closed the door, doing a recall of the same action a couple of months ago when alone, and he'd set out on the Beckside journey which had brought Paula into his life.

'Cynic,' she said.

'Life makes you cynical.'

'Donald,' and she tucked her arm into his as they set off towards the main road and the prospect of a cruising taxi, 'don't brood. Please. You're lots more fun when you don't.'

'Is that what you expect? Loads of fun? Paula, I find it difficult sometimes not to realise life's different without my wife. Don't get me wrong, I'm not criticising you, but . . .'

'Sorry,' she said. 'I suppose I'm overly flippant, being the hard nosed creature I am. Maybe we're both cynics.'

'Maybe. Perhaps that's why we get on so well.'

She stopped, bringing him to a halt with the bag swinging in his free hand. 'Do we get on, Donald? You're not just being kind for the sake of it? Please, tell me?' and her eyes searched his face. 'Please?'

They stood still, in the middle of a London pavement, with the ceaseless traffic running past and the scurrying commuters swerving inscrutably around them. He leant down and kissed her, briefly, lightly, on the lips. 'Give me time, Paula. Give me time,' then he spotted a taxi and waved. 'We've a job to do. Then we'll see.'

అ

The morning went past in a blur as they had meeting after meeting; logistics, wardrobe, timing, and a late change of a second string actor after Booth had a chance to show how hard-nosed and managerial he could be towards someone not toeing the line. Paula quailed, hearing his tirade, and hoped she'd never be the subject of his wrath. She'd been relegated to note-taker at one meeting and vowed she'd never apply for a secretarial job. Back in the office for a very quick sandwich stolen from the buffet table at the last meeting of the morning she endeavoured to make sense of her scribbles. How long before they left? Donald had disappeared with Booth and another guy she'd not seen before and she'd no idea where he'd gone.

She rewrote the crucial bits, gave the paragraphs bullet point numbers, read the pages through and prayed they'd be right. It was all to do with which actor needed to be where and when, to coincide with the best use of the unit's camera time. Slack had to be built in too, and Donald had explained this free time sometimes allowed him the chance to organise background shots, often used to pad out the thinner sequences. Now the go-ahead had been given, the pace had hustled along; there was a deeper sense of urgency, almost as if the unit had changed gear from 'coasting' to 'drive'.

The door opened. 'Ready?' and Donald grinned at her. 'We'll cut and run before Booth gets another mad idea. He's just suggested we move the reconciliation scene to Milan instead of in Rome. That other guy you saw us with? He's got business interests there and, when there's money, there's pressure. So Milan it is. No worries. Got everything down? Lock it away, girl. Let's go.'

He seemed loads happier, Paula thought. Maybe because the project is coming together, or maybe it's because we going up to the Lakes. She clipped the loose pages of her notes, dropped them into a pocket folder and slid it into the desk drawer. Locked, she pocketed the key, giving her another little buzz of confidence, being given this level of responsibility. Nothing here was like her previous mundane job where boredom drowned out all interest.

They walked through the reception area; Pat the girl who'd first given her the security pass waved and said 'have a good weekend' with the broadest of grins, Donald pushed open the swing door and Paula expected a taxi, but no, it was one of unit's plush grey Mercedes.

'Booth said we could,' he explained, ''cos he likes you.'

'Gracious,' she exclaimed, as the driver opened the car's door for her. 'I'd almost believe I was starring.'

She slid across the back seat, tucked her work-a-day cord skirt over her knees and Donald sat alongside. The door closed, the driver got back in, the car started to move. 'You are,' he said.

'I am what?' she asked, not comprehending.

'Starring,' Donald replied.

'What?' She couldn't be hearing right.

'Starring,' he repeated. 'I said about Milan? We'll be using the Grand Arcade, the Gallerie, for the reconciliation scene like I said, but we needed a particular girl to be a distraction. Booth suggested you. So there you are. Happy?'

'But I've never done any acting, ever.'

'Yes you have.'

'What makes you say that?'

'Your fib over getting pregnant. Sorry, Paula, but Booth insisted on checking - we have our ways. Your continuation of employment here wasn't just on my say-so. He nearly had you thrown out when your former employer let slip you must have fabricated the story. I wasn't surprised, because I'd not really thought of you being that sort of a girl.

I had to convince him I'd sponsor you, and it's true, he does actually like you. So you're forgiven, but no more stories, eh?'

'Oh.'

'Is that all? Just 'oh'? No 'Sorry Donald, I was spinning a story just to get back into your life?''

She stared down into the car's footwell. It had been true about her boss and her, always at loggerheads, a consequence of professional jealousy. Ultimately the moment came when she'd snapped, chucked the job and walked out, realised what she'd done and instinctively sought help - or comfort - from the man she'd seen as a role model. What could she say? That she'd been foolish; fabricating the pregnancy story, but it'd been a last minute stupid idea to appeal to his better nature? She'd never once had a man in her bed, believing, maybe oddly old-fashioned, that virtue had its own rewards, and instead she'd spun a lie. Would he forgive her? He must have, otherwise she wouldn't be here. What could she say now?

He reached for her hand. 'Paula, there's a lesson for you to learn here, I think. Thank Mary. And Booth. And your former boss who wanted you back despite your row. I wouldn't let you go, anyway. There's one blessing however - the knowledge that you didn't have an abortion. Not what a nice girl should ever have the slightest cause to consider.'

She could feel tears coming. Why did this man affect her so? 'Sorry,' she whispered, and felt his hand squeeze. 'I'm so sorry.'

'Would you have told me?'

Yes, she'd have told him, when the time was right. Now he knew, maybe things would be different? Better? Closer? Or more distant? She felt small, insignificant, unworthy, a little soiled.

'I don't deserve this,' she said, repeating herself.

He grinned, reached over to lift her chin and make her look at him. 'I think,' he said carefully, 'you've just run up a rock and fallen off. And I'm the guy who's picked you up. I hope there are no lasting ill effects. Let's say no more about it; enjoy the weekend.'

The driver knew where to go, parked as close to the station entrance as any vehicle could get and, in true chauffeur style, had the door open for them and the bag hoisted out. 'Have a good weekend,' he said with an uncomplicated smile.

'Thanks,' and Donald returned the grin, 'we'll try, provided it doesn't rain,' picked up his bag in one hand and guided Paula's elbow with the other.

'I'm spoilt rotten,' she said. 'Never been chauffeured before.'

'Ah well, you have to know the right people. Come on, we've a train to catch.'

'Tickets?'

'In my pocket. Pre-booked, courtesy of our Pat.'

She gave him an old-fashioned look. 'If I didn't know you better,' she said darkly, 'I'd imagine you're accustomed to this routine.'

'This is a journey frequently undertaken, Paula. So yes, it's a practised routine.'

He held a deadpan expression and she bit her lip. Ouch, she thought, I've been thoughtless again. 'Sorry.'

Donald shrugged dismissively. 'This way,' and guided her towards the usual place, the familiar platform. A re-run of two months ago, with one essential difference, he had a girl at his side once more, and one with whom he felt, happily, at ease. *'Well done you,'* - was that Mary's voice in his brain?

Seated opposites, he watched her as the train began to move. Nestled down into her seat, eyes closed, hands in her lap, she looked as if sleep wouldn't be far away. Facial muscles relaxed, with long dark hair now straggled, blouse awry, every inch like the Mary he'd lost in all but a different face. What had he done to deserve this change in his fortunes? After all the pain and tension, the stress and sleepless times, watching his past life unravel with every slow deprivation of Mary's vibrancy dim her former vivacious being into the grey of the shadows, trying to accept every aspect of the joy between them was slipping away, knowing he'd be alone, alone . . .

But he wasn't. He had another woman, a girl, to look after, someone who needed an arm round her shoulders, someone to guide her footsteps along a pathway through this labyrinthine life, a girl who'd slipped into his life within days of the finality of the loss of his previous love. Mary had died. Left him with a ghastly hollowness she'd told him to fill, told him to find another girl. Was Paula that girl?

The familiar backdrop of trackside scenery slipped by, the gentle sway of the carriage as they accelerated out of the metropolis an odd comfort. He closed his eyes, tried to relax and let the residual tension slacken. Over a month, well, nearly two. Paula. Paula. Mary. Paula . .

Mary's Legacy 10

They made good time, or to be more accurate, the journey went to plan. They changed at Carlisle, managed to find decent seats on the local train despite it being the start of a weekend with all the associated seekers after outdoor recreational pursuits, and eventually got out onto the local halt platform amongst the flurry of rucksack burdened walking enthusiasts.

'Whew! Look at them all! And to think I could have been part of that lot.' Paula sought Donald's hand. 'This weekend has a much better feel to it, thanks to you. No Youth Hostel bed - though they are better than they used to be.'

Her bright, earnest, face, the warmth of her clasp, the awareness of her vitality, the knowledge he had of her comforting attitude and her never ceasing appreciation of how he'd given her a new slice of life; all welcoming features of this, the return to Beckside with a woman at his side. A woman at his side, just as it always had been. *Well, Mary, is this what you'd expected?*

'Shepherd's hut?' he pulled her round to face him. This was the moment when he could fall prey to the always-present temptation that had continued to hover like a spectre at his shoulder ever since the day she'd asked to come back to the cottage. *I'm available;* her feminity was saying, loud and clear, even if her personality denied the obvious. *Or my bed* his instinctive masculinity was asking despite the strength of his resolution. *Go on, ask her,* Mary was saying, daring him.

Standing on the station platform, gazing into each other's eyes, wasn't this the corniest thing out?

'I,' and she stopped; her look left him, dropped to the paving.

'Yes?'

'Promised.' She turned her gaze sideways, towards the backdrop of the hills. 'Not yet,' she said, and pulled away, began to walk towards the exit. 'We need to shop, don't we?' she flung back at him.

He strode after her; the tense moment evaporated, but another would occur, and another, like clouds across the sun. The swing of her skirt, the flounce of dark hair, the . . . girl she was. *Not yet.* The promise? To honour Mary's memory. They must collect the Discovery and do the shopping and . . .

✆

The familiar, the routine, like the old happy days when they'd shopped, driven up to the cottage, unlocked, switched the power back on, filled the kettle, wound the clock, opened a window or two, lit the stove, argued - discussed - what to cook for supper, enjoyed a glass of wine . . . *gone to bed* . . . it felt as though Mary had never died, merely taken on a different *personae*. This was weird, and it was happening. The cottage still had the overtones of twenty plus years of lovely times. She filled the role perfectly in all but the one aspect.

'Paula?'

'Donald?'

The thoughts tumbled round his head, the whole conglomeration of circumstances. She sat the other side of the table, as Mary had. She'd helped shop, cook, shared the meal, smiled at him, casual, shapely, *lovable. As a Mary would have been* - and he ached for her, for the feel of her, the expectation of a sharing of the best of emotive feelings. The voice in his head . . . *You've a long way to go, Donald, if you are going to truly love the girl . . .*

'Shall we walk off the supper? Go up the hill? We've an hour till dusk.'

'So long as we don't see an idiot falling off a rock,' and she was grinning at him, aware of the trace of a known euphemism.

'One's enough,' he replied, 'there's a limit to my resources.'

'Don't regret it?'

He gave her an eye-narrowed look. 'So far so good, Paula.' She didn't need to change into walking gear, her sensible tweedy skirt would be perfectly adequate for a stroll; he'd no intention of moving

74

beyond the property's fence line. 'But I'm going to tell Sarah we're here. She likes to know that the place is still okay.'

'You're a very good dad to her. Mine very rarely makes contact nowadays.'

'It's a two way thing, Paula; surely you can phone him?'

She pulled a face. 'Not that easy. Celina's partner acts as housekeeper, she answers the phone and she doesn't like me.'

'Ah. Um. I see. Perhaps you should write, the good old fashioned thing, you know, stamps and envelopes and so on?'

She laughed. 'I send him a birthday card, he sends me one. Don't worry, I'm not. You calling Sarah?'

'Provided the signal's okay.' He pulled the mobile out and looked. 'Sometimes is, sometimes isn't. Okay at the moment.' What should he say? She knew Paula had moved in. There'd been no snide comments for she wasn't that sort of girl; she'd know he was doing his best for Paula. '*Back to Beckside, all okay. Away Italy Tues. How's you? Love, D.*' Tap, tap, message sent.

Paula had moved to the window. 'It may rain. Cloud's low. Shall we go?'

'Yep. Grab your coat.'

'Don't think I'm going without it, do you? We'll wash up when we get back.'

'Right.' She was organising him, becoming proprietorial. No matter.

They followed the track up through the woods, the familiar pathway, overgrown but still usable. Not until they neared the top field when the track widened could she walk alongside. The view across the meadow opened up. The wild flowers were all but over. As before, they leant on the gate, side by side. No walkers visible on the pathway this evening. Scarcely any wind; the dark clouds hung; suggested a threat of rain. The silence folded down around them.

'I love the peacefulness of the place,' Paula dropped a soft comment into the stillness. 'Especially after London. What'll it be like in Italy?'

He turned round, rested his back on the gate and elbows on the top rail, gazed back down the track, remembering, seeing a ghostly image. 'Hectic, mostly. There'll be some slack now and then.'

She looked sideways at him. 'You really don't mind me hanging about, Donald? I mean, we've been constant companions for a fortnight now. You're not bored with me?'

'Paula, if we didn't get on, would you be here? No, I'm not bored with you. I could ask the same question. If you'd somewhere else to go and another job, would you stay around?'

She scuffed her shoes in the soil, looked down at the pattern she'd created, then back to him. 'I'm living with you, Donald. Does it bother you? What do your friends say about me? Am I an embarrassment, seen as a good-time girl, an easy lay?'

He shook his head. 'Nope. You don't embarrass me. I decided to offer you a get-out from your problems, 'cos it was something I wanted to do. It's worked out fine, hasn't it? You've helped me, enormously. And,' he reached round and took her by the shoulders, looked straight at her, 'I've never felt more at home with another woman before, apart from . . .'

'Mary,' she said unhesitatingly.

He nodded. 'Mary.' He leant forward, offered her a light kiss then let her go. 'I have a feeling she likes you. And that's good enough for me.'

'I'm a little - a lot - younger.'

'Which makes you special. Can you imagine me offering an internship to someone my age? They'd want to take over. An art director can be very egotistical.'

'So I'd noticed. Not that it's a problem,' she hastened to add. 'One thing though. You haven't given me the impression of being a very social sort of guy. You've not wanted to parade me, show me off in front of a bunch of cronies, apart from the film lot, so either you're shy or you're hiding me away. We don't go clubbing.'

'Do you want to go clubbing?'

'No!' The vehement reply surprised him. 'I'm a reformed character, remember. This is my real world. Out in the countryside, looking after myself - well . . .' she grimaced. 'You know what I mean. And having a father figure to look up to reminds me of the good times when we were a proper family. I miss that. Really miss that,' and was that a catch in her voice?

He'd relaxed back onto the gate alongside her. 'It feels odd, you know, keeping company with someone who could be a daughter but isn't. Not quite sure what you'd call our relationship. It's not truly father to daughter, it's not purely a man and woman thing, it's not merely a boss cum employee either. A mixture of everything.'

'Does it worry you?'

'Nope,' he said, repeating himself. Could he bring himself to be more definitive? This is where he'd first seen her, striding across the pasture, the two younger girls trailing behind her, walking into his life. If she hadn't appeared then, what would have happened? Didn't bear thinking about. No, she was a present from heaven, a present from Mary. Had he fallen for her? Did she mean any more to him than any other vulnerable girl who might need some support, support he was able to offer? *Let time flow, Donald, let time flow, and don't prejudge the issue, the depth of the feeling between you and her.* One thing was certain; she must feel something of the same conflicts of emotion as he did. 'Shall we go back?'

'Okay. What'll we do tomorrow?'

'Depends on the weather, but I'd like to do my 'get to the top of the hill' thing.'

'Fine by me.

'Right then,' he pushed himself off the gate, held out a hand for her. 'Got the washing up to do when we get back. Happy?'

She allowed herself to be pulled towards him; the inevitable hug, a reprise, a suspension of time as they swayed together, relishing the closeness, the companionship, the awareness of each other, each in their own need. *Let time flow . . .* and they walked on, down the track, hand in hand.

∽

'Sarah's not come back to you?' Paula polished the last clean plate, put it back on the shelf, hung the tea towel over the bars on the top of the stove and tipped the bowl of water down the sink, wiped it round.

Donald had watched her efficiency in fascination, almost with adoration. He pulled his phone out of the jacket pocket, stared at it. 'She has actually. Sent a text message and I didn't hear the phone chirp.' He read it out loud: "*I'm fine, hectic, glad B-S's okay. You're not alone? Love, S x*"

'Oh dear, she's found you out, shacked up with another girl!' She was grinning, pulling his leg. 'Whatcha gonna say to that?'

'Tell her the truth. And I don't like the description 'shacked-up', Paula. Too suggestive. We're not seekers after lust. Are we?'

She coloured up, the first time he'd really seen her blush. 'Sorry Donald. I didn't mean it like that. You know what I meant.'

He grinned back at her. 'Yes,' and tapped away. "*Paula's here, my domestic goddess. Making sure I survive. Speak tomo, arrange see you Paris. L o l, xx*" He read it out to her.

'I'm a goddess now, am I? Ha ha. She'll love that.'

'It'll certainly make her smile. Now, miss, it's past your bedtime. You'll be okay in the hut?'

'Absolutely.' She picked up her coat and slung it round her shoulders. 'I'll leave my things here. See you in the morning,' and he got another light kiss, an acknowledgment.

She closed the back door behind her, he heard the footsteps fade. The room felt empty, hollow, though not quite meaningless. Mary's spirit was still with him, providing a reassurance, a comforting cloak, granting him the strength to maintain that most important of emotions, love. *Love . . . yes; yes he had to be honest, had to admit she was fast growing on him . . .*

78

Mary's Legacy 11

Where was she? The sound of rain, persistent rain drumming on the ceiling - no, not a ceiling . . . oh! Miles away from the familiar - tucked away in the Lakes, a very wet Lake District. Realisation trickled in, like the water cascading down the small window alongside her bedspace. Cosily wrapped up in the sleeping bag, she'd slept well, perhaps too well? What time? Daylight certainly but grey, grey, unpleasantly dim. Shepherd's huts, on warm summer evenings or bright sunlit mornings, may be a delight; but this morning, um, perhaps it might have been better to have borrowed Sarah's bijou room in the cottage. Time to make a move.

She scrambled into her tweedy skirt, pulled on the sweater, shook the bag out, rolled it up, returned it to its shelf. Unworried by the rain, she ran, but the few hundred yards back to the cottage got her soaked by heavy drips from the trees on top of the deluging shower.

The cottage door was ajar; she nearly slipped on the mat.

'Paula, dear girl, there's an umbrella behind the door of the hut . . .' Donald, already up and obviously organised, grinned at her. 'Do you want a bath? There'll be just about enough hot water?'

She shook her hair out and promptly sprayed him with wet. 'And we said we'd go for a walk!'

'It'll clear up. Rain before seven, fine at eleven, so the old wives' tale goes.' He moved across to the window. 'Look, there's a break in the cloud. Let's have breakfast.'

'Got a towel handy first?'

He reached behind the door to the toilet and produced a grubby hand towel. 'Yuck. I'll nip up for a clean one. One moment,' and he disappeared.

She didn't hesitate, peeled off the damp sweater, undid a zip and stepped out of the skirt, to drape them over a chair in front of the stove. The hand towel she used to vigorously scrub her hair dry. He came down to a scantily clad girl with tousled hair. It didn't daunt her, for after all, he'd once put her to bed when incapable . . . He held the clean towel out to her wordlessly, dropped into his armchair and waited while she rubbed at legs and arms.

'Thanks.' She grinned at him. 'Just as well Sarah can't see me - us.'

'She's broad minded, but I know what you mean. If it's any consolation, Paula, you scrub up well . . .'

She threw the towel at him, covering his face. 'Just as well I know you.'

'True,' and unfazed, he gathered it up, folded it and placed it on the other chair. 'How long are you going to stay like that? Your kit's upstairs in my bag. Want me fetch anything?'

'No, I'll go. Don't let my skirt singe.'

'Okay.'

He watched her go, the long naked legs, smooth unblemished thighs, the taut stomach, the well-proportioned full breasted body, and blessed his good fortune in having found a lovely lady who didn't have any of the weird hang-ups about day-to-day happenings like some he knew. A natural girl, with no out-of-the ordinary inhibitions, able to withstand life's rigours and still come out smiling when it didn't quite turn out right. And he'd helped the girl to reach this point. He felt humble and at the same time, proud. She was his salvation.

A couple of minutes later she returned properly dressed, the now familiar maroon cashmere top with its embroidered 'P' over a lightweight linen or cotton skirt in a sort of limestone colour, hair brushed out and silky after its wetting. She twirled. 'Better? Not exactly colour co-ordinated but it's all I've got, other than my walking kit.'

'I know, I helped pack.'

'So you did. So . . .?' The question hung.

'It's still raining. We could drive out somewhere, or sit and read.'

She sank into the other unrestricted armchair, tucked her legs under her, put her head on one side and gazed out of the window. 'This is bliss, Donald. Being where we are, the quiet, the thought that I'm loved, being with you, being . . . oh, I'm a lucky, lucky girl.' Her eyes closed.

He watched her, completely absorbed in the charisma of the captivating concept on view. Without her, where would he be? Her 'quiet' settled around them. Moments like this, precious, unscripted, were all too rare in his world. The professional in him captured the scene, stored it away for the future. Which film, which story?

'I need to eat.' Ever the practical lady, she'd come back to life. 'You mentioned breakfast?'

He stretched, cracked his knuckles. 'Bacon's in the oven. Can't you smell it? Well crisped by now. That and tomatoes? Coffee's made.'

'Yum. I suppose you want me to serve up?'

'In your capacity of domestic goddess, of course.'

She scowled at him. 'What more will you expect me to do? I don't relish becoming house maid.'

'Au pair?' he gave her another speciality grin, stood up and held out a hand to heave her out of the chair. 'Paula, you're growing on me.'

She ducked under his arm to cross over to the stove and picked up the oven mitt. 'I know,' she said, 'and don't think I don't appreciate it. I do, very much so, but I worry about us. You mustn't, Donald.'

'Mustn't what?' He came up behind her as she opened the oven door and brought the bacon tray out.

'Careful!' She turned, he had to step back. She slid the tray onto the top, reached back into the oven for the hot plates. 'Tomatoes?'

'In the microwave. What mustn't I do?'

'Fall in love with me,' she replied in matter of fact tone, reaching up to open the door of the microwave, the only item of modern kitchen equipment that Mary had installed. 'And don't argue because . . .'

He'd waited until the plate of sliced tomatoes was safely on the table before he swept her up in his arms.

She struggled, turning her face away. 'Don't!' and he felt her stiffen. 'Please!'

'Don't what? Hold you? Kiss you?'

Abruptly she let herself flop, sagged into him, to feel his arms tighten round her, to feel his solidarity, his comfort. 'Oh Donald,' she breathed softly, 'we shouldn't, mustn't,' but as she looked up at him, his lips came down on hers and she was lost.

'The breakfast's getting cold,' she managed when she could draw breath.

'Let it,' and he sought her mouth again. Then: 'I have, Paula, I have - and Mary doesn't mind. I can't think otherwise.' He let her go.

Standing there, knowing she'd a flushed face, her hair all straggly, the oddity of the circumstances came in on her. In a backwoods kitchen at breakfast time, with the rain chucking it down, there couldn't have been a more bizarre situation for a declaration - it *was* a declaration? He loved her?

'You have? Have what, fallen in love with me?'

'Truly. Paula, I seem to have,' and he couldn't believe he was saying this, 'fallen in love with you, as a daughter.' Time to be honest with who he was, with Mary, her spirit, with the way life revolved and especially because they were here, at Beckside, where Mary's presence was ever strong. He moved over to the window, watched the pouring rain, thought of the past years, the magical moments, the way life had dealt him the cards still to be played, thought also of the future, the priceless legacy left to him by the only woman he'd ever loved - until now. 'I can't, don't, understand why, but is there ever any logic?'

She followed him, stood behind him, put her arms around him, nestled her head on his shoulder. 'It's never logical. No. But you've recently lost the former love of your life and there's a gap you need to fill. If I'm in the stopgap role as the beloved daughter, then I am, I've no quarrel with that, but I . . .'

He twisted round, held her too, they stood clasped together. 'Do we go on?'

She nodded, gently, simply. 'We go on, Donald. But I'll stay the daughter figure, I think, don't you? While we let time decide?'

'Bless you.' Another gentle kiss. This wasn't tumultuous passion, this was them believing in the possibilities of an abiding, solid, future understanding.

'We'd better have breakfast.'

Their eyes locked in, soul to soul. Then she started to grin, the spell drifting into memory, the moment frozen into time. Theirs; the day, the place, the weather, the time, a moment for ever.

Cold crisped-up bacon went quite well with re-heated tomatoes and toast, rather oddly. The coffee helped.

'It'll be rather different tomorrow.'

'Very true.' Donald drained his mug. 'More?'

She shook her head. 'No. An odd breakfast but memorable. When will we come back?'

He shrugged. 'Once we've got the film 'in the can' as they used to say. Not really appropriate nowadays, not now we film digitally. Lost some of the magic. We don't have 'rushes' either, film once processed in a tearing hurry and fed back to a director by a madcap biker. I suppose it streamlines production but it doesn't feel the same.'

'Who looks after the place when you're not here?'

'There's a woman in the village who has a key, but . . .' and with that Mary's loss came vividly back to cause him to stop, his throat constricted with the emotion. They'd never been away from here for more than a month or two until . . . 'Sorry,' he said, and Paula saw his moistened eyes.

'Donald,' she stretched out a warm hand, took his clenched one from the table and prized open his fingers to hold the hand tight. 'I'm not going to quarrel with how things are, I'm not jealous, I don't want to change you. Please, Donald, if you want to let your feelings show, then do. I,' and this must be another defining moment, 'I love you too, as much as a silly girl like me can love a wonderfully thinking, caring, mature and . . . she struggled to find a better word, 'understanding man.'

Through the distortion of tear-messed-up eyes he saw the assurance in her, the same assurance shown up on the hill with two younger girls trailing behind and an injured person who needed help. Paula, a woman twenty years his junior who was trying to give him the confidence he needed. Why had he succumbed to this expression of emotion when he'd bethought himself strong and firm and able to survive the desperate loss he'd sustained? Was it because he had seen alive in her the same qualities so evident in his marriage to Mary? Or merely because she was available, the first woman to cross his path at the most vulnerable time in his grieving? Time, inevitably, would tell.

She'd let go his hand, stood up and collected the plates, taken them over to the sink. He had a chance to stabilise his thoughts, get back into an organising mode and recover his equilibrium.

She washed; he dried, with not a word spoken for there wasn't any need. The newly declared understanding wrapped round them was all powerful - was it sufficient to prevent any further delving into overly philosophical aspects of who they were, what was going on between them?

'Right-oh. So now what?'

He peered out of the window. 'Maybe it's eased off. I can see a small patch of blue out there.'

She joined him, caught a hand. 'Ever the optimist. So we go out for a stroll and risk getting wet?'

He nodded, squeezed and let go. 'Yeah, why not? Can't see us going all that far, but we could go and look at Stu's rock. As a matter of curiosity, how come you got mixed up with that group? You've not mentioned them since.'

'Local outdoor group back home, casual acquaintanceship, nothing serious. The leader guy, Alan, he wanted to pull a group together to get his certificate, so I joined in. I've not heard from him since then.'

'Not surprising. Bit of a waste of time for him.'

'But not for me.'

'No. Little did you know what fate had in store. Not regretted it?'

She picked up his hand again. 'What do you think?'

They were talking like teenagers, checking up on a blind date. 'Doesn't matter what I think, Paula. What matters is that you're happy and how it's turned out for you.'

'It's turned out fine, and before this gets out of hand, Donald, we're stopping all this analytical stuff. I, we, have started something between us, it's lovely, it's fantastic fun and I for one want it to carry on. So shut up and let's go out.'

There, he was being told. She grinned at him; inwardly he had to agree they ran the risk of becoming so introvert that it might wreck the relationship before it had truly begun. Thinking back, how had he and Mary behaved? Digging into the past wouldn't help, but he seemed to remember a few earnest conversations about how the system viewed them, for linking up inside the production team was often frowned upon in those days. If Mary as unit director had seen him and Paula together in the office, would she have made any comment? Stop it, Donald. Introspection isn't going to help.

'Okay,' he said, with another glance up at the cloud bank - was it thinning out?

She shot upstairs, came down in the familiar walking trousers, slung her anorak on, laced up her boots and stood there, watching him taking his time, lacing up his boots in turn.

The path up, past the shepherd's hut, was sludgy under foot, the tall grasses either side bowed down under the wet, the heavy drips from the pines and sycamores plopping down around them, and once the gate had been reached, the wetting drift of an ebbing rain shower obscured the distant line of the hill.

'Evocative, in a strange sort of way,' Paula said, shielding her eyes as she peered across the pasture, 'timeless and primeval.'

'Grey and dark grey, certainly. And very familiar weather; how many believe the Lake District is always blue and green?'

She laughed. 'How many believe Italy is always hot and sunny?'

'Lots. I hope it isn't going to be too hot. I like the sun but not that much. So today will have to be something to remember when you're roasting. Come on,' and he unlatched the gate for her.

They reached the long-distance footpath within the fifteen minutes he'd estimated. 'Familiar?' he asked her.

'Sort of. It's a while since. Autumn's coming.'

'Aye, leaves are turning. Which way? I'd suggest right, to get onto the farm track as a circular hike. If we go left we'd only have to retrace our steps. There's not enough time to go right round the hill nor is it the best of weather either.'

'I agree. So right it is.'

They strode steadily on with the breeze behind them, and the occasional drifts of sun shone through dissipating clouds to help lift otherwise dampened spirits.

'I don't suppose we'll meet anyone else.' Paula commented casting an eye backwards, 'we're probably the only mad people around, though I'm not complaining. I prefer the hills to myself.'

'So should I go back and leave you to it?' suggested Donald in a jocular fashion, grinning across at her.

She threw him a mock-glare. 'As if you would! No, present company is fine. Despite the weather and the recollections, I'm enjoying the day. Just a pity we have to go back tomorrow.'

'No Italian trip?'

She wrinkled her nose. 'Perhaps I'm being selfish, keeping you to myself. It'll be a new experience for me. Alright for you, mister gadabout anywhere.' She also made a point that had been bugging her. 'You've not talked about the film at all this weekend.'

'I learnt early on to compartmentalise, Paula. Otherwise it can get obsessive, take over your life and spoil things. Mary was good at that too. Beckside is - was - a refuge for both us, somewhere we could live proper lives, not make-believe ones, so no, we didn't bring work here - other than sketching out ideas that appeared, as they do.'

She reflected. Yes, he was right. Another pointer to how decent a man he was and she thanked the gods - or was it Mary's spirit - that they'd come together. Would she be worthy of his declared love for her, even if it was a sort of platonically daughter to father one? The days ahead would be challenging and she vowed she'd make the most of them. In the meantime . . .

'We'll have to have something more than a make-believe lunch. I'm working up an appetite.'

'Even after overly crisp bacon?'

She had to laugh. 'Even so. What about the pub?'

'Another half hour - and a longer walk back.'

'Doesn't matter, does it? We've got the rest of the day and evening.'

'Okay, best foot forward.'

The pub wasn't crowded, no surprise there. That Donald was known was very evident, and she was also aware of the scrutiny she got from the bar staff, a demonstratively busty girl and the pleasant guy who could be the landlord. When handed a lunch menu she kept an impassive face; it was up to Donald to satisfy their curiosity. She asked for a 'proper cider' and got a smile from the girl. Donald went for a local brewed beer; got another smile. She ordered a steak and ale pie so Donald added 'make that two' and paid.

'Table by the window?'

'Suits me. Let me pay for drinks . . .'

He put out a hand, 'No, Paula. Ladies don't buy drinks here when in masculine company. It's not done. My treat.'

'You're always treating me.'

'If it bothers you, I'll deduct it from your wages.'

His grin was infectious. 'Rotter,' she said, and slurped at her full glass. 'If I get any,' she added, darkly.

'Oh, you'll get paid, in one form or another.'

'Um. That sounds ominous.'

They sat in companionable silence for as long as it took for the meals to arrive, then the waitress cum bar girl stood poised. 'Not seen you in a while, Donald,' she said, obviously an opening gambit in anticipation of some gossipy tit-bit. The suggestion hovered; perhaps, Paula thought, this girl wasn't aware of Donald's situation. She raised her eyebrows at him interrogatively and got a small shake of his head.

'Been preoccupied,' Donald told the girl. 'You know how it is, things happen.'

He clearly didn't want to make an issue of it, but she felt left on the edge. Would he explain her presence? Then the girl made a faux pas.

'Mary not with you then?'

Her chance. 'You didn't know that Mary died six weeks ago?' she said with a query and an edge in her voice; 'I'm one of Donald's team helping him sort things out. The meals look lovely,' she added, 'thank you so much,' making it plain that was the end of the conversation.

'Oh, I am so sorry, really sorry,' and the girl beat an embarrassed retreat.

Paula didn't look at him, hoped he wouldn't take her input amiss, picked up her knife and fork and attacked her pie with some enthusiasm; breakfast had been a long time ago.

'Thanks,' he said. 'Absolutely right, Paula. Well done. She couldn't be expected to know, we didn't come in here all that often.' He changed the subject. 'Pie's good.'

She nodded, with mouth full. Another hurdle cleared. Part of his team, she'd thought to say and he'd agreed, so now the day seemed somehow brighter. Despite the long journey, the short time here and the weather; maybe it was worth while, adding strength to the foundations of the rapport between them. Another night ahead. Another day tomorrow, then Italy; when would she be back here again?

Donald laid the knife and fork down; his plate cleared, and downed the rest of his pint. 'Right oh girl, onwards, we've an hour and a half to go. Ready?' and held her chair as she stood up.

A 'Cheerio, thanks,' they got from the barman and a wary smile from the girl and that was that. Outside the sun was cautiously strengthening its appearance; the afternoon was ahead of them.

'Better?' he asked as he led the way across the road to a stile and the start of the path that led slantwise down the slope towards the river.

'Yep, it was good. Did I do right?'

Donald nodded. 'Thanks, yes. That was well handled, Paula, very tactful; you make a good p.a.'

'Thank you! Must be the good training I'm getting.'

He gave her a slantways glance. 'Or you're an avid pupil. Keep it up, Paula. Mary would be proud of you.'

How deep had this love of his been? She had accepted his constant references to his lost love, tried to understand the depth of that loss and it made his acceptance of her somewhat naïve presence all the more precious. To comprehend the comparisons made betwixt her and the memory of Mary she just had to let the days flow, aware she'd never give up on him - he'd have to sack her and kick her out first.

They followed the pathway down to the river bank; before it then sheered off to the right and pursued a convoluted twist and turn through the mature beech trees along the bank.

'One of my favourite walks,' Donald's comment surprised her.

'I thought you were a hill-top guy?'

'Yes, but just look at this; river, tree cover, winding pathway, the way it draws you on, with the sound of water, rustling leaves, being almost alone. We often used to wander along here.'

'Romanticism at its best.' She could almost grasp the mood, so tangible, the knowledge that the woman she'd never known had walked this path with this man. The sheer orgasmic pleasure of the association of idea, mood, and place ran electric fizzes down her back, from shoulder blades, along arms, trickled down thighs. 'And now you've brought me here.'

No flicker of emotion, but he reached for her hand. 'Aye, and I'm privileged to do so; not many ladies of my acquaintanceship would take to the idea of a woodland walk in the wet. So thank you.'

'No, Donald, thank *you*. It's me who feels privileged, and certainly it is a lovely place.'

'Better than the proper footpath that everyone walks?'

'But of course, and another good reason why it's nice to be with someone who shares the same ideas as me!'

They walked on, hand in hand, further words unnecessary, enjoying the vestiges of the late afternoon sun as the clouds began to disperse. Ultimately the path's convolutions brought them out of the trees and up onto the pasture again; Paula could see the roof of the cottage in the distance. The river's course followed the valley bottom, twisting away to the left. Another half mile or so.

They'd been away for nearly four hours and she could feel the pull on leg muscles. Donald seemed unfazed, but then, she knew the older one got - up to a point - the easier it was to maintain a standard of fitness. She'd let herself go since that last hike, the one which had certainly changed her life.

He unlocked, let her in first, watched her strip off her jacket. Once more the striking similarity to Mary hit him, the way she pulled her arm out of the sleeves, folded the jacket to hang it up, every move bringing recollections. She could have been a resurrection apart from the hair colour, the shape of her face, more oval, more Italianate, almost too much to bear. He turned away and took the kettle to fill it, to make a brew, to do something, anything. She went into the bijou bathroom; allowing him a moment to bring some sense back into his mind. *Paula, Paula, not Mary* - but Mary was here, in her spirit, in her constant expressed wish . . . *find a girl who needs you. . . . my bequest to a worthy unknown woman. Bit like a heart transplant,' she'd almost grinned at him, 'for there'll be someone out there.'*

The toilet flushed, a moment's pause, she came out and smiled at him.

∽ ∽ ∽

Mary's Legacy   12

Another lot of déjà vu moments; he could feel the pull, the nagging twinges of mental pain, still desperately unsure of the way this thing was going. Sitting opposite her in the train, the miles slipping away behind them, it seemed so unreal, like a chanced hypnotic dream, having the girl here. Last time he'd done this journey, yes he knew her, however unaware at the time of just how she'd resurface in his life. Then, it had been a simple episode, taking him out of the mire of despondency he'd otherwise have wallowed in, mourning his Mary, grieving at every turn and every aspect of Beckside bringing back the sting of the most precious of memories. Now the pain was different, as though one side had healed only to accentuate another hurt.

Yesterday - only yesterday - they'd walked, talked, eaten, idly discussed random aspects of the future until the small hours when she'd left him, gone up to the hut and he'd slept alone, fitfully, wonderingly, achingly silently alone. They both knew, both intelligently aware, both firmly resolute, that when they did yield it would have to be for ever. Ever is a long time, the time of a life, an inseparable life together and the past would then become the past with whatever spiritual blessing was pronounced.

The shutting of the cottage door, the hiding of the key - she knew where - the closing of the gate the way Mary had closed it that last time with the foreknowledge of her own finality; the half hour ride in the Discovery, the parking, the wait for the local train . . . and all the while she kept close, not letting him brood, clever girl.

She smiled at him across the table. The change at Carlisle had been painless, the brief yet significant interlude vanishing behind them.

'Tomorrow,' she said, bringing his thoughts back into reality. 'Tomorrow you're taking me to Italy, and I still can't believe my luck.'

'Thank Mary,' he replied with her still in the forefront of his mind. 'You still sure you want to trust yourself to me?'

The smile deepened and her eyes caught at him, the depth and the connection positive and radiant. 'Yes,' she replied simply. 'Because I know we'll be good for each other. I've got to work hard at learning how to interpret what's needed, I know that, but I also realise you need someone alongside you can trust, and that's going to be me.'

He had to chuckle at her. There was a chunk of mischief sitting inside her somewhere, not that it'd been too evident this last day or two because they'd been far too intense with each other, letting emotions and feelings run in chaotic circles around them, but as Beckside and its powerful evocative ambiance faded away with the miles and the task ahead loomed ever closer, he'd no doubt she'd continue to find a way to ease light relief in the form of a joke, a pun, a twist on his words.

'So you reckon we'll make a good film?'

She nodded with excess enthusiasm as though she were being interviewed. 'Yes, mister Art Director, we're going to make the best film out. 'Gone with the Wind' won't come anywhere near.'

'Tell Annette. She'll be bucked, being compared to Scarlet O'Hara - though now you say it, there's certainly some similarity and I'd not thought of it before.'

'Hadn't you? Well, I grant you I've not studied the plot like you'll have, but what I've taken on board has echoes. Long time since I last saw that thing though; it's pretty ancient.'

'Very true. And pretty grainy as well with some very old hat scenes; our camera work will be entirely different. There's a plus and minus side to modern film making, Paula. Sometimes I mourn the old ways.'

Paula saw him drift into nostalgia. That was typical Donald, a facet of his character oddly appealing, a tinge of romanticism being part of an art director's make-up. She let it go. Memories could be self-healing.

The hours of the journey south slid by; intermittent conversation, a coffee and a sticky bun to tide them over; finally it was Euston and another taxi. Taxis seemed to be a consistent part of her new life, strangely.

'You don't fancy keeping a car in London?' she queried, having to accept London traffic was awful after the quiet thirty-six hours in Cumbria.

He shook his head. 'Impractical. The flat didn't come with a parking space and I don't like driving in this density of traffic,' he waved at the constant flow of vehicles alongside, 'and it's not as though it's a regular commute.' He lifted eyebrows at her. 'You don't have a car either.'

'True, though I can drive.'

'Didn't doubt it. A girl of multifaceted talents.'

'Flatterer.'

'Realist.' He reached for her hand. 'Paula, I hope this won't end in tears.'

'Not if I can help it.' She gripped his fingers. 'If we fall out over something, promise you'll not let it spoil us? Never let the sun go down on a quarrel was a maxim my father often quoted.' She pulled his hand to her lips, kissed his fingers. 'Please, don't doubt us. There's a guardian angel out there, Donald; you know, I know.'

She watched his face, the way he had to look away, out of the taxi's window, knowing, feeling, the rise of emotion and the suggestion of damp eyes. Another squeeze; she felt the taxi slow. They'd got back to the flat.

He cooked a simple curry that night; she lay, knees up, on the settee and watched, mesmerised. 'Can I help', she'd asked only to get a smiling 'no thanks'; intuition suggested he needed something to occupy his mind. Then they ate quietly, a warm silence, drank half a bottle of a decent wine, smiling together at the Italian label. Donald turned the television on, found a romantic film showing, something in which he'd had some small input years back, only half an hour in from its start and they cosied up together on the settee and let the evening slip by.

Her head rested comfortably on his shoulder, his arm around her, close, warm, comforting. The sound track was soporific, the flat snug, her very presence hypnotic, his mind slowed, the present drifted into the past. Eyes closed . . . dreamt of Mary, his absolute idol, so much his life, for her he'd have given anything; together they'd achieved so much, brought up a super daughter, worked on so many wonderful films with such lovely people, been to the far corners of furthest countries . . .

Paula too, was dozing after a long day, letting her body relax, any residual stress ebbing away, giving her a calmness within rarely felt before. Safe, supported, a soft sensuality flowing through, allowing all inhibitions to drift into such depths of relaxation as she'd never previously experienced. Donald's hand slipped down, rested on her breast. A gentle snore - the man was asleep. She let her mind empty. Time flowed . . .

The film ended; the change in sound must have brought her back to consciousness. Some snatches of weird conversations, some fragments of evenings in her own flat, some recollections of exchanges with advertising customers from what seemed a decade ago, jumbled and stirred into a horrid mix of useless nothingness. Donald was still asleep, bless him. She needed to move and tried moving an arm.

He stirred, of course.

'Sorry,' she said, easing herself from under. 'It's time we called it a day anyway. A long day tomorrow.'

He took a deep breath. 'Yes,' then asked the question she should have realised was inevitable. There wasn't really any answer, for that too was also inevitable.

क्

When morning came far too early and with it the conscious realisation they had a timescale to meet; suddenly the world became real and earnest. He shot out of bed; she awoke to hear the shower running. Dare she join him?

'Hi,' he said, scrubbing vigorously. 'Not much room in here but you're welcome to try.'

So had they turned a corner? Last night must have been one of the best moments in her life; undressed, night-gowned, she'd taken a side of the bed, been carefully held without any thought of lust, then they must have fallen asleep, for no, they hadn't succumbed, at least as far as she could remember they hadn't, and she sure would have known if they had.

She couldn't help the inner shyness. This was all too new, too much of a move towards an achievement she had wondered whether they'd ever reach. Did the morning alter things? Would it be back to a careful dance around the niceties to avoid the obvious? But when he reached for her, pulled her in, the far too soapy kisses must either mean Mary's pull at his sensibilities had lessened or her platonic presence in his bed wasn't a fictional attempt at rationalising their relationship. So, oh yes,

93

she must mean that much more to him now, and the obvious was a very tantalising apparancy. Dare she? The lovely stream of warm water poured down her back, funnelled between her buttocks, flowed around her thighs as he nuzzled at her neck, held her across the shoulders to pull her closer, the strength of him and wiry firmness tight against her tummy, almost . . . but not quite.

He spun her round, gave her the space and stepped away, left her with the cascading remnant warmth of a lovely shower. 'Two minutes,' he said above the waterfall. 'We don't want to miss our train,' added with such a wicked grin.

Within the few minutes it took her to accept she needed to finalise the shower routine and get dry and dressed, he'd made scrambled eggs and a pot of coffee. The grin was still there.

'You're being horrid to me,' was all she could think of saying. Trying to make her body realise it wasn't going to get what nature had programmed it to expect under such provocative circumstances was frustrating and difficult, however, there wasn't an option. Time wasn't on their side and she had the commonsense to understand that he was, after all, being very fair to her.

His eyebrows lifted in that all-too familiar and vexing way. 'Really? And I thought I was being extra nice to you, offering creature comforts and all that.'

She scowled at him. 'If I didn't know you better, I'd say you'd practised the art of winding us females up and then leaving us high and dry.'

He laughed. 'High and dry? Hardly, dear Paula. On a high, maybe, but dry, no. No way. Being very ungentlemanly, I'd say perhaps damp inside . . .' and dodged the tea towel she'd picked up and flung at him. 'Come on. Eat your breakfast.'

∽

They reached the studio by eleven, which wasn't out of the way. Another hour later and after a storming session with Booth in an attempt to put all the missing bits of an intense programme into place, they snatched something of a lunch, Donald did the last minute rounds and they picked up the Italian bags prepared before the weekend.

'All set?' He gave her another Donald style grin and hefted his case. 'Hope you've got all you need.'

'There are shops in Italy, you know.'

'Are there?' The smile turned into a cheeky grin. 'Well, I hope your Italian is up to scratch.'

'Probably better than yours.'

'Now, now, you two,' Pat remonstrated from behind her reception desk. 'The driver's waiting.'

'Okay.' Donald took Paula's arm, steered her through the main doors. 'Here we go. Puglia, here we come. Via Paris tonight and Sarah'll be waiting for us.'

The car dropped them off outside the St. Pancras Hotel; ten minutes later and they were through the ticket barriers at the Eurostar terminal, soon cleared through security and after a brief wait onwards and up the travelator towards the train. A new experience for Paula, and especially being welcomed at the carriage door by the petite smart girl in her Eurostar navy costume, she felt privileged.

'You want the window seat? I've been here before, so feel free.' Donald nudged her in, hoisted their bags onto the rack above them and settled into the seat alongside. 'Enjoy the ride. Paris here we come.'

Not more than ten minutes later, the announcement in both French and English, the almost imperceptible pull away from the platform, the gradual build up to an impressive speed, through the tunnels under London and out into Essex countryside. Donald reached for her hand.

'Okay?' he asked.

She almost shook her head. 'Fantastic,' she replied. 'Unbelievable. Not travelled this fast before.'

A chuckle. 'Wait till you experience TGV - and Trenitalia, the Frecciarossa. Now they *really* travel fast, licensed for over 300km per hour. There's a lot to be said for train travel. At least you can get up and walk about, you can see far more than mere clouds too. And it didn't take us long to go through the terminal, did it?'

'No. Far better than the last time I went abroad, three hours in Gatwick and a choppy flight to Venice. Mind you, it was a while ago. Not had a decent holiday since.'

He squeezed her hand then let go. 'This ain't a holiday, Paula.'

'Feels like one.'

'You wait.' Their eyes met, he winked, she felt slightly embarrassed, with an odd feeling suggestive of being his good-time girl rather than a professional p.a. - understandable, given she'd slept completely and unashamedly near naked in his arms last night. Odd, very odd and her inner girl twitched. The train was slowing.

'One stop here, Ebbsfleet,' he explained, 'then the tunnel. Twenty-one minutes through its fifty kilometres, provided there's no hiccup. Then on to Paris. Gare Du Nord. Not been there before?'

She shook her head. 'No. Never been to Paris.'

'Then maybe I'll bring you back here when we've got more time. Happy?' he asked.

'Never more so. Will we survive, Donald?'

He knew what she meant. In his heart of hearts, he thought, probably yes, we will. Taking her to the edge last night had been a risk, but it had worked. His innermost mind was settling down to accept the dark hole Mary'd left was beginning to close up. Once the raw edges had finally knitted together, then, and only then, would he allow himself the chance of a gamble over her true and genuine inclinations. His own, well, the weeks ahead would say.

He picked up the stray hand from her warm thigh and stroked her fingers, one by one. 'You've not run away, Paula. You could have.'

'You've not pushed me away either, Donald. Rather the opposite. Did you want me? *Do* you want me?' Her expressive eyes caught at him, the depths he couldn't measure.

He wrapped the hand up in his. 'We have a job to do, Paula. And then we'll see. Allow me time - but I'll never push you away. Never.'

Mary's Legacy 13

Paris, Gare du Nord, a bustle of a place, even in the late afternoon.

The journey had been fine. Evidently she'd enjoyed the experience, for there was a brighter light in her eye, as bright as the moment he'd first seen her that time up in the hills. She'd tucked into her lunch tray, absorbed the two little bottles of white wine with aplomb, chattered on about what she knew of her - very - distant Italian family, not that she'd ever met them, and intermittently held his hand, rather, as he happily thought, like a small daughter, which brought pangs of recall over trips abroad they'd made with Sarah when she was still a schoolgirl.

'Well?'

Her eyes couldn't keep still. A place of history, a rendezvous for so many, a backdrop to so many happenings, life-defining moments, and *she was here!* 'Amazing!'

'That's an over-used adjective, Paula.'

'Maybe, but for a simple girl like me . . .'

'Nothing simple about you, my girl. Let's go find Sarah.'

There was something about his use of '*my girl*' that triggered a rush of real affection for him; not a simple 'lust' - and she'd used the word before chastising her mind for suggesting such a thing - but an overwhelming sense of attachment, a feeling of absolute trust in the bond which had developed ever since she'd first seen him, that wonderful day, evening, after Stuart's idiotic fall, the so very silly, simple, yet stupendous event to have brought them together.

'Coming?'

97

She had to do a silly little head shake to clear her mind. Why here, of all places, in the confusion of people all with differing destinations and desires, to have another emotional sensation?

'Paula?'

'Sorry, bit of a déjà vu moment. I know I haven't been here before, but it seems so, so familiar. Where's Sarah?'

'She'll be at the entrance. It's a bit of a hike to her *maison* but better than a taxi. You'll get a flavour of Parisian street life.'

'Will she like me? I mean, if I've rather taken over the daughter role, she won't be jealous, will she?'

'Well, you'll have to see, won't you? Too late now,' and he waved. Paula saw her, it had to be her, the slim girl in a very chic coat, collar length honey coloured hair, high heels - of course - a small clutch handbag and a smile.

'Sarah!' Donald enveloped the girl in a hug, almost lifted her off her feet, smothering any welcoming noises she may have made. Then: 'Lovely to see you, and on home turf. Meet Paula,' he turned towards her. 'Paula, Sarah my daughter.'

Paula felt the cool appraisal, the depth of her dark grey eyes drawing her in. Donald's daughter was certainly a very pretty girl. If his Mary had had this girl's features, no wonder he'd fallen for her.

'Paula,' and Sarah offered her a cheek-to-cheek kiss in true Gallic fashion. 'Lovely to meet you at long last,' and as she turned to Donald, the cool smile turning into a grin, added: 'And I am so, so, pleased you've been so supportive of my dad here. Hope he's been behaving himself?'

The recollection of last night's episode came flooding back; she could feel a blush beginning to warm her cheeks. 'Er ...' but Donald came to her rescue.

'Of course,' he said, 'and she's been absolutely invaluable. Couldn't have done without her. Now, what have you organised for us, darling daughter?'

The moment had passed, her blush subsided and Sarah seemed not to have noticed. But what if she had, what if she'd realised the depth of her attachment to this man and, hopefully, he for her? Would she have thrown a wobbly, told him off, or treated her as a goodtime girl, a gold digger? Sarah smiled at her, an honest '*I think I like you*' smile and the internal tension, the prospect of a panic attack, subsided.

'Karl's been extra kind,' Sarah's cheerful comment, 'so we've supper organised in the Salon, courtesy of the management, though,' her voice dropped in a mock-conspiratorial whisper, 'I think there's an ulterior motive. The staff are on a few days off, post show, so we're on our own other than his, er, discreet boyfriend.'

'Oh? Donald took his daughter's arm; they began to walk round to where the coaches parked, where Sarah would have left her car under the watchful eyes of the gendarmerie. 'Your Karl wants something?'

'Maybe. He'll say.'

'You mean he's hosting?'

'Yes. Very rare, but then, he owes me. Last week's show was *fantastic,*' and she slipped her father's hold and did a twirl; her coat flared and the light pale blue silk skirt below lifted in the draught, carelessly revealing enviable shaped legs. 'You'll never guess.'

Paula suddenly felt dowdy in her travelling skirt, the green velour, the same outfit as she'd worn that life-changing day when she'd ventured into Donald's London world. Donald issued a low whistle.

'Steady on, Sarah. You're not on the cat-walk now!'

'No, but I have been.'

'You mean . . .'

'Yes. Last minute dropout when 'Tasha went sick. No choice but it worked!'

Paula sucked in a breath. 'You've been modeling? Paris, fashion week and all that?'

'Uh huh. And, because I'm so short and *not* ultra slim, got noticed. Watch this space, daddy mine,' she nudged her father as they reached the car, a smart looking grey metallic Peugeot. 'Paula, you'd look good on the catwalk too, I can tell.'

'Me? No way. Not my scene.'

The car unlocked, Sarah slid into the driver's seat, Donald slung their bags in the boot then held open the other front door for Paula. 'Here, you take this one. I'll sit in the back. Go on . . .'

Sarah wouldn't let go, after a few moments whilst she took with the car away into the frenetic traffic she carried on with her comment, eyeing Paula despite keeping up with the road speed. 'With those Italianate looks of yours and such a super slim figure you could wow them. What do you say, dad?'

He had to agree. With the more intimate knowledge he'd gained fairly recently, having platonically put the girl to bed once and having her - for comfort's sake - in his bed too, he'd be churlish to disagree. Paula turned her glance back to him, gave him a look as if to say 'yes, I know what you're thinking' then remembered what he had actually said in the car before they went up to Beckside. The decision to put her in the film?

'Your father,' how strange that sounded, 'has said they want me to appear in one of the film sequences, in Milan's Gallerie. I'm not sure why.'

'Wow! Like I said, 'cos you're a natural,' and laughed at her. 'Paula, one of the tricks you learn in this game is never under estimate your own capabilities. I got my first real exposure to the fashion paparazzi last week and had to take it on the run. Now I'm hooked.' She adroitly swerved around a large Citroen van that suddenly decided to park, accelerated to the next intersection and turned left. 'Nearly there.'

If she didn't know differently, the Salon's tall exterior gave no impression it was one of the better establishments. An anonymous worn stone façade, though a wide gloss black door and the polished brass handrails lining the crisp stone steps impressed, as did the discreet plaque alongside the door bell push - *Karl Largouman Couture* - which said it all.

As Sarah drew up at the step's foot, the door opened, an urbane young guy in a dark tailored jacket appeared. 'Jacques will park the car,' she said, sliding out of her seat and opening the rear door for her father. 'He'll sort the bags and take them up. There's a mews round the back.'

Like entering a different world; into the rarified rather suave atmosphere of haute couture where the décor emphasised the concept "if you have to ask the price, you can't afford it". There wasn't another soul in sight; as per Sarah's account though she'd already explained Jacques' presence as an extremely discreet butler. Paula felt inconsequential, as though she didn't exist, whilst Sarah led the way across the marble tiled floor and up the broad stairs to the first floor gallery. She could see Donald was impressed, although she felt sure he should have been here before, it didn't seem like it. He must have been into many exotic places so probably took it in his stride, whereas the extent of her trespass into the realms of high living had been the drab main London office of the publishing company she used to work for before she'd walked into Donald's world.

At the head of the stairs Sarah stopped, said, *sotto voce,* 'Karl will be still working, he hardly ever stops, so don't take offence. He'll be sketching away . . .' she tapped on an ornate double door, opened it without waiting, held it to allow her father and Paula to enter.

The tall, white haired aristocratic man rose from behind the huge desk at the end of the room. 'Welcome, welcome to my world,' and advancing across the deep carpeted floor with, Paula thought, one of the most pleasantest smiles she'd seen for ages, Donald excepted.

'It is a great pleasure to meet my wonderful Sarah's father, and . . .' he paused, allowing Sarah to introduce her.

'Paula is my father's latest conquest,' she said with a cheeky look at him, 'he picked her up on some lake district hillside a couple of months ago. A waif and stray who is repaying her board and lodging by acting as a personal assistant.'

'So! Romance is never dead!' He eyed her up and down; she didn't feel embarrassed but honoured for this was a man who dressed some of the most exquisite ladies in France. *'Pardon moi, mais tu est très, très . . .'* and oddly, hesitated.

'She is,' Sarah added in a more solemn voice, 'still finding her feet. Working with my father in the film world is likely to be fairly demanding. She's going to have a small walk-in part in the latest film too, more than I'll ever get.'

'Mais, tu . . . a arrive,' soothing her feelings, then he relapsed back into English. 'Then she will succeed in obtaining the great *attention.'* He took her by the arm and spun her round. 'Sara,' using his *nom d'amour* for her, 'this *mam'selle* is worthy of a Largouman dress. Go; put her into something - you will know and choose - for the evening. We will wait for you. Go!'

Paula felt faint, as though the world was spinning away from her, but allowed Sarah to shepherd her out of the room. Donald watched her go, this 'waif and stray' who he'd adopted, the woman who potentially fulfilled the role of her *"find a girl who needs someone like you . . ."* his beloved Mary's last words.

'Now,' Karl said, 'we talk. Please, let us, as you say, take it easy,' and led him through to the room next door, a sumptuous sitting room with quality soft chairs in a deep grey velour around the low walnut tables already set with a collection of buffet plates, glasses and wine - champagne? - in silver coolers. He waved a hand at the two-seater settee. *'Asseyez vous.'*

Once comfortably seated, Karl wasted no time. *'Les girls* will be back soon.' He paused, briefly, then: 'I am grateful for the chance to say to you, *en confidence* about your Sarah. My *Sara.* She is invaluable, one of the best *directrices* I have ever had, and she has taken to the position in the most admirable way. I do not wish to lose her but I fear she is unsettled. Your dear lady wife, her death was the most upsetting for us all, my dear - I may call you Donald? - a tragic loss at such an early age.' His appearance and tone amplified his expressed feelings in genuine consolation. Donald nodded; that so many friends and mere acquaintances had followed this line of support was indeed comforting. 'But,' Karl continued, 'her mother's loss has affected her work, we have noticed a smidgeon of sadness, though I will hasten to say it will not prejudice her position here. There has been reference to a *'legacy'?'*

'Paula,' and Donald took confidence in owning up to his knowledge of the girl and her role in his life, appreciating this great man's openness. 'Mary left me with an obligation,' and he repeated the phrase now etched into his soul *'find a girl . . .* 'My wife's spirit still burns, wherever she's gone; Paula is the personification of her wish and maybe the legacy of which she speaks.'

'So? You love this girl?'

Donald nearly shrugged. This was all a fraction raw; he had not wished to air his private thoughts for both he and Mary's *alter ego* had still some fair mileage to travel but in this company, perhaps easier. 'I will admit to a deep care for her,' he replied guardedly.

Karl smiled understandingly. 'Ah, that is good. But, and this is the point I wished to make, our *Sara* needs reassurance that all is well with you, for I fear her grief has come out in this way, in her care for you? Once the matter is settled, perhaps she will come back to me in the better attitude. I am sorry; this may appear a little, how do you say, *garbled?'*

'No, not at all. I can understand, though Sarah's never shown her concern to me in quite the way you suggest.'

The other doors opened, the two girls had returned, so Donald capped the conversation with: 'I'll see what I can do,' and there the matter rested.

Karl gave a quick nod. 'I am grateful. Now, *Sara*, what have you found? Ah, *oui, exactement . . .*'

Donald's heart leapt. His girl had a glowing face, an expression of uninhibited joy and spun, twirled in the most beautiful long dress in a shimmer of pale gold and ivory. She'd brushed out her hair too so it flowed across her shoulders in a wave of chestnut brown and the hints of gold. Gorgeous, no other word for it. He'd seen some beautiful women in his time too, but Paula - *Mary's Paula,* a glorious girl and the emotion rose, brought the foolish yet unstoppable tears.

Karl lifted out of his armchair, dispassionately eyed the girl up and down, pulled at a sleeve, lifted the skirt's hem and examined the underskirt. '*Oui.* A good choice, *Sara.* How do you like your new dress, Paula?'

'It's so-oooh lovely,' her reply; perhaps an inadequate comment, given she'd not taken on board the full implication of his question. 'An absolute privilege to see the collection and to actually try a few on - I didn't think I'd stand a chance to get into one, let alone find it fits so well. Thank you so *so* much. What have I done to deserve this?'

'By looking divine, of course. And because you are providing happiness to my dear *Sara's* father, *that* is the most important. You would like to keep this dress?'

She was flabbergasted. Brought to Paris, en route to Italy, welcomed into one of the small yet exclusive top Paris fashion Houses by the man whose name was revered by so many, allowed to model one of his latest creations and then asked if she'd like to keep it? She cried, tears flooding down her cheeks, unable to believe what was happening to her.

Sarah understood. In the short time she'd had to appreciate what her father had achieved, finding and supporting a girl who must have had a large gap in her own life, the concept of bringing the woman out of the girl, the real three dimensional person out of an everyday one was going to be mind-blowing, in the same way she'd experienced the feeling when initially taken on by this famous House and ultimately walking the platform only last week - and in this dress, well, tears were inevitable.

'Of course she'd love to keep the dress, Karl, but . . .'

'I know, my dear, it's special, but only *really* special to the woman who wears it and wears it well. That is what we do, *Sara,* make women special. It is my delight to see such happiness, such pride in the artistry of their body and their *feminity*. This Paula, she wears my dress to perfection, gives it the life it deserves, therefore it is hers. We can design another one for Sachkia. Now, we must sample our chef's handiwork. Come, Paula, dry your tears, sit alongside your *patron* and allow him to feast not only on our food but also on your beauty.'

Surreal. Totally surreal, with the candle sconces lit, the curtains drawn, the conversation, half in French, half in perfect English, Donald's eyes constant on her, Sarah's smiles, Karl's far too repetitive adulation, she must be dreaming and a dream where the presence of another woman's spirit enhanced her confidence.

'Has Mary ever been here?' she asked in tentative voice.

Donald's eyes were steady on her, Sarah gave a soft smile, Karl looked impassive as Sarah replied, 'yes, she has. And sat where you are sitting now; I was allowed to show her where I worked when she came to Paris for the last time,' then her voice broke. The buried grief suddenly surfaced and she cried in her turn, sobbing, before Donald stood, went to her, lifted her from the chair and folded her tight in his arms. They swayed gently together and Paula remembered how she, too, had been held in similar fashion, way up on the pasture above Beckside. Mary, the most wonderful of women; she'd been here, had sat here, left her indomitable spirit for them all to absorb, each one in their own way. Sarah grieved for her mother, Donald for his wife of twenty plus years, and she grieved too, because she'd not known Mary personally but oddly, now believed in her spirit, a soul who'd never ever die whilst Donald needed her.

Then Sarah gently slipped out of Donald's embrace and returned to her chair. Donald's glance towards Paula said all; Karl reached for the champagne and filled four glasses. He stood, held his aloft. *'A Marie, bonne femme, her memory undiminished. Bon chance, mes Amis.'*

Glasses clinked, a minute's silence, a moment transferred into memory.

Donald glanced at his watch, attempting to induce practicalities. Sarah caught his look. Her petite penthouse suite beckoned; though small, it oozed comfort. 'We must thank you,' he said, 'for your immensely generous welcome and hospitality, Karl; it has been an evening of pure delight.'

Karl gave a little bow. *'Mon plaisir*, Donald; and Paula, you must visit us again. Wear your dress with pride and always remember who gave it to you, with love.' His eyes twinkled. '*Sara*, I believe you have a wonderful father.'

✍

This was another most odd experience, trooping up the stone staircase of a eighteenth century building, walking the corridors in the attics, the golden dress swishing round her thighs, to be able to glance out of the windows and see the lights of Paris below and hear the subdued hum of continuous traffic. Sarah unlocked her door with a comment about 'sleeping above the shop', showed them the bijou flat. 'You have a choice,' she said, with an unrestrained grin. 'Either Paula and I share the double bed, luxury, and dad, you'll have the couch, or you can choose which girl you'd like to sleep with and the disappointed gal has the couch.'

A mischievous damsel; this daughter of his. 'You choose,' he said, ducking out from under the decision.

Paula protested. 'I don't mind the couch, but . . .'

'Neither do I. Though I can't remember if dad snores.'

Paula hadn't heard him. 'Shall we toss a coin?'

'Ha,' Donald replied. 'Though's there's another option. How wide . . .'

The thought of a threesome appalled. 'No way!' Sarah grinned at him. 'No, if Paula's okay with it, I'll take the couch. Been there before.'

So Donald had the option of the warmth of his lady once more, but first the dress had to come off. 'I can't believe Karl has been so generous,' Sarah's comment as she carefully undid a dozen hooks and eyes from around the waist line to allow the material, a stiffened silk, to relax. Then a concealed zip allowed the top to fall away from the fullness of Paula's breasts, finally to give her the freedom to step out of the pile of shimmering fabric left in a heap on the floor. 'You do realise how much this would cost, assuming you could find a retailer who'd stock one?' Sarah carefully picked the dress up, shook the folds out, laid it on the bed and smoothed the skirt across the duvet.

'No, and I daren't think about it otherwise I'd faint with embarrassment.' Paula stood there in merely a decent bra and pants with no concerns, looking across at Donald sitting, legs crossed, arms folded, watching the floor show. 'This must be the third time you've seen the near naked me.'

105

'Third time, dad? Is she . . .?' Sarah raised her eyebrows with a remarkable if perceptive sanguinity.

'First was a necessity, 'cos she'd virtually flaked out on me after a night at Claridges, then - well, never mind. She's growing on me ...' and blew a kiss at her. 'Best get into bed, girl, we've along day ahead of us tomorrow and it's nearly that already.'

'Right. I'm for the couch then. I'll leave you two with it,' and she picked up the dress, inserted the shoulder padded hanger and hung it on the picture rail. 'Be good,' she added with a knowing grin and went next door.

'I could get used to this.' Paula unfastened her bra, slipped on the soft cotton nightdress she'd pulled out from her bag, shimmied her pants off from underneath and slipped under the covers, turned away from him and closed her eyes.

Donald dimmed out the light; within half a minute he too was flat out, barely aware of the temptation to cosset her, but - was that a girly version of a snore? Morning would be here all too soon . . .

∽

'Hey! You want to catch that train?' Sarah was shaking his shoulder, 'Paula's up and dressed, time you were.'

He squinted at his watch. 'Gracious! How true! Okay, give me five.'

He'd slept so well; Sarah's borrowed bed was lovely, girl or no girl alongside and without any recriminations either. First the small bathroom; he'd love a shower but looked forward to one in the hotel tonight. He dressed in his travel kit, lightweight trousers, sweat shirt, the woollen jersey top. His bag packed and zipped, he joined the girls in the kitchen. Paula had a lovely smile on her. Sarah looked solemn.

'It's been great, dad, having you here, meeting Paula,' she caught the girl's look. 'We've had a chat whilst you were still dreaming. I've no hang-ups about you two, father mine. You want to work together, that's good, and,' she coloured up, 'if you want her to take over some of mum's role, then that's fine. Really. I've got good vibes and the dress did it. Karl's got talent, spotting how frocks work. So look after her, love her, and mum'd be ever so proud.' Her voice had caught; she picked up the dirty plates from the table and turned away.

Paula's eyes brimmed once more. Mary's legacy; how could she possibly live up to what these two, husband and daughter might expect of her?

Donald, with perfect intuition, knew. 'We'll survive. And we'd better go. Catch up with brunch on the train. Will you drive us, daughter mine, or shall we taxi?'

'Oh, I'll drive. No probs. You will keep in touch if the schedule allows?' knowing he probably wouldn't, not until after the location work had been completed.

'Of course. Look after the dress.'

'I'll bring it over once you get back. Promise.'

'Thanks. Paula?'

'Okay. I'm ready.'

They clattered down in an antique lift to the rear mews, slung the bags in the Peugeot's boot and Sarah drove. Drove like a Frenchman, Donald said, to make her laugh. Drove to the Gare de Lyon, drove as close as she could to the imposing façade, let them out, kissed her father, kissed her dead mother's choice of legatee and watched them go, hand in hand with bags in other hands, and cried. Cried for her loss and for her gain.

Mary's Legacy   *14*

Once ensconced in the luxury of the TGV Donald felt he could relax, with a lengthy trip ahead of them down to Milan. Paula - and being now so familiar with her moods and attitude to new experiences he could have predicted her reaction - sat tight to the window and absorbed everything around her. The all-too brief interlude with Sarah and her *haute couture* employer had been a phenomenal lift for the girl; he welcomed the relaxed yet educational aspects of Karl's hospitality and especially the surprisingly generous present of a bespoke dress from a recent collection. This gift, from the show where Sarah had taken her debut steps on the catwalk, could never be matched, for the intrinsic value was way beyond reckoning, far more than the mere financial. Left wrapped in acid-free tissue in Sarah's own wardrobe, he hoped they'd be able to collect it on the return trip; the prospect of seeing her in the Largouman creation at, say, the film launch, would be utterly fantastic.

A hour into the journey; Paula was nearly asleep, no doubt lulled by the extra smooth rumble of a train now travelling at well over two hundred kilometres an hour, and not really surprising after yesterday's eventful evening, capped by the near spiritual night spent sharing a bed. It could have been construed as commonsensical for he and she were fast being seen as an 'item'. His daughter's own analysis might be even more logical with her intelligent view of how this girl had, perhaps in an unorthodox manner, helped diminish the nagging and still continuous pain of Mary's absence. However, it was time to marginalize the development of a hang-up, physcological or no, about whatever 'relationship' they had. He must try to treat her more as an employee now they were en route to the film location.

'Paula?'

She jerked, looked surprised and then a little sheepish, pulled herself upright to manage a proper girly smile.

'Sorry.'

'Nothing to be sorry about, you're entitled to a doze after all yesterday's excitement. Today might seem tame in comparison. You won't have done a long rail trip before?'

She shook her head. 'A learning curve and all that. It's a nice train.'

'The French know how to build railways, even if the rolling stock is getting travel weary. I think we've lost the knack back home, or can't be bothered with the aggro when we need to upgrade them. But don't let me bore you. Kip if you want to. I'm going to go through my notes.'

'Can I do anything?'

A question that suggested many answers; he grinned at her, suggested: 'stay looking pretty?'

She stuck her tongue out. 'You know what I mean. You've brought me with you for a positive purpose, not merely as eye candy. Or have you?'

There had to be a serious side to this and he knew it, ignoring the eye-candy jibe. 'I want you - no, I'd *like* you to give me a candid reaction to the ideas I come up with. You've got an incisive eye, a broad view of life and a refreshing honesty which may cut through some of the overly rosy glow used to coat my set-ups. We need to get this right, for everyone's sake.'

'Including Mary's,' and her comment brought matters back into focus.

'Yes.'

'Did she give you honest opinions too?'

'Why, or how, we survived the flak, you mean?'

'She must have been a great girl,' and Paula's voice had an edge to it. 'Donald, am I the right person for this? Can I truly become someone she'd be proud of, because that's what I'd like to think was possible?'

He leant across the table and took hold of her hands resting there, captured them in a firm grasp. 'Paula, during the past few weeks or so we've philosophized over your role a fair number of times, and I doubt it'll stop, but at every moment when I've looked back, at every time when I've thought about losing Mary, nothing's ever suggested that I've done wrong in taking you on board. So, provided you can see what's needed, do what's asked, and importantly, say what you think, then I reckon there's every chance you'll come out of this project with head held high. Sarah likes you; you've made one hell of an impression on Karl Largouman; moreover, Booth is paying me to keep you on as a p.a. So don't worry.'

She didn't say anything, merely turned her hands round so she could hold his, then mouthed three silent words, *'I love you'*.

His eyes crinkled in wry humour, wondering if he dare go that one step further, thought briefly and then copied her style and her words with one addition '. . . .*too.'*

Her look softened, her fingers stroked the backs of his hands, the image of her across the table blurred into the familiar picture of his partner, wife, companion, lover of twenty plus years. Mary, dearly beloved Mary had blessed him with her vision, her dying vision of his future. So onward, onward and upwards. *Paula, dearest girl,* his thoughts firm in his mind, *when and if it's right, perhaps we'll take the next step . . .*

In the meantime they had a job to do. In the capacious side pocket of his bag, the expensive bespoke bag Mary'd had made to her own design by a firm in Bedfordshire's Lavendon, discovered when they'd explored around that county, and given to him after what turned out to be their last film together, there sat a copy of the script he'd ignored these past two days, together with his sketches, his storyboard comments and, most importantly, the thumbnails on the actors - and actresses - he hated the way modernism had dropped the feminine cachet, a demeaning mannerism best left to male chauvinists. Packets of potential, as Mary had once called a similar collection of his, prior to a film shoot way-off in Latvia. He grimaced, recalling the biting cold of the month out there. This one - *au contraire,* they'd likely be perspiring despite the autumn season. He stood, reached up for his bag, extracted the packet and shoved the bag firmly back on the rack above them.

'Have you a copy of that?' Paula nodded at the bulky collection of paper. 'Otherwise . . .'

'No, only in my head.'

'So if you lose it?'

He narrowed his eyes at her. 'Then I'll blame my personal assistant.'

'Oh.'

'That all? Just 'oh', when you stand a fair chance of getting fired should the worst happen?'

'I'd guess you could redraft the whole thing in your sleep,' she retorted. 'Unless you were distracted.'

'Now then, miss.' He scowled at her then grinned. 'You're probably right. I tend to get obsessive. Feel free to criticize if I neglect you. And before you say '*I don't think so*', I can assure you I might. It's the only time Mary and I got anywhere close to having a row. She was,' and another inexplicable and sudden rise of emotion caught at his voice, 'she was,' he repeated, 'a straight line girl; never raised her voice, never got cross unless I forgot her goodnight kiss, which I sometimes did when thinking too much about the next day's shoot.' His eyes took on a distant look, a gaze into nostalgia, and couldn't help his next query. 'Oh, Paula, Paula, why did she have to leave me?'

She got up out of her seat, slid onto his side and cosied up to him, snuggled her head onto his shoulder, extremely thankful they had the foursome seat to themselves; the other travelers around them didn't seem to matter. His arm came round her, the train's motion and the subdued roar of wheels on the high-speed line lulled them, silent and thoughtful. He closed his eyes, felt the warmth of her, the evocative scent now a well-recognised pheromonal attribute.

She could have been Mary. Without her, where would he have been? Was she an angel - or, as Mary would have had it, a spirit - in a realisable, feminine, human shape? The train sped onwards, the steady low roar, the miles - kilometres - flying away behind them. Reluctant to disentangle from her, necessity had to take precedence.

'Okay?' she asked, straightening up. She brushed her hair back, a strand escaped and in the tenderest of gestures, he reached up and tucked it behind her ear, drifting his fingers across her ear lobe. She shivered, wishing and wondering about the wish.

A brief hold of his look, the depth of it, the way instinct was bringing secret parts of her body stirringly awake from over-long dormancy, a gathering of emotion into a potential storm of irreconcilable desire which brought a flush to her cheeks. 'Give me a moment,' she said, pulled her skirt clear from its trapped state below thighs and fled to the toilet.

By the time she returned, Donald had the papers spread over the table, sifting them into an order of film shoot locations; the tumult of thoughts subverted below practicalities.

She slid back onto her side of the table and leant her head on her elbow-supported hands. 'Where do we start?' she asked, her voice a fraction croaky, but then, her five minutes of deep breathing alone in an attempt to regain practicalities hadn't resolved the problem, only postponed it. Another question: 'Where do we stay tonight?'

'Milan, of course. Hotel's booked. Same as when we come back so it'll become familiar.' He moved one clipped sheaf into a different pile. 'We'll trawl through Milan City tomorrow, meet up with some of the first unit who'll be flying in overnight, poor things, I don't envy them.' He gave her a wry smile. 'You'll begin to wish you hadn't come back into my life when reality sets in. It's not a glamorous job, you know, making a film. It's hard work, long unsocial hours and under trying circumstances. Chatting up the big names and seeing lovely people becoming harassed might be a reward, but it certainly presents an opportunity for dubious fame if you get it right. Or being buried in anonymity if you get it wrong or the cinema-going public doesn't like it. Still okay with this?' and he ran a careful hand over the table's content so as not to disturb the arrangement. 'I want you to look through this schedule, get to know what's happening and learn it. You'll be my ears and eyes, to let me know if someone's not happy.' He picked up a set of the clipped papers and handed them across. 'All right?'

She took a deep breath, accepted his offering, relaxed back into her seat and started to read. This was the reality he spoke of, not the high adrenaline rush of affection but the necessity to work consistently together and achieve results. His attention was back with the plot, she could tell. Her role in his life would rock back and forth from very nearly a lover to very much a working girl. So be it, she'd survive.

He left her to it, made his own journey to the end of the carriage. Now firmly launched into the new-style adventure with a girl who he'd come to love but who wasn't a Mary, wasn't his life, wasn't someone he could yet fully open his heart to, would the whole *raison d'etre* of the trip come good? It had to, being his bread 'n butter, his job, his own personal creativity and what he'd never once doubted was all he'd ever really wanted to do.

When he came back, having diverted to the buffet car and collected a couple of salami and cheese bruscetta to get them in the Italian mood together with two small bottles of Chianti, he found her in far more practical and serious mode.

'This one,' she pulled out a cream coloured sheet which signified it was the base plan for an important part of the action, 'Don't you think it'd be good to have a roving view of the bay first? The reveal seems to be in the town's streets, doesn't give you an idea it's actually close to the beach where she's going? Annette, I mean; what's her screen name again, Maria?'

He slid in alongside her, putting the bruscetta bag and the bottles on the only spare space on the table.

'Oooh, lunch!' She twisted round and gave him an unheralded quick peck on the cheek. 'Glad you're looking after me.'

He took the sheet from her, read it through. 'Annette's not Maria,' he said shortly, to add, 'you've missed the previous day. Where the bloke she's trying to avoid walks across the beach and stands looking out to sea; he moves back to the hotel through the same street - but yes, we could try a dawn shot, provided the weather holds good.'

'Perhaps a little local colour - or a more precise venue for her? A café or something?' and she was to remember this suggestion.

He nodded. 'You're getting the hang of it. That's what the recce is all about, walking the ground, doing an appraisal, making sure it'd work. How about the Milan bit, where we'll be tomorrow? Puglia comes later. Here, have a bruscetta.'

They worked solidly through most of the plot; discussing, amending a few minor points as the remaining hours slipped by and France gave way to Italy, the journey's time condensed into a happy build of increasing rapport.

Paula relaxed back into her seat, closed her eyes. 'I didn't know how much was involved,' she said, 'or how much I'd enjoy all this.' A moment passed, she re-opened her eyes and began to clip sets of pages back together. 'The story's pretty well engrained in my head. I'll dream about it.' Her tummy rumbled. 'Those bruscetta didn't go very far. Hope the hotel's restaurant is up to scratch,' and was about to ask about the timing when the train began to slow. The country had given way to houses, factories, warehouses, the rail lines began to multiply into sidings with all manner of rolling stock mostly covered with graffiti, and then, almost abruptly, they'd arrived. 'Milan?' she asked a rhetorical question.

'Milano. Where you'll become a starlet.' He grinned at her. 'But don't think you'll get your name in the same size font as Annette's. I wonder what dress they'll find for you. Or maybe it'll be jeans and a scruffy tee-shirt,' before suddenly having a surprise idea he'd not reveal, confirmed by her next comment.

'Huh. Whatever it is, it won't match Karl's creation. That was astonishing, and I still don't know why I was so lucky.'

'It was,' and here he was being truthful, 'because you came over as the girl with something different about her, and Karl has a passion for dressing women with character. You wait, he'll be asking you to model on the catwalk next, alongside darling Sarah. And you're very pretty, when you want to be.'

His jocular tone wasn't lost on her. 'Am I not always pretty?'

'Depends,' he said, keeping his options open. 'Now, grab your bag. We've a hotel to find.

Mary's Legacy 15

So much to see; her world was expanding beyond belief, the streets, the people, the art, architecture. Yesterday, Paris, today, Milan. And it wasn't going to stop here. Donald apparently knew where to go, striding out with bag swinging, offering encouraging smiles at every other step. He was a fast walker too and she struggled to keep pace. Should she have abandoned heels, even low ones, for something less trendy? But this was Italy. Where she'd never thought to ever be, certainly not as p.a. to a film production company's art director. This was no dream either; this was for real and in true earnest.

Leaving the comfortable nest of their seats in the TGV to join the bustle and tumult of the throng in the vast station, hurrying to keep up as he threaded their path through the travelling crowds, out of the concourse and into the streets, now enroute to the hotel, she could only switch to autopilot - and that was Donald. He seemed to know where he was going; she'd have been totally lost had she been on her own. And the Italians - goodness, how did they manage to speak so fast and understand each other?

Round another corner, across the street, avoiding the Fiats and the Minis - there seemed to be lots of those - and into an hotel. Swanky? How did it compare with others? She didn't, couldn't possibly know, but the ambiance grabbed her, folded her in its warmth and sumptuous grandeur, she could only stand and gaze around. Donald was at the desk, signing in; beckoning her, bringing her into the reception girl's orbit, she who had the smile, the '*buona sera!*' and her key card. *Her* keycard? She caught his eye; he nodded, picked up his bag and gestured towards the elevator.

In the quiet whoosh of the lift, dare she ask about the room? No. His choice, and not for her to either suggest or compromise; maybe their cosy togetherness wasn't to be extended into the professional world where Intrepid would pick up the hotel tab. She'd live on her dream suppositions that Mary, the late dear Mary, wanted her to be around but not to take over, not to impinge on the life they'd lived together in this film world. Maybe Beckside was too much the dream, the London flat the much too practical, logical obviousness; perhaps on location she was supposed to become quietly efficient, no more.

At least they were on the same floor, albeit opposite sides of the corridor. He helped her through the manipulation of the sometimes quirky key card, watched her into the room, smiled, said; 'See you in the lobby in half an hour,' and turned away. Left on her own, oddly, as now it came to her, it was the first time for weeks.

A double bed though; probably standard in all rooms, with a soft and fluffy duvet, then two armchairs, a small coffee table, a decent if plain carpet, a window with slatted shutters, clothes shelves and hanging space by the door into the en-suite. There she found the elegant fittings, the complexity of toiletries, the towels to the same high-fluff spec - and here she was, a simple girl with a smallish woven bag, not the high fashion leather one she'd own if she was truly going to star in this romance-with-moods movie. She turned back to the bed and spread-eagled herself, wishing and wondering. Half an hour, he'd said. No time to shower though she'd love to, barely enough time to strip and get into a dress.

Leaving her alone in her room was, he knew, going to change her mood, and he wasn't sure about his inner reaction. So used to having her around, part of his life, constantly planning for the two of them, meals, transport, work-load, spare time - going to the theatre, the films, walking the rounds in the park, all the little things that they'd unconsciously done as if, and here he had to take the deep breath, they were man and wife. They weren't. He was the widower with an unbroken love for his deceased wife, she the needy lonesome girl with a mixed-up past and no longer a true family life. Yes, she'd slept alongside him, but that was a comfort and a practicality, not a demand for sexual relations though glory knows, they'd been close to nudging each other over that fine line between a cuddle and copulation. Only his

116

inner strength to treat her as a woman in her own right and the firm devotion for his and Mary's past togetherness kept them that essential yet miniscule distance apart. Or was it her? Would Mary's spirit have screamed at him if they had succumbed to reality? Or smiled from whatever ethereal platform she floated on and put herself in Paula's place, taking his true loving to luxuriate in her own pleasured satisfaction? What thoughts to have! He'd better come back to sanity and the knowledge he'd got a job to do and, heaven help him, a need to come out of it with an unblemished reputation, lovely girl in tow or not.

He managed a quick and efficient strip-wash, found a clean shirt and the better chinos, combed his hair and stared at his double in the en-suite mirror; he'd be on show; presenting a professional image to the world. He'd not enquired, but fully expected Ronald to have flown in by now, probably with two or three of the others. The previously simple life alone with Paula and his memories would take on a different pace. How would she manage? No sign of her in the lift lobby; should he wait for her or go on down? He didn't want to risk her room - then her door opened and she looked lovely, absolutely lovely.

He had to; it was expected, to take her into his arms, to carefully kiss her as the recognition of her subtle scent raised the ante. 'You look pretty,' he told her, a careful understatement, well below his actual feelings.

Her eyes shone at him. 'Thankyou, but it's only a simple dress I shoved in - you saw me . . .'

He silenced her with another kiss. 'Simple it may be, but simplicity sometimes does the trick, Paula. Perhaps I should have said 'delicious', like good enough to eat - but,' and he put a gentle finger on her pursed lips, 'we'd better go on down. Ronald may well be about.'

'Ronald?'

He nodded. 'Work starts in earnest, dear girl.'

'Oh yes, so you said, sorry.' and she sought his hand as they walked down the corridor to the elevator door.

'Logistics can be boring. He and a few of the others were flying in and the kit will be on its way together with the tech guys. They'll gather everything together whilst we go on south tomorrow,' and he gently declutched his hand to call the lift. 'You okay with another train journey?'

'Of course,' and voiced her puzzlement. 'I thought we were looking round the city tomorrow?'

He nodded. 'Mmm, we are. Then tomorrow night we'll catch the sleeper down to Lecce. Another experience for you.'

'You didn't say?'

'Sorry. Our Pat does all the bookings. You'll have to learn to talk with her and get the lowdown on the logistics.' The lift purred to its stop and they were back to the foyer. Donald took her arm to walk her over towards the lounge - and yes, there was Ronald and three of the other lead people who she'd seen in the office, the two blokes, Peter and Jon together with a blonde girl, wasn't she the one who Donald had kept at arm's length? Yvette, wasn't that her name?

Handshakes all round, a kiss on the cheek from Ronald - he was entitled - she felt the admiring, perhaps envious looks from the other three. Were they going to be part of her day-on-day co-workers?

They made substantial inroads on the excellent meal, downed two bottles of Chianti and the conversation was lively, free ranging and, Paula did have to admit, stimulating. A far cry from the Claridges evening; she wasn't going to make that mistake again, even though she'd survived the aftermath it was more by luck - and Donald's care for her - that it hadn't ended in a bad memory.

Ronald leant towards her, lowered his voice. 'How do you like working alongside our art director then, Paula? Not driving you too hard? What do you think to our little project?'

He had a nice manner, this director chap Ronald, with the crinkled grin of his beneath the cropped grey curls. She liked him. 'It's amazing,' she said, not finding another word and having to admit to her constant refrain, 'I feel so privileged. He's been very good towards me,' and saw his glance across the table at her, likely aware of Ronald's inquisition. She lowered her voice. 'I hope the unit's not fazed by us being together?'

Ronald's smile deepened. 'Oh no, Paula, most of us think you've been the saving grace, if you aren't concerned by the description. Losing Mary like that - it was a blow, not just for him but for all of us. She was a great director.' She watched his eyes grow distant, the pause palpable. 'And a lovely woman too. A sad loss, very sad.' Then his smile ebbed as he voice dropped. 'Make sure you look after him. He's brilliant at what he does; the project wouldn't be same without his eye.

And your help, girl. Thank you for what you're doing.' He straightened up, tapped the table. 'Boys and girls, let's toast the project. We have a title, a generous and apt well-thought one, arising from a long and serious consideration of the well established plot,' his look around homed in on Donald, 'and by a strange and coincidentally appropriate set of circumstances we may have wished happened otherwise. Donald, Peter, Jon, Yvette, and our new protégé Paula, the very best for us all; here's to 'Maria's Legacy', may it be the best film of the year.'

Paula was stunned. She caught Donald's eye, aware no one knew of the agreed title before; it'd only been Project Puglia on the paperwork. Oh lor, how would he take it? The glasses were raised, clinked where possible, sipped and *'Maria's Legacy'* echoed round the table. She felt the chill working its way down her spine. She, the girl from nowhere, blundering down off a Lakeland fell, insinuating herself into an unknown man's life, following unseen, unknown forces, was *that* legacy. Given credence by the intensity of the spirit of a woman who'd been this man's life, thrust into a world of near make-believe, it had every feeling of unreality yet, and she quivered inside, knew it wasn't make believe. It was them.

Mary's Legacy   16

Breakfast was to be taken early, on late night instructions from Ronald, 'to make the best of the day'. Donald appeared to go into a distant, misty mood after the lovely meal last night; she went up with him in the lift but there was no conversation, just the familiar nice soft smile of his, a mere peck on her cheek at their parting at her door, a simple 'good night' and that was all. Was she disappointed? Perhaps, perhaps not, knowing she really had to switch her mind into work mode, to leave their association at an uncomplicated straight-forward level. The naming of the film at dinner must have had some impact on him, especially the 'Maria' bit. Flicking through her recall of the film's plot, she could see it all now, the way the word 'legacy' worked. No-one else would know the significance in the way she did. The 'Maria' role, as far as she knew from her reading of the plot, was a still-to-be cast thus unknown, un-named Italian girl, unless Booth was being ultra devious, for Donald had already said it wasn't going to be Annette or any of the other names. When she got a chance, she'd tackle Ronald - he, above others, might give her an answer as he seemed to like her, and as Booth wasn't likely to appear on set at all, directing matters from Pinewood, she couldn't ask him.

The chance came sooner than she'd thought. She entered the breakfast lounge before anyone else - had she been too keen? As she drifted around the buffet table in selective mood, Ronald appeared and of companionable disposition, so once plates were laden she'd no objection to his suggestion she joined him at a table.

'Not often I get a chance to have the pleasure of a pretty girl on her own,' his comment said with a cheeky grin and one she didn't see as flirtaceous. His look pinned her down. 'I watched you and Donald when I revealed we'd finally given the movie a title.'

'Was it that much of a secret? Donald didn't know?' Why was she asking? Would he guess?

Ronald pulled a face. 'You're concerned about a possible significant connection? Your being around must be a great help to him. So my thanks.' He reached across for the coffee jug, 'just so you don't think we're being deliberately insensitive to the way things are. This idea of a title was mooted some long time ago, whilst the original script was being chucked around. The first option was far too blitzy, 'Maria's Secret Hazard' or something similar. But,' and the coffee jug went back on its stand, 'Mary's death brought it very much into focus and probably meant our bosses gave the project more credence. Our Mary has had influence even after her very tragic loss,' he sipped his cup reflectively. 'I had a great deal of time for her, she was a lovely woman. I hope it won't affect him too much.'

'I wouldn't be here if wasn't for her.'

He raised bushy eyebrows at her. 'No? Well, what makes me surprised? You stick with our Donald. He's a great guy and deserves all our support. You love him?'

The question took her by surprise, or did it? This Ronald was as astute as they came. She stared at her plate, at the luscious croissants with her lavish spreading of apricot preserve. Love him? Between her and Donald they had a precious understanding but hadn't reckoned on it being too public an affair. No, not an *affaire*. A rapport. Dare she declare her feelings, if she could put them into real words?

'You do. Otherwise there'd have been an instant denial. He's a lucky guy. A very lucky guy. Don't you dare mess it up, Paula.'

The inference was plain. She shook her head. 'No,' she said carefully, 'I won't. Mary wouldn't let me.'

The eyebrows went up another notch. 'Mary?'

'She's looking after him - in fact, both of us now. Her 'influence', as you say, is still very much around.'

'Lordy! You believe in the afterlife?'

'I hadn't given it a thought until something odd happened. I was with Donald and stupidly, very vulnerable. He,' and she hesitated, would this be going to be a step too far? But Ronald was very much like a father confessor style figure so she pressed on, 'He didn't, if you get me. She was *there*, in a sort of spirit way, protective of us both,' and added her honest appraisal, 'I reckon I've been more the daughter figure for him. Yes, I know we've lived together,' - *what an admission* - 'but not in the way most would see it. This film, movie, project, whatever it's called, will likely decide what happens and Mary must agree. It's her,' and gave him a wan smile, 'legacy to him, for him to find a new woman in his life to replace her. So you'll understand how odd I feel over it, the film's title I mean.' For a brief moment the silence hung, before she came back to reality. 'Who's going to play Maria?' There, she'd finally managed her question.

He reached for her hand, resting lightly on the table, and gently held it. 'What you've said, Paula, I didn't know, and that's a truly honest admission. Thank you for sharing your confidence with me and I'll keep it so. In answer to your query, I don't know either, not yet. She's out there and we'll find her. To be correct for the film, she has to be innocent, vulnerable, beautifully presented in an Italian way and unaware of what's happening, for only then will we get the right sense on screen. No professional actor - actress - will give us quite what we need. And Donald knows it, I'm sure. He'll have the instinctive feeling - one of the reasons why we hired him.'

'With Mary's help.' The statement came without thought; for Paula knew with certainty that was the way it would have to be.

Ronald looked straight at her, serious now. 'With Mary's help,' he agreed and let her hand go. 'Look after him,' he added and got up. 'I have a meeting with the Gallerie management. See you later,' and he left her.

Donald joined her within minutes; as though he'd instinctively waited till Ronald had gone. 'Sorry,' he said, pulling out the chair alongside her. 'Overslept. You okay?' and reached for the same coffee jug. 'Someone's been at this. You've had company?' and beckoned the ever-watchful waitress for a refill.

'Roland.'

'Ah. He's a nice guy.'

'Yes, he is. And hopes you weren't fazed by the title announcement. Seems it was on the cards long before . . .' and her voice dried up. The emotive side to all this hadn't gone away.

He nodded. 'Commonsense suggests this project's been running for some long while, though I'm not going to deny his pronouncement last night threw me. A night's reflection puts it perspective. Mary's still with us in more ways than one.'

'I know.'

'You've wondered about Maria, who she may be?'

'Yes. And asked Roland. He doesn't know either, says we'll find her 'out there' and reckons you'll know the right girl when she does appear. I said Mary'll find her for us.' She heard him take a deep breath. 'He agreed.'

Another deep breath from him. 'Paula, lass, this is going to take some working out.' Then he had a flashback, to that weird dream he'd had, ages ago. 'You know, I'd agree with you. I've some inkling we'll find her too.' The coffee jug came back in front of a charming smile. 'Thanks,' and he beamed at the young waitress. 'Fetch me a croissant like hers? Please?'

Paula's second apricot croissant had stayed untouched during her exchange of views with Roland. Now she felt the appetite return. 'Feels like more of an adventure than a project. I'm a happier girl, Donald, seeing your smile again. I did worry, that perhaps last night's revelation might have thrown you. I didn't get my proper good-night kiss!'

His sideways glance with a grin made her inner girl squirm, with an odd flush of what, desire? *Paula,* her mind said firmly, *behave.* The little waitress girl reappeared with a plate and *three* croissants. Temptation took a different slant. Apricot croissants could be her downfall . . .

⌁

Milan, from a tourist's point of view, would be fascinating. From an art director's viewpoint, full of potential, and they could have spent more than a day wandering through the city but there had be some logic - and that was firstly, importantly, a visit to the Gallerie. Donald had his large sketch pad - and his camera. Paula wasn't sure what she was expected to do, but had also collected her own sketch pad and little camera from her room, just in case. She'd have loved to have explored La Scala, or the Duomo, but assisting Donald was supposedly her work - and intriguing work it could be too - which, of course, was why they were here.

It didn't take them very long to get there, Donald with his athletic stride and her trotting along to keep pace, despite avoiding wonderful

123

old trams running along the streets paved with multicoloured granite setts. Entering the Gallerie, she was amazed; she'd had no concept of the size, the extravagance, the vast colonnades under the curved glass domes, the beautiful terrazzo patterned floor and the famous names tastefully inserted over the windowed facades of the shops with their artistic pendant globe lighting. Shops? What else could she call them? There was one unforgettable memory of barely a few days ago, of wearing a Parisienne *haute couture* dress, one that could have been created in just such an establishment as those facing her now. This was one of those *ethereal* places, where Donald's Sarah would be so very much at home.

Donald had come to a halt, she could regain her breath. Out came his camera. 'Paula, ideas please. What strikes you most?'

'Pure size - the length, the height. It's overwhelming!'

'That's what we need to capture. The scale of the place.' She was treated to another of his fantastic smiles, 'and you're going to be here, on camera, to be seen as a figure walking towards the couple we're featuring; a swivel round the vastness then a close-up with you expressing 'intrigue'. Our main guy will turn round; see you and you'll grab his attention then we'll catch Annette's feelings, try to get the atmosphere - you can feel it now - a camera whirl, the argument, a pan away to see the couple walk off, your surprise, even disappointment, a shrug, then you carry on down the concourse and the out-focus to bring it to a close. Get it?'

She sensed his enthusiasm; how his mind had become inspired at the scene, now merely a simple virtuality. 'Where's the Maria in all this?'

His face clouded. 'Ah. Been and gone, I'm afraid. It's Annette who becomes his Maria in the end; the 'legacy' of the title. The viewer doesn't know it at this stage. The clinch we might do up in the hills, you know, umbrella pines, olives, scorched grass, soft rug and a bottle of Chianti . . .'

'Blue sky and distant sea?'

'You've got it. Shall we explore?'

A fascinating experience and she was living it; living it to the full. She saw a different Donald, the one who was wrapped up in the project. Still she found it difficult to continue the process of naming the film in her head. The newly released title, '*Maria's Legacy*', as a parallel to their intimate knowledge, was too raw, too close to home. She wondered about the plot, of what she'd read in the story line and was surprised she hadn't seen how the whole project turned on the way an as yet unknown girl caused a change in their character's mindset. It was subtle; that much she could understand and, providentially, nothing like the run-of-the-mill soppy romances. But was there a twist she hadn't seen? She'd have to curb her impatience and let events take whatever course they may.

They spent the rest of the morning roaming the esoteric depths of the vast building, Donald continuously using his very swish pocket sized camera. Later on he seemed to want to wander off alone - had he become bored with her, possible inane, comments? She found a convenient bench seat so she could use her sketch pad to salve her conscience, be seen to be innovative. A particularly interesting window display which, with the surrounding architecture and constant flow of passers by, caught her imagination and provided her with a challenge. No-one appeared to take any notice of her and she became absorbed. Time passed.

'Happy?' She jumped, startled, surprised, and suddenly aware how long she'd been parked on the bench. 'You're enjoying the experience?' Donald, leaning over her shoulder and studying the sketch. 'That's very good. Shame it has to be so small.'

'Thank you.' She stretched her back and he moved to allow her to stand. 'Got all you want?' she asked him.

'Yep. I've been into the square too, seen a couple of angles to expand on the run-away. We can go back to the hotel if you wish.'

'We've had no lunch!'

He pulled a face. 'Sorry. Habit of mine, forgetting to eat when on the trail. Mary . . .' and he stopped.

She knew, instinctively, what he would have said, like 'she kept an eye on me' a relic of the way the pair must have worked together and she felt it. Was it a jealous pull, or a twist that she'd not been able to foresee the basic need? Trivial it may be, but essential. Part of a p.a.'s job. Damn . . . why hadn't she taken the initiative? She got a small smile from him, an acknowledgement of her unspoken concern. However, no words were necessary as the intuitive thought-read was already there.

'You're okay, girl. No probs. Best get back?'

'Sure. You said we're heading south tonight?'

He took her free hand. 'Yes.'

'A sleeper train?'

'Yes.'

'Should be, er, an adventure then? Or am I being naïve here?'

'Bunk beds, but in the same compartment. Hope it's not an embarrassment but it saves a few euros and I can keep an eye on you.'

She had to laugh. Him and her, together, aware and each with a smidgen of a hang-up, a different mind-set, slung together like it or no because of the paucity of the unit's expenses fund? Or was it because of the devious or mischievous mind of the reception girl who did the bookings? Whatever. She'd go naked for him any day without a worry - so her mind said, to then immediately chastise itself. The expression suggested more than the essential companionship that was, at this point in their relationship, all that mattered. He took her hand; together they walked out into the Italian sunshine.

ॐ

Dinner with all the film production team in the hotel was another light-hearted affair, last night's numbers augmented by two more of the technical types, Andy and Bill, and the very prim and proper Evaline, she who kept an eye on finances. Evaline kept eyeing her. Why? Donald didn't take much part in the conversation; was he under some sort of stress with this woman present? Once the meal drifted to its lengthy close and Donald glanced for the nth time at his watch, she felt his vibes. *Time to get up and go, girl . . .* she stood, he got up too, he said their farewells and with a light hand on her shoulder, steered her away.

'I know,' he said, once they were out of hearing and into the lift lobby, 'you wondered about Evaline. Past history, but she never liked Mary.'

'Why?'

She saw his lips purse, the slight frown deepening the lines on his forehead. 'I shouldn't tell you. Too . . .'

She cut him off, with a female's intuition. 'She wanted to join your fan club?'

That produced a chuckle as the lift doors opened. Inside, to her surprise and joy, he took her in his arms and *really* kissed her.

'There,' he said, letting go, 'I've wanted to do that all evening.' His smile warmed her right through, down and down . . .

Practicality; keep hold of your emotions, Paula, girl. 'To spite her?' she suggested, hypothetically.

Another chuckle. 'Perhaps. Now, grab your bag. There'll be a car waiting downstairs. We can't afford to miss the train. It's a long way and there won't be another until tomorrow.'

Mary's Legacy 17

How long had she slept? She must have had an hour or three. The constant reverberations of train, track, wheels, windage, the feel of fast travel, the warmth of her oddly comfortable bed, suspended, vaguely aware of Donald's closeness yet remoteness.

Joining the train had been yet another facet of this adventure; adding one more experience, happily accepting her mentor's presence, his guidance; taking the welcome offer of coffee and intriguing biscuits from the steward, trying to understand rapid-fire Italian and failing despite her ancestry, but liking the man's broad open smiles, building her memories into an enormous patchwork of unforgettable happenings, all becoming part of her life. She could even have wished it'd go on for ever, but now the train was slowing.

According to the timetable, there'd be another hour before reaching Lecce, time enough to breakfast in the buffet saloon. Would there be more apricot croissants? An odd query crossed her mind.

'Donald? You awake? Are we on our own here?'

He stirred, rolled over in his bunk. 'I can't see anyone else.'

'Not what I meant.'

'I know. There won't be anyone waiting for us if that's what you're worried about.' He pushed the bedcover to one side, swung his legs out and slid to the floor. 'Did you sleep?'

She sniffed. 'Off and on. You?'

'Yep. Like the proverbial chunk of timber. Can you manage another day without a full sleep quota?'

She took a full breath. Could she? After a night of odd dreams, occasional interludes of half consciousness? After the drift of thoughts reappearing in her mind, of the moment she first saw him, of the much debated decision to inflict her concerns into his life, of that time when she realised he'd actually put her to bed after the Claridges debacle - and not being upset that he'd sensibly unhooked her bra for her as part of the process. Most importantly though, that her presence here dictated work . . . of course she could manage.

'Yep. Provided there's breakfast - and coffee.'

He stood up, stretched, and reached for his chinos, shrugged into a clean tee-shirt. 'I'll leave you the cabin for ten minutes. Do what you have to,' grinned at her, blew her a kiss across the gap, pushed his feet into the deck shoes and left her alone.

Lecce, a southern Italian town at the edge of the - her - known world, was to be the place where Intrepid would create a new style of film art, where personalities would merge, separate, swing back together, hover in the abstract beauty of the place, absorb its ambiance and translate actuality into a virtuality that cinema-goers would revel in, talk about, try and emulate - therefore a place travel companies would take more to their hearts - and emphasise the location in their holiday brochures.

They took a taxi to their hotel in the middle of town; again she marveled at the ease of his approach to the reception staff, a fluidity of actions she found impressively sexy - and cuffed her female mind for such a suggestion. Work; my girl, this is work and he's good at it. A room by herself again; oh well . . . yes; perhaps just as well, it'd give her a respite from the intensity of it all.

Mid morning and it was hot. She looked at the small collection of clothes tipped out on the bed. What to wear? The travel skirt was crumpled and underwear unspeakably over-used, especially after sleeping in her knickers. Pondering over the heap, she scarcely heard the knock at her door; but without ceremony there was Donald, already changed. Maybe she shouldn't have taken her top off, but he didn't stare, merely sifted a hand through her untidy heap on the coverlet.

'I didn't think you'd packed enough,' his critical comment. 'Sling that tee shirt back on and we'll go shopping. You need clothes, I need exercise and we have to get a feel for the place. Come on.' He moved to the window, opened the half shutter briefly to peer out and a waft of warm air entered the room. 'It's busy out there - at the moment. We'll explore. It'll quieten down in an hour or two, siesta time, so it'll be easier to get about later. Okay?'

Whilst he talked she did as ordered, wished she'd a lighter skirt too, but 'shopping' sounded good. 'You mean 'shopping' as in proper shopping?' putting the emphasis where she knew he'd react.

He grinned at her. 'I enjoy dressing women, but it's usually for the screen and, generally, starlets do as they're told. To practice on a girl who'll answer back if I get it wrong will make a nice pleasant change, especially if she gets what both she and I want.'

Dare she? Probe into a sensitive area? 'Did you shop with Mary?' and watched his face change.

There was a nod, no more. 'Ready?' he asked.

She nodded back; they left the room with no further comment. Had she upset him? Surely not - they were too close for that sort of a concern.

The hotel was right in the middle of the town centre; it didn't take long to discover what looked like the right woman's wear outlet, good clothes in the window, an uncrowded sales area, assistants with smiles and excellent posture - she recognised class when she saw it, and Donald didn't hesitate either.

Language wasn't a problem. The girl who came forward to greet them switched straight into faultless English from the initial '*boun giorno!*' once they'd revealed where they came from. Paula was quite prepared to stand up for herself and explain what she wanted, irritatingly she found Donald taking the lead, asking about skirts . . . *as though she was a daughter. Then that's what she was supposed to be. No worries.*

She couldn't stand meekly by. 'Not too short,' she said, 'and pure cotton.' The sales girl caught on, gave Donald her gorgeous smile and led Paula towards the rear of the shop towards racks of lovely things.

Within twenty minutes or so she'd tried on three or four, chosen a simple yet understated dress in a swishy floral pattern with lacey sleeves, a skirt, added a pack of silky pants and a lovely apricot coloured silk top she couldn't resist. And Donald paid, bless him - but then, he owed her, didn't he? Though she was working for him, she'd yet to see any reimbursement for her services so it was about time she had some solid recognition; it was a perfect opportunity for him to make good. She took advantage of the shop's facilities, changed back into the newly acquired skirt, a fully pleated below-knee length in a wonderfully light straw shaded cotton, before they left the girl and her effusive thanks to plunge back into the heat of the day.

'Thanks,' she said, swinging the bag in what she saw as a jaunty fashion. Life was on the up.

'That's okay. Need to keep you up to the mark. We'll drop the bag back into the hotel. Don't need to carry that around all day, do we?'

What was in store for her? Could she see herself like a 'kept' girl, with travel, accommodation and, now, clothes paid for? She must keep it clear in her head about maintaining the sexual distance between them. *Mary, what do you think?* The mentally posed question thus had its own tinge of euphoria; was a spirit's presence looking after her?

With the clothing bag deposited at reception, he didn't suggest a pause, instead they continued to gently amble around the town, to discover the old ruins, the park, to admire the beautiful buildings and the statues, to catch an assessment of the busy life of the town before, as he'd predicted, by an hour or so after noon, all appeared to go uncannily quiet. By mutual, unspoken consent they turned back into the gardens; walked slowly on to reach a tree and palm girt central building in white stone between two ponds, a central fountain playing over the depth of clear water, truly an architectural gem.

'Beautiful!' She stood still, mesmerised, hands gripping the railings, soaking up the feel, the quiet warmth and romance of the place, the magic of it all. Alongside her, he stood absorbing the same experience, conscious of how well he'd be able to use this place in one of the more emotive sequences of the film. Absolutely right for a dialogue between the two main characters; instinctively aware it was a perfectly apt location - could they film when the place was all but deserted, during the same time in the day, siesta . . .?

'Back to the hotel?' They'd covered a lot of ground, she'd be tired. Her presence was now so natural that his care for her wellbeing was second nature.

She glanced sideways at him; she couldn't help the grin. With eyebrows raised her reply opened an opportunity. 'If I didn't know you better, I'd take that as a proposition.'

He chuckled at her. 'Be flattered, girl.'

'Hummph,' she made a mock frown. 'Now if you were a young sexy Italian guy . . .'

'Fed up with the old-stager, are you?' and he made the comment in similar jest, unaware of how she'd react.

'No!' and the strength of her denial surprised them both. 'No,' she repeated. 'Never,' and sought his hand, caught his eyes, snatched a deep breath and took, on a silly whim, a gauche chance, for the attraction conceived was undeniable. 'If you want me, want me the way I'd love to be wanted and . . .' without warning an inner emotion took hold and tears squeezed out of hot eyes, choking off what she would have perhaps added, 'if Mary would smile at us,' but she couldn't, couldn't, couldn't.

His strong hand gripped hers, his arm went round her, held her waist tight, held the warmth of her supple youthfulness close to him, breathed softly into her ear 'one day, maybe,' kissed her first on the smooth skin of a low neck, then, as she turned her face upwards in hope, on her lips, the fullness of her young soft, kissable lips, felt the surge of feeling for her expand and nearly choke him with a dangerous desire he'd scarce thought ever possible since that last time with Mary, his Mary, his love of a lifetime. 'Oh Paula . . .'

She twisted out of his hold with an inner strength, denying her wantonness, realising how close they both were - yet again - to precipitating a drastic - and possible - disaster and the demolition of all that they'd achieved; with the sanguine effect of necessity she managed to regain sufficient common sense to cool her thoughts. Mary, she kept saying in her head. Mary, Mary, Mary - help me?'

'Sorry,' she said instead.

He gripped the railings to squeeze his emotions back into check. What was he thinking of? This young girl who he'd absorbed into his life, allowed her, given her, a part of his soul, was vulnerable, far too vulnerable; he was nearly twice her age and he had - unfortunate term - used her, yes, he had to admit the euphemism free transgression, if that's what it was, used her constant presence to dullen the ache of his always attendant sense of loss. How far down the path of that transgression had they gone?

The water jets of the fountain in front of them swayed in the quirky breeze and splashed down closer, the drift catching the edge of the terrazzo sets of the pavement where they stood. Instinctively they both stepped back and collided. He caught her once more, held her firm in his hands. It was inevitable, the fatal echo in his head 'find a girl. . .' Had he really found her? The question hung in the warmth and against the backdrop of water and blue sky.

'Let's go back.' Her decision, her's the choice, but truly the common sense had insidiously crept in, he'd got what he wanted, scenarios locked away in his head, places to use, appropriate aspects for the plot.

'Right-oh,' he agreed, as a return to logic.

He took her hand as they walked down the path between the statues of Italian notables, the dark green of the trees contrasting with the swathes of lawn, the emptiness of the place strikingly odd. Regent's Park at this time of day would be plastered with couples, families, escapees from myriad offices. She swung their clasped hands.

'Are we winning?'

'The plot thickens,' he said, in a theatrical voice.

'Are we succeeding then? Oh, you know what I mean!'

'I'm happy with what we've achieved; does that answer the question?'

There are two ways of interpreting the comment, she told him, and added 'you're irritating!'

He gave a little sniff of amusement. 'Whichever way, dearest Paula, you want to make the interpretation. I'm sure your instinct will tell you. What do you think?'

They got to the gate; the hotel was less than five minutes away. She pondered on how to return the euphemisms without getting into trouble.

He took pity on her, appreciating the silence. 'I've got what I need, Paula. There'll a fair amount of homework to be done, getting it all into the storyboard, so it'll be a boring evening, sorry.'

'Can't I do something?'

'Oh yes, most definitely. That's why you're here - well, partly, other than to keep my coffee mug topped up, my pencils sharp, to divert strangers from the door, that sort of thing.'

'Now you're laughing at me!'

'Not really. You'll see.'

≈

One of the hurdles to be overcome whilst being in Europe, Paula found, was the general inability of any establishment to brew tea in an acceptable English manner. The first thing Donald said, entering the hotel lobby, was 'I could do with a nice cup of tea' and so, in her role of p.a., she needed to oblige and tried her English on the man at the reception desk.

They sat in the small lounge behind the lobby and waited - in due course along came a waiter with a tray, cups with Yellow Label teabags and a jug of hot water. 'No teapot?' she asked.

A puzzled look, then a rapid Italian explanation before his departure.

'So what was that all about?'

Donald chuckled. 'They don't understand the 'boiling water' bit. Never mind. It's a 'do it yourself' exercise. Seasoned travelers always carry their own teapot - and kettle. You've noticed we've no room tray.'

'Stick to coffee then.'

'Which is what Italy's all about, girl, as you should know if you've ancient connections. Coffee, more coffee and the stronger the better. Tea is not something in their psyche. Come on, make the best of it.'

So she poured less than hot water over teabags and sat back in her chair to sulk. Donald took it in his stride, eased back in his comfy armchair, crossed his legs, sipped at the cup, placed it back on the small table alongside. 'So? How's it so far?'

'What do you mean?'

'Overall impression of being involved in the film world. What you expected, what you felt might happen?'

She stared at him. 'Donald? What's this then, a staff appraisal? Odd place, odd timing?'

'Oh, I don't know; end of a working day, relaxed over a cup of tea . . .'

''You're not regretting dragging me along?'

'No, not at all. *Au contraire,* you're a delightful addition to the expedition. But,' and she saw his expression take on the thoughtful look she actually was becoming quite used to, 'as we're getting into the thick of things, I want some reassurance that we, sorry, *I'm* not taking advantage of you,' and a frown appeared.

'Why ever would you think that? It was me who 'took advantage', relying on my reading of your good nature to help me out of an impasse. I'd got myself into a hole, you pulled me out. Therefore,' and she put her cup down, settled back in her chair to pull a knee up and couple her hands round it. Her new light cotton skirt rode tantalizingly up her thigh and she ignored it, staring across the room at paintings on the opposite wall, 'I'm indebted to you. And because you hadn't assumed anything and we seem to understand each other . . .' She released her knee, pulled the skirt back into place, 'why should either of us worry? Let's do a good job with '*Maria*' and see what happens?'

'You won't hesitate to tell me . . .?'

He got a lovely smile from her. 'No, I won't. But,' and she reached out a hand to rest it briefly on his knee, 'it's unlikely. You're too much the gentleman. And,' she added reflectively, 'still in love with Mary,' at which point she got up. 'I'm going to have a shower before dinner. See you upstairs. Give me half an hour.'

He watched her go, her skirt swinging, her shoulders back, head up and feet straight, a perfect walk an actress would envy. And heard Mary's voice in his head "*she's a very nice girl*', and '*Yes, she is,*' his mental reply.

Mary's Legacy 18

Weird, that evening after dinner, or so she thought, was the time spent in the small lounge browsing through the 'thoughts from the day', as Donald called his sketches. They'd showered, dressed to relax - and here Paula's feminity came to the fore, playing with her acquisitions from the day to choose the most flattering new frock - to enjoy a quiet meal as any friendly couple would.

'Tell me about your school days,' he suggested, but she didn't want to be drawn. The claw back of claustrophobic days spent in classrooms at Roedean, with abrupt teachers and awkward moments, P.E. periods when she'd be forced to run around draughty playing fields in her navy knickers, no, not times she'd wish to remember let alone talk about; definitely not, her previous life was something she wished to push into the dim recesses, preferably never to surface. Here was the future, alongside one of the nicest men she'd ever had the blest fortune to meet - and all down to the woman who still kept the key to his heart even beyond the grave. Would she ever get access to that key? Stop brooding, woman, she told herself, shook her head, brushed her forehead and smiled at him.

'I'd rather you told me about yours.'

'Okay. What do you want to know?'

'Where you went to school, siblings, what your father did, how you got into films, that sort of thing?'

'Nosy,' he said, not meaning it.

'You know more about me. I've told you about my family, where I went to school.'

He nodded. 'But I needed to know; I couldn't take any odd girl into my entourage. I was giving you a job . . .'

'Not then you weren't and I didn't apply for one either, I . . .'

He waved a hand at her. 'Okay, okay - though you did apply for a position in a round-about sort of way. Never mind. I've no brother or sister, perhaps sadly. My father was an accountant, though a highly paid one,' and he mentioned the company.

'Wow,' she said. 'Them!'

'Yes, them, which was how I got to Marlborough, though public schools aren't always nice places if you're an individual, perhaps Roedean . . .' and again she cut him off.

'We have something in common then. Don't tell me; ragged and bullied, yet came out with five 'A' levels? And we are both individuals, I admit that. Did you go to Uni then?'

He nodded. 'U E A,' expecting her to query the mnemonic, but no, she knew.

'Media studies?'

He nodded again. 'Seen by some as the easy option but I was all too serious a student and didn't rag about like lots of my contemporaries. It's a rite of passage for far too many who use - misuse - their time to shag around. Not me. I made a decent little arty film which got me noticed. So a job offer came along; with a small production company who did work for a television channel where I helped make a landmark series and that got me head hunted by you know who and, as they say, the rest is history.'

Was that feeling one of an odd sense of pride in association? Partnered with a guy who'd actually made the most of what life threw at him, whereas she'd messed up, not caring and, as he'd truthfully said, misused her time? At least she hadn't been in the 'shag around' circle though she'd known some who had - did - and one or two much the worse for wear as a consequence. Pride that she hadn't - or did she felt oddly belittled?

'We're wasting time. There's a lot to plough through here. Shall we get on with it? Tomorrow we go north, along the coast.'

'Oh?'

'Next stop on the itinerary, Vieste, which is where life begins in earnest. The troops will join us there and then it's *'cameras roll'*.

'Blimey,' she said, 'when we've only been here a day?'

'Occupational hazard, girl. Can't hang about. We'll get the Lecce scenes wrapped tonight; the guys will take them all on board when we give them the plot late tomorrow, while they're getting sorted we'll try and find our Maria and she'll be the starter. We'll be back here in a couple of days or so if it goes well, then you'll really see how it all happens . . . ready?'

She had to swallow her feelings, get on with why she was here, put her mind to more constructive use, and started to sift through the pile of notes he'd made; Donald ignored her and began to sketch on his lovely cartridge paper pad. She vowed she'd hide a few of these sketches away once they'd been scanned and when a future opportunity occurred, frame them to allow memories to have some substance. How easy would it be to allow these moments to slip away into obscurity! The day's rambles took on a better meaning - she reached for the big chunk of script notes to help her ease some of his jottings into appropriate places. Within moments it began to make sense, the scenes in the script and the locations they'd spotted. An odd sense of delight and euphoria trickled through her, a sort of spine tingle of an entirely different flavour, as the pieces in this weirdest of jigsaws started to fall into place.

'Hoi! Paula - does this one work?' He showed her his pad and immediately she knew where they were, back to the fountain, the Lowry style figures included could well have been them rather than cast members doing their thing though his artistry gave the picture a deeper significance.

'It fits here,' and she moved her carefully positioned pages to open up the appropriate wordage so his picture would slot in.

Donald peered at the papers, initially said 'Um,' and sat back, hands behind his head, stretched. 'Time to pack it in, Paula. We've done it. Good work.'

'That's it?'

'Don't you think so? Not a scene missed. You're good, you know. I'm glad I hired you,' and a lazy smile grew, 'for you've done most of the work. All we need is the storyboard artist to offer accolades and who knows, Booth may even offer to pay you himself. Come. It's bedtime.' He eased out of his chair and began to carefully stack the sheets. 'Wouldn't do to lose these now.'

She watched, seeing the deft way he managed to put them in correct order for shooting, despite her having sorted them initially. *Don't be hoodwinked by his casual manner,* her mind said, *he's brilliant at his job.*

'If you hadn't become an 'art director',' she asked, the question out of the blue, 'what would you have done?'

He chuckled as he slid the wad of sheets into a clean folder and dropped it into his briefcase. 'Probably been an interior designer - or decorator. Boring. I may have had to advertise in that magazine of yours.'

Her turn to chuckle. 'Then we may have met in a different way.'

He zipped the case tight shut. 'Likely, Paula. The fates had it in store for us. Coming?' He hefted the case and offered her a hand.

She took it; he pulled her close; together they went upstairs.

Mary's Legacy 19

Once Donald came slowly to the surface after - as far as he could tell - a dreamless night, the thoughts about the day started crowding in. First, the necessity to travel along the coast; that journey would, in itself, be a fantastic experience, then finding the hotel where, if the logistics had worked, Peter's unit would already be; Ronald would be there, the admin lot coming in later. Did Vieste know what was in store? Had the public relations team done their thing? How long would it take them to shoot? Two days? Three? Annette and the other guys would be chauffeured in tomorrow; they needed to have everything in place - big names wouldn't stand for delays, neither would Booth appreciate the loss of time. Having a star hanging around cost loads of money even if they were on lump sum payment; one had to maximize the time available and it was a large part of his job to ensure the scenes were shot in logical sequence. Mary was always good at that. He missed her, saw her image on the hotel room ceiling, could sense the warmth of her alongside, the neat pile of her clothes on the chair, the whisper of her 'good morning' in his ear, the feel of her arm across his chest - he missed her, missed her. . .

A tap on his door - heard in his imagination as an echo, the reverberation of a past moment, or the girl? Could she ever fulfill the suggestion of being Mary's 'the girl who needed him'? The door handle tried - it'd be her.

'Donald?' Her voice, so yes, Paula. And yes, he loved her but how deeply? Nothing for it; get out of bed, sling on the dressing gown and let her in.

Dressed, the vision in the doorway . . . . 'Donald? I thought it time we were down for breakfast; you said we're moving on?'

'I slept too well. How about you?'

'Not sure about my dreams, Milan, the Gallerie, scorching hot beaches, that sort of thing. And, of course, getting your shooting schedules right.' She looked pensive. 'So when do we leave?'

'After breakfast. You want to go on down? I'll only be a minute.'

'Did I get you out of bed?'

He shrugged, 'yes, but probably as well. You're as bad as my daughter - she always pulled me out of bed when a teenager.'

'You've not spoken to her lately?'

'She knows not to call when I'm on location. She'll be fine.'

Paula's expression relaxed. 'I did wonder.' She changed topic. 'How do we get to where you said - Vieste, wasn't it?'

'Hire car, the hotel should have it organised. Best way, means we're not reliant on public transport and quicker. So, can I get dressed?'

She grinned. 'Okay boss, see you downstairs,' blew a kiss at him and shut the door rather too firmly behind her. Donald shook his head, muttered *'women'*, but it didn't take him long to progress through the bathroom and dress appropriately. Today was the true start, when the pace hotted up and he was looking forward to it, to get back into the thick of the shoot, an adrenaline rush, a sense of urgency followed by the euphoria when seeing the first play-backs on the screen. What he did, he did well, whilst living the fulfillment of a constant dream - except for the ever-present gap?

'You'll be fine,' he heard in his head as he flung things into his bag, *'I'm behind you all the way. Look after the girls.'*

Girls, plural, what did she mean? *Mary,* he sent the thought waves soaring, sure the beautiful spirit of his past love would know, wherever she was in the cosmos, *'what d'you mean, girls?'*

'Ah, you're looking for a Maria, remember? You'll find her where you least expect her. Keep her safe . . .' the message seemed to say before it faded away. Too much interference, he said to himself and managed a grin. What would Paula - or Sarah, come to that - think of this odd phenomena? He zipped the bag closed, left it on the bed.

She was waiting for him, the lovely girl that she was, in open blouse, her light cotton skirt in the patterned light green and white. Summery, refreshing, smiling, *his protégé; Mary, is she the one?* No answer - a hint he should make up his own mind? *Come on, Donald; get on with the day . . .*

The hotel receptionist smiled at him as he asked the question about the car, picked up the phone; he heard the rapid burst of Italian before she repeated her smile when the phone went down. 'Your coupé will be here within the hour,' she told him. 'An Alfa Spyder, as requested. More expensive than a Fiat, but,' and her eyes narrowed down with a sideways look at Paula standing across the entrance hall, 'more the *correto* romantic *auto* to travel in with a companion,' as if she were wishing to take Paula's place. He gave her his own polite return smile and rejoined *his* girl. 'Breakfast?'

Within the hour they'd breakfasted, cleared their rooms and were waiting with bags packed in the hotel lobby, poised at the start of another chapter in the unstoppable saga.

'We look forward to seeing you again soon,' the pleasant girl had said as he'd signed the bill. 'Your car will be here soon. I hope you'll have a nice day.' *She wouldn't know . . .*

Five minutes later the open-topped bright red Alfa Romeo Spyder was duly delivered; Donald signed the paperwork, slipped the delivery driver a ten euro note and that was that. Their bags neatly stowed in the boot, Paula nestled into the passenger seat and, at the start of another sunny day, it was theirs to enjoy.

They looked at each other. 'Happy?' he asked with more of a meaning than the immediate one.

'How could I not be?' her reply, instinctively aware of the significance of his simple query, 'I chose to go on a hike in the Lakes, and now look where I am, sitting in an impressive Italian car!'

'Yes,' he said briefly. 'Hope you won't regret it …hang on to your hat, it's a long time since I drove left-handedly and the Italian driver isn't always forgiving.'

'I haven't got a hat ….'

He flashed the big grin at her, suggested she ought to have one once the sun got to work, slipped the Alfa into gear and trusted to instinct. Vieste was northwest and his in-built sense of direction took him correctly out of the town to cross the ring road and away onto the Strada 16.

'It's a fair old way but we'll play tourist. Stop off here and there. In this game, adding value to a journey comes second nature. Places we see, views, buildings; you never know, they might come in handy.'

'So how far?'

'Three fifty K or about four hours or so, but it's stunning scenery from all accounts.'

She settled down into the snug little seat. 'Hope you don't get us lost.'

'Fat chance. This ain't the UK, it's Italy.'

Ten minutes later and they were out of the town - city - happily the traffic was light. Donald kept the Alfa down to a steady eighty kilometers per hour and the car ate up the distance. She stayed quiet whilst the journey got really under way then couldn't resist it.

'Lovely car. Bit different to the Discovery.'

He laughed. 'True, but horses for courses, if that's the right cliché to use. Intrepid pay the bill so I make the most of it. Next stop, Brindisi.'

The route turned out to be straight forward; Brindisi came and went, Donald found the turn onto the coast road and Monopoli was in their sights. Paula kept quiet, enjoying the ride and the scenery. What else? As often expressed perhaps, with a wry thought, too often, she still had odd feelings of euphoria mixed up with disbelief allied with twinges of anxiety over the outcome of this adventure. This journey along the coast road - would it be another move into the unknown for her? Donald seemed happy enough, she could tell, with a casual hand on the wheel and lips pursed in a soundless whistle. Happy with her, or the thought he was obeying a final injunction, come what may? The sun was certainly doing its thing; the sea sparkled, with the Turkish coast a grey line on the visible horizon. What lay ahead? Should she, dare she, suggest a lunch stop? Perhaps she should have suggested a picnic basket, and as this more logical thought bubbled to the surface of a wandering mind, so Donald turned his head away from the straight and empty road ahead, caught her eye and winked. 'Lunch,' he mouthed, his foot came of the pedal, the car slowed and with the opportune incidence of a layby, he brought it to a stop, switched the engine off, let the quiet descend. 'Phew,' he said. 'Half way or thereabouts; we should have brought a picnic.'

She couldn't help the wide grin. 'You and I with common thought. My fault, I should have been more switched on. I've a few biscuits I nicked from the breakfast buffet.'

'Ah, another commonality. Better than nothing. I've got some too,' and fished in his pocket. 'Shall we go and look at the sea, stretch our legs?'

'Okay. The car'll be alright?'

'Not much about. Should be.'

The road ran parallel to the shore; a small fence, a hundred metres of rough ground, a few shrubs, then the beach - a ten metre wide strip of coarse sand stretching north and south. Not a soul about. A wave-worn and weathered old tree trunk provided a perfect seat. Paula crunched on her biscuit. 'I suppose this is the lull before the storm?'

'Reckon. Three or four days of frenetic film making. You'll love it. Then back to Lecce, on to Milan, do much the same before the return to London, see the studio work and watch the in-filling. You'll get bored.'

'Is that a promise or a threat?'

'It'll lose its appeal after a while. Becomes routine. Once it's all in the can, metaphorically speaking, we sit back. Editors take over.'

'Aren't you involved with that?'

'I'll look at the rough edit, in case we need to add a shot or two to keep continuity. If I've got it correct then there won't be very much of that.' Paula watched his eyes go distant, reflective, a stare across at another country, across the Adriatic. 'Mary,' and he heaved a probably unconsciously motivated sigh, 'and I had an instinctive feel for things. This'll be the first on my own. Hope I get it right for her sake.'

She couldn't add any comment. He knew, she knew, it was still a raw wound despite her input, her presence. She hoped she was some small comfort - a close physicality helped, her feminity told her that, but it had yet to erase all the hurt. He must have mind-read and reached for a hand.

'Just be here for me, Paula, be here for Mary. Please.'

'I will. Whatever you need, Donald, just . . . well, ask; suggest - whatever. Me, if you want - or not, you won't offend me. We're awfully close.'

He gave a sort of amused sniff. 'Some of the crew will have their own ideas about us. Ignore them. Oh; and never worry about the other girls, Evaline, Yvette, they mostly don't mean anything. Mary kept them at bay. One or two may try it on if they think I've lost my bodyguard.'

'I could play the jealous girlfriend quite well.'

The sniff was repeated with a following chuckle. 'You may have your work cut out.'

'I'll enjoy it. Watch me.'

Another chuckle. 'I will, don't you worry. You're very watchable.'

'Flirter.'

He leaned over, flipped her hair sideways and kissed her cheek. 'We'd best move on. Still a-ways to go.'

She got up, turned, leant down and kissed him gently on the lips. 'Love you,' she said and walked back to the car.

They drove on, back onto the main road and away from the evocatively named *Via de Torre Testa,* Donald's apparently careless one handed guide on the wheel suggested he wasn't at all stressed and that made her happy, stimulating an almost forgotten ability to whistle an oddly out-of-character phrase of an old pop tune. He recognised it.

'Strangers in the night, Paula?' said above the car's steady rumble, with his now characteristic sideways grin at her. 'Not a Freudian slip, surely?'

The grin was returned. 'How can it be?' a plain reply but underneath she felt the emotional pull. *She'd slept in his arms . . .* perhaps it was a psychological connection and therefore best suppressed. What else? Somehow that catchy old song from '*My Fair Lady*' appeared in her head: *'I could have danced all night'. . .*

Another grin. 'Remember '*Oklahoma?*' There's one which may be more appropriate - *'Oh what a beautiful morning...'*?

'Except it isn't morning any more.'

'True. Sorry I can't think of a more appropriate tune for you, not being a pop fan. I'm more into classics. *'Moonlight Sonata'* perhaps, or something composed by Rachmaninov.'

'Not Elgar, his *Introduction & Allegro,* or Vaughan Williams and *'Lark Ascending'*?'

'I'm impressed. A girl who knows her English composers!'

'I have my moments.'

'So it seems. I'll ask the sound track people to talk to you.'

Back on the dual carriageway of the *Strada Statale 369* Donald pushed the pace. Though used to continental driving it'd been some time since he'd last been this far south; the heat of the day had been building and this part of the route was boring, endless flat landscape, white stone, dry earth and best put behind them. The best bit was still to come. 'Ever been in the Alps?' he asked.

'Gracious, no. What's that question to do with today?'

'The road does wind around rather, or so I'm led to believe. Maybe we'll have our couple drive it on their way up so we can say it's part of the research.'

'You're very devious, mister. You didn't tell me.'

'Ah well, have to maintain interest.'

'You do that already. Rather more than I can take in sometimes.' She pushed further back in her seat and stretched her arms above her head, letting the windage fling her hair back.

'That's a very Marlene pose, though she'd have a scarf too. And, if I may say so, a lower and more prominent frontage.'

'Huh,' and she brought her arms down. 'I'll refrain from further comment,' and watched his expression crease in a grin.

'This is the Strada Adriatica,' he said, tactfully changing the topic, 'a logical name,' then lapsed into silence to concentrate on another junction. Barietta came and went, followed by Manfredonia and the road began to climb.

'I see what you mean,' she allowed, wondering how good he was at manipulating rather tight bends as the twists and turns took them up and into the hills. She got no answer, he was obviously concentrating. A large truck suddenly appeared coming the other way, she winced as the car squeezed to the right but there was more room than she thought and she could let her muscles relax. Then they were out of the trees and - surprise - there was the sea, stretching out blue as blue though a long way down. A glimpse of cliffs, white against the water, more bends, and then they were running down towards the town, along the line of beach restaurants, the wide stretch of sand. Donald eased the car to a stop, looked at his watch. 'Five hours, give or take. Not too bad I suppose. You okay?'

'Stiff. Be glad to stretch muscles. And hungry.'

He smiled, 'yep, I'll go with that. Short walk along the beach, before we find our hotel?'

'Yeah, why not?' Out of the car, she took his hand. 'It's warm, isn't it,' and stared across the width of sand at sun loungers, parasols, at the amount of naked flesh on display. 'I didn't think to put a cossy in.'

'Not overmuch time to sunbathe, Paula. But,' and she felt his hand squeeze, 'you'll look good in a bikini.'

She swung their conjoined hands, feeling light headed now the journey was over, the work was about to start, and with the lovely relaxed atmosphere of the place surrounding them, what more could she want? Ah, a leading question . . .

They strolled along the hard-packed sand towards a sort of unspoken marker point, the tall white rock pillar to the north, silent, comfortable together, to then veer off and walk back along the wave edge, smiling at each other as they hopped back to avoid wet feet. Somehow it felt so natural, so much them, carving out new facets of a different life, for her, for this man who'd offered a new reason for living. *Bless you, Mary.*

Mary's Legacy 20

The hotel was buzzing. Familiar faces smiled, unfamiliar faces were introduced; Donald was in his element. She got a hug and a cheek-to-cheek kiss from Ronald, a handshake from this person and that person.

'Dinner at seven, folks, we've Annette and Marco, with Rosina too. Oh, Jon - can you make sure our Italian people are okay?'

It was all happening. She felt like a spare part until Ronald came back to her, asked how their journey went, had they sorted out all the Lecce locations, was Donald happy with things, could she ensure the shooting schedule was as she thought it should be, and she did know she'd be in charge of the continuity team?

She had to put on the proverbial brave face, hoping Donald would fill in the missing bits of her knowledge, and again asked about the mysterious unknown girl, the other Maria, to divert his attention.

'Still to be found. I've faith in this, strange though it might be. She'll appear. We've a day and a half till we need her. Beach scenes we'll shoot tomorrow, early, before the sun-worshippers get out there. You okay with that?'

'Sure,' she replied, with more confidence in her voice than she felt, 'looking forward to seeing the cameras roll.'

She got a chuckle from him then. 'Good old fashioned phrase, that. Cameras don't roll like they used to. Film, yes, digital, no. Shame really, losing something of the magic. Makes a lot of it easy, but . . .' he tailed off and she sensed he could descend into nostalgia like most of the other veterans. Then Annette appeared and away he went, off to meet and greet the others who'd come in with her. The 'stars', she assumed, and looked around for Donald. The other side of the room, locked in avid conversation with Peter, waving his hands, as animated as she'd ever seen him. He must have sensed her need; he broke off, looked across the room and caught her eye. She saw him pat Peter on the shoulder, nod at the other guy with them and then headed straight for her. He put an arm around her waist, steered her off to the side.

'You surviving?' A cryptic query but a valued one.

'I think so. Ronald's told me I have to look after the continuity team - and something about the shooting schedule?'

He nodded at her. 'That's simple - it's what we did the other night. I've discussed it with Peter in principle, he's happy, and we can fill in the detail whilst the main beach scene is boxed up tomorrow. Continuity - well, Yvette's no amateur and she'll keep on top of it. Ask her for her crib sheet and watch the cast assembly, knowing you, you'll soon spot if one of 'em's got the wrong frock on.' The grin, oh that grin ... 'detail's everything though. Nothing so bad as an email from a viewer telling us a character's wearing three different pairs of shoes in the same scene. I've every confidence in you ...' He dropped a smart and unexpected kiss on the tip of her nose, briefly gripped her hand and pointed back across the room. 'Yvette - go and grab her.'

Paula did as she was told, fixed a smile in place as best she could and, before she'd had a chance to decide what to say, found Yvette welcoming. Oh, relief!

'Hi there! Paula, you lucky gal, how's you with our Donald?'

Caution, girl . . . 'Good,' all she managed to say before Yvette went galloping on.

'Let's get in a huddle first thing. You check over my sked while I get going with the cossy gal. Found Maria yet? No, thought not.' A brassy laugh. 'Donald's good, he'll catch her. Annette'll give her the once over when we do. Marco, now he's a pain; had him on the last shoot. Rosina's okay. Nice legs. I'm envious . . .' she stuck a jean clad leg out, 'I wish,' paused, looked her up and down. 'Paula, I didn't like you at first sight 'cos . . . well, Mary, you know . . . , but I've seen the way our man's been soothed . . . I worried, we all did but reckon you've a magic touch. Keep it up. Now, I must pop to the ladies, too much Prosecco. See you at lift off,' and she scurried away.

Peter she found alone and had a chat with him; revealingly he admitted to some pre-shoot nerves. 'Surely not?' she managed, got a wry grin back.

'I'm okay once we're under way, Paula. Beforehand I'm always worried - perhaps concerned is the better word - that the kit's working; that the Grip - especially as he's new - knows what I need, the right weather. It's a long way from home if we need replacements. Booth's generally good on things like that, though, even if he's remote. Most things fall in place. How's yourself?'

The number of times people on the team asked her if she was 'okay'!

'I'm fine, thanks. Provided I don't mess anything up, 'cos its all very new.'

His stare was unnervingly direct. 'You won't,' he said. 'Donald won't let you,' giving her a single unexpected wink. 'He's fallen for you, everyone can see, plain as plain - no,' as she opened her mouth to protest, 'don't concern yourself. We knew Mary, we all loved her and we miss her, all of us, but our Donald would not have been the man for this film without a gal to fill her shoes; I reckon you're doing alright. Keep it up,' he added, echoing Yvette's rejoinder, and that nearly brought her to tears. Ronald, Yvette, Peter, all saying the same. So was she truly the 'legacy' talked about? The repetitive query wouldn't go away.

Over dinner, a buzz of chat all about the shoot, she had a chance to watch this Marco - who seemed full of himself - and Rosina, a slight girl with fuzzy bronzed hair, quite what role the girl would play she'd yet to discover. Donald sat opposite; he'd hardly patronized her at all since they'd got to the hotel other than at the networking session; he'd seen her to her room, made sure she was comfortable then left her to it so he could see to the car hire people and let the Alfa go.

So? Was it a turning point? He wasn't watching her; she got up, slipped quietly out of the room with the idea she'd go up and have an early night but, and for no reason, she crossed the lobby and went out into the street. In true southern Italian fashion, the evening street was heaving with people, couples hand-in-hand, young people in threes and fours, the older ones still swathed in dark coats and scarves whilst she felt the embrace of the warmth. Social hour - the cafes were full, the shops with open doors, the pavements alive. So different, so friendly, so much of what the place was about. With no particular motive, she wandered with the flow, shop window gazing, people watching, catching the glimpse of building detail, of fashion, of incomprehensible conversation. Her distant family on her mother's side hailed from this country; remember that, Paula girl, her thoughts swirled. Shame she'd not been given more of the Italianate flavour in her upbringing, perhaps offered a chance to acquire a greater familiarity with the language. She didn't feel out of place, on the contrary, very much at home. What would tomorrow bring? Where were they going to start in the morning? How much impact would the unit make on the place? How did the logistics work - the technical kit, the necessary wardrobe, catering - star's caravans; she assumed they'd have somewhere to go between shots, she couldn't see Marco wanting to lounge around in a deckchair - or Rosina, come to that, though knowing a trifle more about Annette, guessed she'd manage if she had to. Would there be other and lesser stars? Her wanderings had taken her down towards the water, across a bridge, towards the harbour. Fewer people here; more strollers enjoying the evening's cooling. Across the water the quay curved away towards a lighthouse tower the other side of the harbour entrance. Too far - she turned and retraced her steps along the street, absorbed in the atmosphere. A statue took her attention, the winged bronze female figure holding a wreath erect. A small truck passed her, a three-wheeler barely bigger than a wheelbarrow. Where was the hotel? Past a small square, the pavement cafes still full. Past a lovely clothes shop - and the memory of that fantastic evening in Paris, Karl's gift of a couture dress she'd still to wear. Ah, here it was. She pushed through the swing door, no one she knew in the lobby; up to her room - found a card on her pillow: *"Have a good night, Paula, D xx."* So Donald had missed her? Maybe.

Tomorrow . . . to be the big day. She undressed slowly, finally stretching naked arms above her head in front of the mirror, stood teetering on pointed toes and wondered about her role in the film, in his life, in Mary's memory. Tomorrow . . .

A knock on her door. She'd overslept? The time? Another knock, Donald's voice. *'Breakfast, Paula, on set at ten!'*

'Coming,' she managed in a croak, lordy, it was gone eight.

No way was she adopting the uniform dress of jeans and a muddy coloured tee-shirt. The new light cotton skirt, the lacy blouse over a modest vest, naked legs. If a mischievous breeze lifted a hem, it did. No bikini knickers today, gal, proper ones. Combed her hair out, no make-up other than a touch of lip-gloss. Keep out of the sun. Maybe she'd buy a floppy hat? Breakfast . . .

'Morning Paula! Lovely light today.' Ronald was cheerful. 'Donald's had to go early, I'm afraid. You can come down with me; I had to wait for Simon.' He wheeled round, beckoned to the tall, youngish guy in slacks and a violent pink shirt topping up his coffee cup. 'Simon - come and meet Paula, Donald's right-hand girl. Simon's the boss-man's gopher,' he explained. 'Keeps an eye on things from the State's perspective. Flew down to Foggia late yesterday.'

She got an expansive smile and a handshake but then she didn't know him at that point. 'Hi Paula,' he gave her a speculative up and down look. 'Lucky ol' Donald. Did I hear you're his guardian angel?' He retained her hand rather too long; no, she wasn't going to be looking at him in *that* way.

'Still learning the ropes,' she retorted brusquely and recovered her hand, to turn back to Ronald. 'Sorry I overslept.'

'No problem. It'll take the gang awhile to get organised. Donald said to bring the schedules; so I take it you *do* have them?'

In her room, in the desk, carefully placed there yesterday, she should have read them through last evening instead of wandering the streets. Oh dear, was she letting her dreams get the better of her? 'I'll go and get them now,' wheeled round and headed for the stairs.

'Nice girl,' Simon commented in his transatlantic drawl as she disappeared round the corner. 'Lovely legs.'

Ronald narrowed his eyes. 'Yes, she's one of the best around and, Simon, definitely not on offer. She's Donald's girl, very much so. When Mary died, he was distraught, we thought we'd lose him but he found Paula somewhere up in the Lake District and they've been together ever since. Brilliant arrangement, and though she might be new, young and maybe naïve, it'll work. More to the point, she's brought Donald back to life and we're the winners. You watch.'

'Okay, okay, I get the message, hands off, but she's still a pretty girl.'

Ronald wasn't prepared to go further, shrugged, beckoned the waiting driver. 'Once Paula's down with the schedules we'll go.'

It took her three minutes; she checked all the files were there, clipped the folder shut, cast her eyes round the room, yes, reckoned she had everything, sped back downstairs and joined the two men. 'Ready,' she said, mentally praying this first day of live action filming, her debut, would work, not just for her sake but far more importantly, for Donald. Was that Mary's voice in her head, *'You'll be fine,'* or her imagination?

The car, a sleek grey Lancia, took them down to the northern side of the harbour, down the road she'd walked last night, but further on and, as the car turned down the beach road, she saw the huddle of vehicles, the caravans parked on the road, the dozen or so people busy doing whatever - with a surprising number of onlookers too. All this, in no time at all? She'd wondered in her head quite what would happen - but still surprised at how it'd all come together. Perhaps Ronald had been right about Booth. The driver knew what he was doing, turned through a gap in the beach wall and drove without concern across the hard sand towards the melee of people.

The driver did his chauffeur job, slid out, opened the rear door for her with a shameless *'boun giorno'* added to his grin. She didn't wait for Ronald, he'd be preoccupied with keeping Simon happy; she cast her look around - Donald, where are you? There he was, standing with his hands on his waist, chattering on to - yes, Peter. With the papers firmly tucked under her arm, she walked up to them.

'Ah, Paula, good. Can you check on the approach scene?' he asked before he went back to his conversation with Peter, demonstrating with his hands - presumably indicating width of the camera shot. No smile, no 'hello', no 'good morning', so . . . never mind. She flipped through the file, found the sheet, the sketches of the beach, the figures and the weird diagrams of the walk-through. Behind her the camera rails were being laid, the light reflectors positioned, the props people laying out the rug, the glasses on a small table, the book left on the rug. All there on her diagram; expanded into the storyboard - suddenly it clicked. Mentally she ticked the boxes. Ah, no cushion.

'Cushions!' she said out loud - and the prop girl heard her. 'Coming, Paula - red or green?'

'Red,' she answered, instinctively. 'And a bottle - a spritzer needs lemonade?'

'Sure thing. Do you think we need anything else?'

'Sun cream lotion? Something for Annette to fiddle with?'

Donald had finished; Peter was getting back behind the camera on its trolley. Ronald had appeared, Simon was standing back, Annette in her very trendy bikini, large towel across her shoulders, was coming across from the caravan, Marco behind her. The sound guy with his boom microphone and the two others with recorders waved 'okay', Jon's query *okay Annette?* her wave back, then quiet descended as Annette took her lounging position on the rug - picked up the newly placed sun-lotion bottle with a quick grin at Paula, Marco had strode off to his start point, Ronald held an arm up, nodded at Peter. The clapper board snapped, Ronald's arm dropped. 'Action!'

She watched. Marco's walk across the sand, the swagger, the poised stance over Annette, her careful use of sun cream, her look up at him, the script words perfect and she felt rather than saw Donald behind her. Not a word between them, just the dialogue from the actors, then Marco, bending down, reaching for Annette's arm, pulling her to her feet, the table going over, the glasses crashing down . . .

'Cut!'

A brief silence. 'Peter?' Ronald waited. The monitor in its big hood had been unused, unwatched - all eyes on the real action rehearsal.

'Not sure, needs to be wider. The glasses - I can catch them if Marco is slightly further round?'

'Okay, Take ten, then we'll have the first proper take, folks. .'

'So?' Donald, from behind; Paula felt his hand, gentle on her arm. 'The first run through? What you expected?'

She shook her head. 'Don't know what I expected. Well, perhaps. Scary-ee. How many takes does it - take?'

He chuckled. 'As many as it takes . . . usually three, sometimes four, occasionally just the one. Ronald'll watch this next one on screen; I reckon this second one will be okay. Your sun cream suggestion was good.'

'Yes?'

'It's what you're expected to do, Paula, think on your feet. Don't hesitate to say, either, for the more positive you are, the easier it becomes, the more people respect you. And I'll back you, all the way.' His hand squeezed. 'We'll get it right, together,' and he moved away.

She watched the second take, saw the improvement, heard the word 'Wrap' with relief, turned to her crib sheet, found the next scene where Annette would be more in dialogue with Marco and where the extras should play beach ball behind them, checked through the story-board sketch and began to gain greater confidence. The day would work; she knew it would, for from her spirit world, Mary'd said so. Confidence, girl.

And it did. The unit worked through the morning's shooting schedule with enviable efficiency, all three main actors came up to precise expectations and even the extras did as they were told. At the lunch break Donald sat next to her on the beach wall. 'What d'you reckon?' he asked, munching on his panini; the catering unit in its large Fiat van was performing well.

She swung her legs, stared at her skirt before turning her look towards him. Should she really say what she thought? He might not approve. 'I'd say the story line's a bit drab. Not a lot of sparkle.'

'Honest opinion?'

She nodded. 'The scene's okay, if rather stereotyped. The 'boy meets girl' on a beach scene is played out everywhere. Isn't it?'

'Hmmm, perhaps.' He mulled over her remark. 'Actually you'd be right if it was seen out of context. It's how the sequences are cut that matters, how one mundane scene can act as backdrop to the more intense one. I'll have to say 'wait and see', but I do take your point, Paula, and thanks for being truthful. It's what I'd expect from you, so well done. Look at this afternoon's scenes; if there's anything there you don't like, say so. Jon can change things around. Ronald will be intrigued too, he likes you. It won't affect my side 'cos I merely give the guys a set to work in. Feel free. Now, 'scuse me, I have to take a walk,' and he heaved himself off the wall and strolled off.

Did she feel lost without his continued metaphorical arm around her? No, oddly, on the contrary, quite happy; she reached into her floppy bag and pulled out the sheaf of papers.

Ten minutes later and she'd had an idea. One scene - previous in the plot to the one already 'in the can', was where Marco would be mooching about on his own, doing a reflective 'wonder where she is, what's she doing' thing before he sees her sunbathing, the bit already filmed. The story board concept was to see him walking along the edge of the waves. In her mind it'd look flat - so surely he could go into a café place, whatever it was, buy a take-away coffee or something, then maybe collide with an extra before storming out - then he could mutter a 'silly, clumsy, idiotic' phrase to show how moody he was? She jumped off the wall and went to find Ronald.

Within ten minutes there was another on-set conference. Peter, Jon, Donald - and Ronald - Ronald, listening to *her, her!*

'I'd agree with Paula,' and he attempted to excuse himself. 'I should have seen it but too concerned over the as yet unknown Maria. What d'you think, Peter? Jon, not too much wordage to change? Donald?'

Peter shrugged. 'I think it's fine and Paula has the new girl's eye, so it's good.' Jon nodded an unspoken approval. Donald put a protective arm round her shoulders. 'More brownie points. Earning her keep already. Yep, I'll go with it.'

Ronald reached out and shook her hand. 'Well done, girl. Let's go,' and so the mini-committee meeting broke up, each one to sort his aspect of the revisions.

Donald kept Paula tight to him while the other three strolled off. 'So which café then? Have you one in mind?'

'Not really. Have we time so we can do a recce?'

'If you want; can't be too long, an hour at most, there's the bit where Annette does a runner coming up. We have to ensure there's no traffic to spoil the middle distant shot; it's scheduled for mid afternoon while the siesta period's at its best.'

She nodded; having gone through the master copy of the call sheets not half an hour ago, she knew. 'Perhaps the other side of the harbour?'

Hand in hand, and how lovely it felt, they walked the length of the harbour wall, around the headland and into the next bay; somehow time vanished, the afternoon's sun brushing the pile of terracotta and white houses with a luminous glow. The drooping fronds from the palms offered a shadowed contrast with the warmth from the multicoloured paving below their feet. She swayed against him, relaxed, at home, wanting the gentle feel never to go.

'There,' he said, pointing. 'That do?'

Under a trio of cone-thatched sunshades, a few tables, the evidence of a café, quiet and empty at siesta time.

'Perfect.'

Seen close up, this epitome of the promenade coffee shop even had a 'Lavazza' sign to prove the point. The door was open. 'Shall we?'

The dim recess wasn't large; a counter to their right, three tables nestled on the left, all sorts of touristy things hanging from the ceiling. The woman behind the counter was assiduously polishing mugs and saucers, a half-hidden girl crouching in front of the large fridge with its door wide open appeared to be cleaning the shelves.

A quick burst of Italian accompanied the instant smile triggered by the anticipation of a paying customer, rare at this time of day. Donald did his best though it'd be guesswork and intuition on behalf of the middle-aged woman - owner or employee - that achieved the assembly of cups, the dexterous use of the espresso machine and the reaching into the display unit for a couple of delectable pastries. Then the girl crouching by the fridge finished her work, stood up, closed the fridge door and turned to face them . . .

> . . .*that night, months ago, when a furious pot-pourri of a sketched scenario had brought to mind the frighteningly real image of a girl, a girl like Paula but not like her, too young, too - innocent?*
>
> *Long gloss black hair in two distinct woven tresses down her back, the full simple blouse with short sleeves, a rounded semicircle of neckline above a fulsome bust, a neat waist above a knee length skirt in, yes, the usual black, with naked shapely legs bearing a sun-kissed tan, heeled open shoes, she was high cheeked, dimpled, her slanted deep brown eyes smiling a shy welcome, a picture of youthful beauty at work in this shore-side café.*

Donald turned to Paula and her expression echoed his amazement. Was *she* their *Maria?* This girl, he'd estimate her at twenty, a year more or less, the girl he'd seen in his imagination, the exact description. And smiling, no trace of awkwardness but a slight uncertainty, a modicum of reserve. She'd be absolutely right. Perfect.

He needed fluent Italian and mentally cursed the lack. She met his look and it was if she were poised on her toes, her elegance sublime. Was the woman who had set out their coffee and pastries her mother or employer? How did he ask her name? Would it be seen an intrusion?

Paula tried, with a flashback to early schooling. '*Come si chiama?*'

The girl's smile deepened, she moved forward from behind the counter, away from the fridge and into a better light. 'I am Michaela,' she said in stilted but clear English, 'I help my mother here. You are *inglise?*'

'Yes,' said Paula and added '*si,*' which made both women smile again. 'We are,' and prayed this Michaela would understand, 'making a film here,' did the typical hand-turned camera action and pointed back through the door at the promenade behind. 'My friend,' - what else could she call Donald, now holding his mobile phone to his ear, - 'is the art director. *Direttor d'arte.*'

'*Ah, si,*' Michaela's mother replied, pulling out two chairs and beckoning them to sit at the small round table where the coffee cups sat steaming, and directed another burst of quick Italian at her daughter. The girl blushed beneath her tan.

'My *mama* says I should be a film *divo.*'

A perfect opening. 'Yes,' Donald said, pushing the mobile back into his pocket. 'You should. You wish to be?'

The blush didn't go away. 'But I am not known. I work here, with my mother. I like my work. I meet people.'

'Like us,' added Paula. 'Michaela, we are looking for an Italian girl to play a small but important part in our film.' She made eye contact with Donald, looking for encouragement.

'I've called for Mario to come round. He's a fluent Italian speaker,' he explained then tried his coffee. '*Perfetto,*' he added to achieve another beaming smile. So far, so good, and the odd dream he'd had ages ago and now coming into astonishing reality was surely a consequence of Mary's timely guiding spirit.

Michaela's mother exchanged more words with her daughter, a questioning tone, accompanied by hand gestures. The girl sounded conciliatory, before turning back to them.

'She asks, what is this film about and where is it,' and gave a charming smile as she added, 'and if I accept a part, how much do I get paid?'

Donald looked at Paula. 'You tell her.'

Paula took a deep breath. Was she going to assume a Booth-style role here? Interview, select, hire? She tried to recall how the 'unknown Italian girl' was to act, where they would do the reveal and how long they'd allowed in the schedule and hoped she'd get it right, hoped she'd retell the story sufficiently simply so this beautiful young lady would understand. Donald stayed impassive, sitting and sipping coffee.

'It is a love story. There is a complication. Here, a man and a girl are staying here on holiday in separate houses, the man who is the male lead falls in love with this girl who plays hard to get. She has a dark past. He meets this girl several times, on the beach, in a restaurant, in the street. She knows he wants her but won't admit she likes him too. Then the man sees another local girl who he also likes because she is so pretty and a true Italian, so he decides to use her to see if the first girl becomes jealous. It works for a while but then they have to return to their own lives. When the same thing happens again in a different place, the girl's past is revealed and it affects their relationship. He has to decide whether to dump her or pursue her; it gets more intense each time they meet; always there is the shadow of this other girl and . . .'

Donald put up a hand. 'Enough, Paula, you'll confuse the girl though you put it over very well. *Comprendere?*' he asked the girl.

She nodded, her face alight, '*Si, si, affascinante,*' and appeared to re-tell the story to her mother, though Paula was sure she'd embroidered it, before asking: 'You are looking for a pretty Italian girl?'

'We've found her,' and gave her the full smiley treatment.

'*Mi?*'

'*Tu.*'

The girl's eyes were alight; they'd surely made her day. All they needed now was her mother's agreement - if she was prepared to let her away from her café duties.

'*Madre?*' the girl asked.

The mother appeared to go into a trance. Maybe, Paula considered, she was wishing *she* was young again . . . then she gave a little shrug, her face creased into a beaming smile. '*Quanto tempo?*'

'How long?' Paula looked at the daughter and passed the query on towards Donald.

'If we get it right, not too many re-takes, less than the day.'

The girl understood and relayed the answer back.

'*No problema.*'

And that's how it was. Marco turned up shortly afterwards and once briefed, must have done a sterling job on filling in the details, adding in the expressed wish to film a small scene actually in the *caffe,* interpreting the queries and relaying Donald's replies. Meanwhile, Paula took the girl away from the intensity of her mother's involvement, walked her along the edge of the esplanade under the palms, found a bench and sat her down.

'You're a very lovely girl, Michaela, and you speak very good English. You learnt at school?'

'*Si* - yes, also I study at home and learn from the *tourista.* This film, what is it called?'

'*Maria's Legacy*'- and you will be Maria.' She watched the girl's expression, incredulity followed by burgeoning delight. It would be a life-changing experience, paralleling the way her own life had been changed by a similar unique experience. What was so profoundly intriguing was the way the discovery of the girl had occurred. Donald - and Roland - must both have had sublime faith that such a girl would be found, though what they'd have done had she not been was incomprehensible. Gone to an agency, hired in the best looking youngster on the books and prayed she wouldn't be so hard-bitten as to give the wrong impression, for the script - storyline - called for naivety, innocence shown in every way. Now it wasn't going to be necessary to import anyone, Michaela was exactly right.

'Have you a boyfriend, Michaela? And do you always work for your *mama?*'

Michaela shook her head. Paula was envious of the way her shimmering long black hair flicked round her shoulders, emphasised by the off-the-shoulder white silk blouse. The girl's boobs were truly magnificent too, not overly large but proud and wonderfully shaped under an obviously expensive bra. No boyfriend? Gracious, how strange.

'My *mama* is, how do you say, *protettiva?* And there are few Italian boys I could like around here. I am happy working for *mama*. Maybe I know you will come,' and the girl gave another of her huge smiles. 'It was *ordinare.*'

Paula knew exactly what she meant. Ordained, as was Donald's response to the accident up on the Lake District fells, her involvement with the walking party in the first instance; as though the jigsaw pieces were laid out exactly in place. What else would happen?

'Can you act, Michaela? Have you perhaps done something at school?'

'Oh yes, I loved to be an *artista.*' She laughed a low, musical chuckle. 'I was always, how you say, *scema, divertirsi,* oh, playing silly things. This film, is it funny or serious?'

Serious for some, Paula thought. 'You have to be serious in a light-hearted way,' and she went on to describe exactly how she felt about the relationship she had with Donald, not that Michaela would realise how therapeutic it was, expressing her situation to another girl. 'I feel as I have known you for a long time,' she ended, and was tempted to put a protective arm round the girl.

Michaela snuggled close. 'I have no friend other than my *mama*. *Pardre* is,' and Paula sensed the hesitation, '*morto*. But,' and her voice softened, 'I love the caffé.'

'We will be friends, Michaela. This film, it is important for me too, as I have said. We will both take comfort from the success we will have, yes?'

'Yes. *Grazie*, Paula.'

Then it became serious. Marco, having explained the way he would play the 'reveal' scene and the follow-ups, was commissioned to go and find Roland, to give him a digest of what had transpired, while Paula, following a discussion with Donald, arranged to collect Michaela from the café in the morning; she'd be pleased to act as chaperone.

They walked back. Donald slipped his arm round her. 'You know what this means?'

She nodded, all of a sudden she'd felt emotion building so it took a few moments and another three or four hundred metres walk before she felt she could reply.

'Michaela? Part of Mary's legacy? Here, in the middle of nowhere when we least expected it?'

Donald stopped, held her. 'There's an unanswered question here, Paula,' and searched her eyes, 'and it worries me.'

It clicked. *Find a girl* - which girl? Her - or *Michaela?* Oh, oh dear. They walked on, silent, each lost in thought.

Paula knew she wouldn't lose Donald's friendship, but what would he decide? He'd said he loved her, but how deeply?

Donald knew he didn't want to, couldn't, lose Paula, but after Michaela had stood up from her crouch by the fridge in the café, had shown off her phenomenal beauty, poise, grace and smile, the undeniable artistic attraction had kicked in. She - Michaela - had something deeply magnetic he couldn't analyse - younger than Paula by a year or three, maybe an only child and now fatherless, with a protective mother, true, but otherwise nothing but a job in a seasonal café? Was she another girl who needed the loving, caring, supportive person, the one Mary who had commissioned?

᪥   ᪥   ᪥

161

Mary's Legacy

Paula couldn't forget her, not even for one moment that evening. Michaela - *Maria* - a lovely lass, the epitome of an Italian *signorina,* exactly as she should be, poised, graceful, assured, and Donald's dream. She knew she'd been eclipsed in some manner, for at dinner that evening he'd been unable to stop chattering on about how this girl had appeared in his quiet thoughts, that she'd fired up his enthusiasm for the film, that he'd had no doubt he'd find her.

'But if I hadn't come up with the café idea for Marco ...' she interjected at a suitable point, '. . . you and I wouldn't have gone for the walk, discovered her.'

He'd hardly heard her, for Ronald was adding his accolades. 'The project's taken on a real significance,' she heard, and that suave creep Simon was climbing on the same bandwagon, no doubt relishing the thought of getting close to Michaela in the morning. Not if she'd anything to do with it, she vowed. The whole unit had been fired up by the way Donald had gone back and extolled all the girl's virtues. Virtue - yes, untarnished, an *innocente,* Michaela fitted the script definition perfectly.

Somehow the evening came to an end as different parties drifted away; expressing some aspects of tiredness for truly, it had been a long day. Three more scenes had been shot after Michaela's reveal. Somehow Paula managed to keep some sanity, admittedly got fulsome praise from both her mentor and Ronald but nonetheless definitely felt she'd been relegated to second string. Did she care? Well, yes she did, given all that Donald had said, the way he'd dressed her, feted her, admitted his *love* for her. Not lust, *love.* So did he lust after Michaela? Probably not, for if she'd become another candidate for the legacy girl she'd be held sacrosanct; but somehow it was if she - Paula - had lost the edge. *Mary - please sort it out?*

She hadn't felt she could wait for him to say 'goodnight' - he was still wrapped up in conversation with Roland; it wasn't as though they'd ignored her, just not bothered to include her in whatever was the topic of the moment. She slipped upstairs. Would he notice she'd gone?

She'd almost finished undressing when there was a knock on the door. It could only be Donald. She slipped on the hotel's provided towel robe and opened the door.

'Sorry,' he said as she stepped back to let him in. 'I came to apologise. Is it convenient?'

Donald, apologising? Perhaps the odd feeling now creeping along her back was some relief that he'd not completely gone off her since Michaela's appearance on the scene - or was there still some jealousy, or even a slight tinge of malice? Very unlike her.

She shrugged. 'You seem to be preoccupied. The dream coming true?' and sat down on the edge of her bed. No, she did *not* want to be compromised at this particular moment and hugged the bathrobe tighter round her.

'Sorry,' he said again, 'if I've neglected you, but the girl will be an absolute marvel if she performs and Ronald's cock-a-hoop. It's exactly what the film needs, a fantastic opportunity.' His voice, his facial animation, the body language all indicated how carried away he was. 'You will look after her tomorrow, won't you?'

'What I'm going to be paid for?' and couldn't help the cynical tone of voice.

It went straight over his head. 'Of course. You're the only person I can trust to see what we need. And you'll be able to keep her away from Simon - and Marco, other than from his scripted involvement. I thought I'd let you know how much I'm depending on you. Okay? Now, I'd best go. Wouldn't do to be seen coming out of my best girl's bedroom.'

'*Best* girl, Donald? You mean I've not been given second place now you've got the Italian dream girl?'

He stared at her. 'Eh?' It still hadn't clicked.

'When we found her, you said about the question, the one that worried you? Well, it worries me too. Which girl, Donald? Which girl does Mary think is right for you?' The query brought on emotion, unstoppable watery eyes and she sniffed, had to wipe her eyes with the back of a hand.

'Oh!' He stopped, his hand on the door knob, as though he'd frozen. Silence between them, though seconds, an eternity. Then he hesitated, mumbled 'I don't know,' as if it didn't matter and went. The door closed behind him and she fell across the bed and couldn't help the onset of tears.

⤎

She couldn't sleep. The situation, the query, the images of the beautiful Michaela and a reprise of the precious moments she'd had, shared, built hopes around, swirling around in the grey muzzy depths of her mind. Finally she put the bedside light back on, pulled herself up against the bedhead and tried to be rational, to catalogue the ifs and buts, the logic - if there ever was any - of what had gone betwixt her and Donald.

She'd precipitated the relationship, phoning him, calling on him, declaring silly untruths to persuade him she needed help, spinning the tale about her flat and the lies about a pregnancy. Nevertheless he'd taken her on when he could have said 'no, go away' or even 'get lost'; he'd taken her to Pinewood, given her a job, they'd lived together in platonic harmony pretty well ever since, with the wry thought that they'd done everything a couple could do except for one thing. He'd not used her, and for that she could feel both relief and disappointment. Still virginal. Was Michaela? Probably - she had an air of delightful innocence about her. No matter, for neither would be vulnerable whilst out on set. So what now? Pretend to be hurt - though not much pretence needed - or ignore the situation and try to carry on as normal? There were plus points. She had a job - though still unsure exactly what she would be paid - she was on an expenses paid trip, she'd met some wonderful people and gone places she'd never have dreamt of visiting. Then there was the very expensive haute couture dress waiting for her back in Paris - and she'd made a friend in Sarah, who had been left *incommunacado*. And she was down on the casting list for the Gallerie scene in Milan. Donald wouldn't sack her; send her home, she was ultra confident about that. So the film would be made and provided the edit was good and the bosses liked it, would go on general release with her name amongst the credits. *You're being foolish, girl,* she told herself firmly after this half hour of introspective self-analysis, so she put the

164

light out and slid back under the duvet, not that she need warmth, it was warm enough. Ten minutes later she was asleep.

She went straight to the café after breakfast, avoiding complications. Donald had waved a 'good morning' to her from his seat on what she'd cynically thought of as the 'high table', Ronald, Peter, Jon and the jerk Simon. One reason, now she looked back, why she'd left coming down to the last moment. They'd have been discussing the crowd scene at the car park; she'd checked on the shooting schedule, and it wasn't anything on which she'd need to provide an input. Loads of extras were coming in by coach from Foggia. Yuk! At least there was a bright side, the irksome Simon had stood up, bag in hand, obviously satisfied the way things had come together, said his farewells and gone, so that was some small blessing.

The promenade was quiet, the perfect azure sea below also quiet under a cloudless sky; the sun not yet pushing the temperature up. It'd be a lovely day, shifting spirits up a notch. Deep down, she realised she'd not lose Donald's affection, they'd travelled too many miles together, but it was the depth of that affection under review. Never mind. Mary'd sort it. Her shoulders went back, she stretched her lungs in and out, swung arms, the crisp walk wonderful in the solitude. What would it be like, living here?

The *caffe* was already open, unsurprisingly, Michaela's mother busy polishing the counter. The girl herself wasn't there. Oh dear, and she'd not be able to converse with the mother? Then, in a flurry of flirty skirts and unconfined hair, she appeared as if from nowhere.

'Paula, *caro,* is it still true? That I am to act in your film? It is not a *scherzo,* a joke?'

'No joke. It's real. You ready?' Paula smiled at the mother, got a cheerful '*buona fortuna!*' from her. Michaela took her hand and walked her away.

'Better we go,' she explained, 'before *mama* changes her mind. She has to keep open the *caffe,* it is how we live. Maybe she will come later, at *siesta* time. You stop for *siesta?*'

Paula had to chuckle. 'No - it is when it is easier for the filming with less people to watch.' She changed the subject. 'Will you always work in the *caffe?*'

165

Michaela nodded. 'Of course.'

'Even when you marry?'

Michaela laughed in her turn. 'Marry me, marry the *caffe*,' but her voice changed. 'I am not interested in men.'

Oh dear. Surely not . . . Paula couldn't believe this lovely creature wouldn't appreciate the finer aspects of the other sex - however Michaela had intuitively guessed her companion's inner dismay. 'Not while I am still learning about life. Perhaps later,' she explained and smiled that expressively beautiful smile.

They turned the corner; the crazy arrangement of vehicles with the huge reflectors and the camera dolly were scattered over the northerly promenade.

Paula steered her towards the monitor truck. Donald would be there; she felt a stab of unease; would he manage to play this right? He saw her coming, moved away from the screen and, surprisingly, greeted Michaela with a handshake whereas Paula felt sure she'd have been more likely offered a full-blown Italian greeting had she been alone.

'*Buon Giorno*, Michaela. Are you well? We are so very pleased we found you, couldn't have wished for a nicer Maria.' He must have seen her puzzled look and explained. 'In the film you are Maria, the romantic idol that the main male lead falls for. All you have to do is follow the walk we'll show you and then when you see Marco, pretend you don't care for his attentions and perhaps expect him to pursue you. It'll take three or four minutes of screen time.'

Michaela didn't disappoint, expressing the usual surprise at how short an amount of time it would take in the film. He explained few people realised that half a day's filming often came down to minutes when it was edited, smiled at Paula with a hand's brush across her arm and took the girl away.

What should she do? Follow them or use the monitor to watch progress? The dilemma was resolved ten minutes later.

'Paula!' the shout came from behind the caravans, 'Need advice here!'

She eased out of the folding chair and went to see. There was Marco, looking very dapper and suave, a slightly bemused Michaela with Annette whispering in her ear. Roland stood back behind the camera dolly with arms folded. Donald met her.

'If you were Maria in this context, how would you deal with Marco?'

She drew breath. Rephrase that, Donald, she said in her mind - *if I was Paula, how do I deal with Donald?* She had to grin as her thought went straight back to the Lakes; remember she'd asked for the same sort of help then?

'What does he say? I've forgotten.'

Donald thumbed through the script, pulled a face but read it out: '*Hi lady, you're a smart looking girl. Can you tell me where I can get the best meal round here?*'

'Rather naff,' she said. 'He needs to look woe-begone, to say something more like '*scusi, is there someplace good to eat around here?* Then she'll respond '*Sure, we've a lovely little caffe just five minutes from here*', and not knowing he's already been there, there'll be confusion. He'll discover that she knows his query was a chat-up line. Then it's up to you to decide whether if she takes him there or gives him directions.'

'If it were you?'

'Me being me, I'd take him. Michaela?'

'We are a friendly people,' she said. 'I would take him, but I would be careful not to walk too close.'

'Done,' Donald looked at Roland, got the nod, switched his look at Jon and it was sorted. Jon took Marco to one side, script in hand; Paula, ignoring Donald, took Michaela away out of hearing.

'Are you sure you are happy with this?'

She got a wry smile and a head side-to-side nod. 'It is a new experience for me and one I can boast about! This Marco, he seems 'okay'?

'As far as I know, Michaela. I've only known him on set. Don't . . .'

'Be taken as too easy a girl?'

She nodded. 'But Donald is fine. I've known him a while.'

'You have *comprensiva* - an understanding, I think.'

'How did you guess?'

'There is something between you, the way he looks at you, the little gestures.'

A comforting thought, but: 'you have an advantage over me, Michaela.'

'How can that be? We only met yesterday!'

Paula drew breath. How was she going to explain? 'It is complicated. He lost his wife a few months ago and they were very close. Apparently she said, told him, before she died, that he was 'to find another girl who needed him'. He found me, accidentally, and we have, as you have seen, a good relationship but not perhaps in the way many might think. He also had a dream about finding a girl . . .' and she couldn't help the tight emotion, 'who is very much like you. He has been knocked off-balance by our discovering you, which is so much like his dream.'

'Oh.' Michaela's face went blank. 'It is not good for you. I should . . .,' she struggled, 'perhaps say I do not like him?'

'You cannot say what you do not believe. And for the film we need you to fulfill the role. It is what everyone has hoped for. We had to find the right girl; she had to be a film virgin and Italian. So you must, please, play the part?'

Michaela reached for Paula's hands, held them together in very touching gesture. 'For you, *Cara mia,* I will, but I cannot, er, *distruggere,* break up, your *rapporto. No, mai in vita mai,'* and she shook her head. *'No!'*

'Thank you,' was all Paula dare say. The girl was brilliant, understanding, lovely - and encouraging. 'Let's go and see how we can get this shoot done and then maybe my Donald will relax?'

Michaela nodded vigorously. *'Si.'*

She took the girl back into the melee, paced out her walk; at first got her to follow, then to have her do it on her own. Donald, Peter and Roland followed her movement; Marco stood nonchalantly at the side, leaning up against the camera dolly. The rest of the crew watched, some impassive, some interested in this novice girl, one or two enthusiastic, even, surprisingly, applauding. Certainly she had the sway on her, the shoulders back, chest out, a small sideways toss of the head, toes in parallel line. When she reached the appointed 'rendezvous' position she stopped, poised, turned to look at her three main critics with a lift of eyebrows. *See,* she was saying, *we Italian girls know how to walk.*

Roland separated from the triumvirate, crossed over towards her, shook her hand. 'My dear girl, you're a natural. Do that while we've the camera running and it'll be fabulous. Marco,' he added, turning back to the suave star, 'you'll take it from there?'

Marco nodded. 'It'll be a real pleasure. You're damn right, she's a natural.'

Annette must have been watching from the rear of the assemblage somewhere, she came forward to put an arm round the now silent girl. 'I can see I'll have to watch out for the competition, honey. You may be on the threshold of something big here. Now, take lots of deep breaths, swing those lovely arms of yours to get some of those muscles relaxed. Can't have you too tense now,' and she dropped a light kiss on the girl's cheek.

Ten minutes later Michaela did her walk once again as the camera rolled, Peter behind the viewfinder this time rather than trust it to his second cameraman. Marco stepped forward, said his new lines, the pair were into close up, the expressions perfect.

'Cut!' and Roland had a happy smile on his face. 'That's it, folks. It's a wrap for here, so another half hour before we can get the *caffe* scenes set up that Paula's organised. Onward and upward. Back to Lecce tomorrow. Donald - a moment?'

As Roland had predicted, the scenes at Michaela's café were easily shot, mostly on close up without the need for repetitive takes; it was all falling into place. The last scene shot, Marco's exit from the *caffe* and colliding with a rather too smart extra was also done. The familiar and welcoming cry 'it's a wrap' followed the last 'cut!' and brought a short eerie silence before the scramble to get the kit disassembled and into trucks. The Lancia took Marco away; Annette and Rosina had already gone. The frenetic two days had come to an abrupt end with no need for the allowed third day in case of problems. Lecce here we come . . .

Paula, obeying instructions, had managed to persuade Michaela's mother to let her daughter accompany her back to the hotel for a debrief. Now the two sat in the lounge whilst others of the party shuffled back and forth with cases to jam into the two minibuses booked to take them across to Foggia, the railhead and the late train down to Lecce. Tomorrow would be a fully scheduled shooting day; time was pressing. Annette, it seemed, was under pressure to fly back to the States at the end of the week.

Michaela looked tense; out of the blue she posed a query. 'They will let me go back home soon? My *mama* does not wish to be on her own of an evening. I was *non male?*'

'Not bad, Michaela? You were brilliant,' Paula patted the girl's hands where they rested in her lap. 'I've got to do something similar in Milan, in the Gallerie, so you've given me a stunning example to follow. I'm not sure what Donald wants, he's chatting to Roland in the bar. I'm sure he won't be long. *Pazienza!*'

Less than a minute later, Donald came out of the bar, plumped himself down close alongside Paula and put a welcomed arm round her shoulders. 'My two brilliant ladies together. Michaela, how are you placed for a spot of foreign travel? Roland would very much like you to come to Pinewood - that's near London in the UK - the week after next for some on-set shots. He'd ask you himself but he's gone with the minibus. Your mother can come as well; there's a chaperone budget. What d'you think?'

Paula could see what effect that had on the girl, her eyes opened wide, her lovely mouth dropped open, happily she didn't go pale - otherwise she'd have said she'd have gone into shock. 'Why, that's terrific, Michaela!'

'*Mama* may not wish it. We have a *caffe* to run. What will we do - we cannot close it for so long, our friends will forget us?'

'Isn't there anyone who'd run it for you?'

Michaela pondered; obviously, thought Paula, she hadn't dismissed the idea out of hand. 'We will have to think about this thing. May I consider your *proposta* - your proposition?'

Donald stood up. 'Shall we walk you home, Michaela, and discuss this with your *mama?*'

Much later that evening yet just before dusk, when the hotel had quietened down, Donald persuaded Paula to take another walk down to the harbour; it would be the one of the few times they'd have left to themselves and he desperately needed to restore sense to his relationship with Paula. Fully aware of the complications that had arisen following Michaela's insertion into their lives he must urgently put matters right between them. He took her hand as they crossed the street and strolled on down the slope. The sky had a few streaks of cloud, now tinged with red from the sun's fall into the Aegean, that sea now a dullened pewter. It wouldn't be far off dark, barely another hour.

Once they reached the harbour, they had a choice; along the new quay or up towards the old town. Without discussion they took the quay, along the curved wall in front of the boutique shops and offices created as part of the town's re-generation, some occupied, some not. Further on, a solitary large yacht lay moored, abandoned, derelict. Another few hundred metres and they came to the curved neck of the pier head, the harbour's protective arm guarded by a copper statue with extended arms, poised over the jumble of huge blocks of stone.

'Relative of yours, Paula?'

'What do you mean?'

'Look at the inscription. *S Rance Co Da Paola.* Paola.'

She grinned, comforted by the statue's presence. 'Not that I'm aware of.'

He swung her captive hand. 'I think I'm over Michaela's sudden appearance, Paula. She's very sweet, rather too beautiful for her own good, but she's not my Paula. I'm sorry if I . . .,' and she knew what he meant without the sentence completion. 'But I'm exceedingly glad she'll do as we asked. Her mother's very adaptable.'

She shook her head. 'No need to apologise. Anyone could fall for her, and they will, though she's got to be strong to keep her head above all the flattery she's getting.'

'Will you look after her?'

'If I can, and when it's necessary.' A moment's silence, then she asked, 'you care for her?' and she didn't mean as a mentor.

'Yes, I do. But I've searched my conscience too, in a few quiet times I've asked myself what Mary would have done had she been here. Michaela has a doting mother, a lovely business, and, if it all works out, maybe the prospect of another career - if she wants it. If we hadn't come along, that wouldn't have changed. What we need to do is ensure her exposure to the film world doesn't go wrong for her, and that's what we'll do.'

'There's more to Mary's bequest than simple old me.'

He chuckled, a good sign. 'You're very perceptive,' paused and added, 'and understanding too. Paula, I love you, you know that. You came into my life by sheer coincidence and I've not regretted it for one moment. Stay with me?'

They were standing on the curved foot block of marbled stone below the statue. Above them, the outspread arms, an embracing gesture. Across the water the lights of the old town twinkled and shone, the water below them a gentled lap lap against the pier, the sky now a deep dense purple against the black edge of the hills beyond. She shivered;

he wrapped his arms around her, felt her warmth, her steadily beating heart through the thin silk and cotton blouse, rested his head against the softness of her hair with its alluring fragrance, and lowered his lips to kiss the pale length of her neck. 'Stay with me?'

She couldn't put her answer into words. She'd become used to him, his ways, his irritations, his caring, his obvious passion for his work - and for the ever-present memories still too raw to avoid. Mary was still around, even now, especially now, when a legatee was wrapped within those arms which had held and loved another woman. He rocked her gently, swaying and holding her, firm and confident. She felt the care, the confidence, the concern, and hoped the passion would follow when Mary would allow. Her arms came up of their own accord, to tighten their hug almost into pain. She could only attempt a nod within the embrace, no more, but enough for him to sense her answer.

'Bless you,' he said, and kissed her once more.

Mary's Legacy 22

A lovely three days back in Lecce. A reprise of the time, barely a week ago, where they'd spent a happy time idling hours away, pottering round, making notes, taking the ideas back to the hotel and drawing out scenarios which had now been fully exploited, sending the town into a mini frenzy with the filming action here and there. As the scenes were shot, mostly without a hiccup, Paula could see Donald becoming more and more comfortable with the way it was coming together. Even Peter appeared more relaxed as sequence after sequence worked. Her own input, checking the props, the costumes, and giving the continuity girl Yvette a helping hand, was now becoming second nature; relaxed and happy with the way she was moulding into this strange life.

'We're about there,' Ronald said at the last dinnertime. 'Reckon it'll hang together pretty well. Annette,' and she looked up from her *pasta,* 'may I be so bold as to admit you're the best gal we've worked with in this *genre?*'

She didn't exactly blush, it wasn't in her nature, but the smile said it all. She tried to play it down. 'Marco's been good too. And Rosina is a very good stand-in,' her remarks falling into the hush of the oddly quietened table. 'I'd also like to offer Paula a word of praise as well; despite being a new girl she's fitted into our ways very effectively. Sorry if I'm making you squirm, Paula, but it's true. And I reckon our Donald would have been lost without you.' She caught his eye and winked.

He coughed, quietly, as if to clear his throat before a reply, but Paula beat him to the rejoinder. 'It's been an absolute pleasure, Annette, and a privilege. I'd never have thought I'd be part of a full blown feature film, not in million years.' *Cliché,* she thought, but pressed on. 'I've sure learnt a great deal, meeting all you wonderful people.' *Except Simon,* she added silently. 'I'm here largely because of Donald's appreciation of just how lost a girl can be without an anchorman. I'd raise a toast to that, and publicly express my thanks for all he's done for me.' *There, I've committed myself.* She picked up her glass, looked at him across the table. The others followed suit, '*To Donald!*' and assorted add-ons came from Ronald, from Peter, even from Yvette who'd rejoined the group.

'You're too kind,' he said. 'It's me who should be thanking you, Paula. I know,' as she appeared to want to continue her own explanation, 'that you're all aware of how great a loss I've felt, still feel, and the doubts I've had about coming back into the world in which we were both so happy. Well, Mary told me, in her last days, and which some of you may already know, that I should find another girl, someone who needed me. A bequest. It's an odd coincidence; at least I think it is, that our film has the title '*Maria's Legacy*' and we found our Maria so easily. I believe, though I'm not a religious sort of guy, my Mary's spirit has been with me - us - to guide us along the way. I know,' he repeated, 'that some of you might scoff at this, but if you believe in something deeply enough, perhaps even pray often enough, it may well happen. I believed in Mary, the thought her spirit would guide me, and Paula came into my life. I've not for one moment regretted it.' His voice cracked, the emotion all too evident, the sudden silence round the table nearly too smothering. Then Roland lifted his glass once more. 'To Mary!' he said.

'To Mary!' and Paula heard at least one say '*may she rest in peace*', her own unsaid wordage was a simple '*thankyou*'.

An anticlimax followed. The group slowly disassembled, a few had decided to go that night rather than stay on. 'What'll you do, Donald? Milan the day after tomorrow. Will you be okay?'

'Sure, Roland. Paula and I'll say our goodbyes to the place in the morning then head upcountry. Should be back in the hotel tomorrow night. That okay? You going tonight?'

'Yeah. I like these overnight trains. Lulls you asleep, no time flat,' he patted Donald on the shoulder, blew a kiss at Paula, and went. They were on their own.

'Last walk round?'

She nodded. Back to the fountain grotto place, where they'd come close, oh so close, to precipitating an unstoppable and very human passion? Being the people they were, commonsense had gotten in the way. Had that been right for them? They were still fencing, darting, lunging, trying to score yet not score - and she chuckled inwardly at all the mixed-up metaphors - or were they similes? So if they went back to the place, would the same thing happen? She wasn't sure, not yet; whether she felt she could get to the edge, the precipice, and summon up the courage to seduce him.

'You've got a very thoughtful look on you. Doing a reprise of the week? It's worked, you know. I'm happy, Ronald's happy, the crew hasn't moaned. We've made another little girl rather happy too. Are you?'

'Happy? I suppose so. I haven't messed up, have I?'

'No, you've come out of it rather well, lots of compliments flying about.'

'You haven't regretted having me on board then?'

He managed to get her into a hug, dropped a light kiss on her neck, a familiar gesture.

'You're flirting again,' she said, ever so quietly.

Another kiss; 'habit of mine,' he said and she felt his hands move further down. 'Paula,' and this time his voice dropped into a husky murmur, 'will we come out of this alive?'

She pushed herself free, shook her hair and smoothed it back into place. 'It's Milan tomorrow. Then back to Pinewood I suppose.' She tried to keep her voice matter-of-fact but inwardly her heart was racing and nature was beginning to get organised in a not entirely unexpected way. This was neither the right time nor, in her too rational mind, the place. So he got his answer, another quietly spoken affirmation, '*yes, Donald, I think we will,*' and with that she took his hand in a firm grip and walked him round the garden in companionable silence before it was time to return to the hotel and back to their separate rooms.

Mary's Legacy   23

This time she could appreciate the scenery, travelling in daytime, a relaxing way to move back up-country. There wasn't any doubt in her mind that Donald's aversion to airports and the associated nausea was something she could well understand, and his addiction to long haul trains she could definitely get used to, especially travelling *di prima classe* For one reason or another she didn't feel particularly sparky this morning, quite content to tag along behind him as they strolled, yes, *strolled,* towards the *stazione.* 'You're very quiet,' he told her as they waited on the platform for the train to arrive.

'Anticlimax perhaps; that or a reluctance to consider we're on our way home. Don't mind, do you?'

'Nope. I quite understand.' He had hold of one hand, bag in the other. 'At least we can relax for a few hours. There'll be another briefing dinner this evening, ready for the fray tomorrow.' He pulled her round to offer a light kiss on the nearest cheek. 'Have I told you how nice it is to have such a pleasant travelling companion?'

'Not explicitly.'

'Well, it is. Quite like old times.'

'Can't be the same, none the less.'

He shrugged; she could see the far-way look again, the *'I remember Mary'* gaze into the past. She squeezed the held hand. What could she say? Nothing; they both knew where they stood.

Then the train arrived, precipitating a few minutes quick action, checking the reservations, stowing bags, settling down. Nice to ease into the comfortable depths of the seats of Trenitalia's Freccia Rossa, the superb red train that felt like a land-based aircraft, to allow muscles to relax, to know she didn't have to worry about anything during the journey north. Within minutes, with the train up to speed, she felt drowsy, her mind slowed . . .

�

He let her sleep, understanding the way brains went into a sort of relaxation mode after a stint of - relatively - frenetic activity. There was something about the film world; either all action, the push and shove of getting sequences shot, or boring inactivity whilst logistics were sorted, hours spent waiting around or in this case, getting from one place to another. Way back, on one feature that fortunately did generate a fair amount of box office receipts, he - and Mary - had days and days of not a lot happening after what must have been over a thousand miles of travel. That had nearly seen them resign and move onto another production company, but sense prevailed and the money rolled in. Then, on the flip side, there'd been a thing they'd done in London, on the doorstep, took less than a week and gave them a Bafta nomination. Would this one get anywhere? It might. That Michaela - a mentally stirring reprise of her artistry in form, flair and flashing eyes - she'd wow the audiences and get them hooked on the concept. And Paula? Would her walk across the Gallerie terrazzo floor produce the same vibes? Little did she know he'd a surprise lined up . . . his late night call to Sarah a couple of days ago, her affirmative reply last night . . . how she'd laughed at him over the phone line, clear as the proverbial bell, told him he was an old romantic and her mum would be proud of him. Oddly, her remark had settled his flexed thoughts and he'd actually slept well. Unlike Paula, if her subsequent languorous state was anything to go by. Over three hours to go . . .

They must have woken simultaneously; she stretched, looked at her watch, blinked and her eyebrows went up. 'I've slept for ages. Missed all that scenery. Damn!'

The train was slowing, buildings appearing. Milan. 'Won't have done you any harm. I've dozed as well, given there wasn't any lively conversation coming my way.' He grinned at her. 'At least we should be all bright and perky for this evening's session, and from what I remember, it's an early start in the morning. With his connections, Booth's organised a deferred public opening of the Gallerie so we can get your sequence in without too many gawpers,' bethought himself about the 'surprise' and hoped it'd work. 'Annette will be looking for an early fix so she can get away. She flies back to the States from here. Marco'll stay on; it's home territory for him.'

'Rosina?'

'Not sure. She might come back with us, who knows. We'll have a day or three to get rid of travel stains before we shoot again at the studio. There's a whole raft of sequences to fit in. Not much for me - us - 'cos it's mainly close-ups. A few interiors that are easy to set up, though, yes, we do have to look at the detail . . .'

His voice changed; getting carried away with the enthusiasm she recognised as part of him, what he was, the dedicated professional and fully involved, why Booth wanted him on the team, and how therefore she'd become involved. And all down to that casual 'yes, okay' agreement to join the hiking party she'd made to Adam in the pub following a workout session in the gym after work. Another world - she idly wondered where the guy was, and Stuart, come to that. And those two young girls, Susan and Marianne?

The monologue went on, his description of what would happen, the fill-ins, the voice overs, the use of library footage if there weren't enough backdrop shots . . . but her mind wasn't with him, it was back in the Lakes, in the damp and the chill and the greens and muddy browns and the shepherd's hut and the ancient Discovery and how she'd sensed some hidden rapport which she wasn't going to let go at any price.

'You're not listening.' He'd stopped the diatribe and she coloured up, he was quite right, she'd switched off.

'Sorry, Donald, still asleep, it seems. Forgive me. What was it you saying?' as if she didn't know, it was sure to be about the filming back at Pinewood.

'Doesn't matter - it'll keep. Probably boring you. We're here,' which was very much telling her the obvious, especially as the train had smoothed down to a stop. He heaved the bags down, one after the other, they moved along the passageway with all the other passengers, out onto the platform - and she was back in Milan.

A brisk ten minute walk to the familiar hotel. For an unexplainable reason she was not looking forward to the 'cast and crew' dinner. It'd be too conversational, an irksome blend of bonhomie, technical stuff, queries about this and that. She wanted to continue to relax even after the hours in the train; she'd love to spend the evening curled up in

Donald's arms, just him and her, letting the strains of the past week go, but it wouldn't happen.

The same room; and alone; somewhere inside her there was an ache, a hollow, unfulfilled ache. Collapsed on the bed, shoes kicked off, she let her mind go blank . . .

Donald, with Paula escorted safely into her room - he didn't doubt she'd stay there - checked with the hotel Night Manager. Had there been a special delivery for him? Yes sir, in his office. Would sir like the parcel delivered to his room? Donald cogitated - decided no, but in the morning, he said, it was to go to Room 204, Paula's. At precisely nine o'clock? Absolutely sir, I'll see to it myself before I go off duty.

Donald relaxed, rejoined the others gathering in the anteroom to the dining room.

'No Paula?' This was Ronald.

Donald shook his head. 'I think she's switched off filming. Whether she stirs for a meal is doubtful - we ate on the train between naps. Anticlimax or something.'

Roland was sympathetic. 'Happens. Never mind. Her day tomorrow.'

'Yes. And I've got something up my sleeve she doesn't know about, so beware hysteria. It'll be good though. Peter better be at his best.'

'Do I hear my name in vain?' Peter had overheard. 'What's all this? Paula strutting her stuff on camera a.m. tomorrow? I know, so what's so special, other than it's her debut and Annette will be watching?'

'It'll spoil my surprise if I tell you. Another Michaela moment. There's bound to be tears, which will work well, so close-up shots, Peter?'

He got a non-committal shrug. 'If you say so, mister art director,' then returned to the comment about Michaela. 'The little Italian is coming to Pinewood, I gather?'

Donald nodded. 'Her mother will bring her. She's been to London once before, which helps. Should be fun.'

'I look forward to it. Pretty girl. And sincere too, which makes a change from the 'I know I've got tits and a bikini wax' hard nosed open-legged gal.'

'And you'll know all about them, Peter?' Donald half grimaced, half smiled, knowing it'd be seen as a rhetorical question. Far too many women had trodden that route to an unwanted catastrophe or early wrinkles. He'd been well blessed in his choice of lady - Mary kept him sane and well away from the syrenic attractions that crept into the less savoury media corners. Peter nodded and moved on, towards the buffet. Jon and Marco followed him; Donald hesitated, wondering about Yvette and Rosina, had they come down? He decided not to wait and went after the others. It'd be a dreary evening without his girl, but there was tomorrow to look forward to . . .

Mary's Legacy   24

The dining room, transformed into a breakfast buffet servery, hummed with chatter. Bursts of cheerful laughter, bright smiles everywhere. It was Gallerie day and the climax of their location work. Despite the early hour, even the waiting staff had caught the buzz with grins nailed into place.

Donald, after a reasonable night's sleep, had managed to rouse himself at six, gone for a brisk half-hour walk through deserted streets to clear his head before his usual and traditional continental breakfast, unfazed that Paula hadn't yet surfaced. Half seven, he'd another hour and a half before the rendezvous with the parcel fresh from Paris. He half hoped she'd have been up - and as he wished, so she appeared and made a bee-line for him.

'Morning!' Bright and breezy, thank goodness - the prolonged rest must have swept the lethargy away - or she'd summoned up more energy, given it was going to be *her* day.

'Morning, Paula love. You rested?'

She nodded. 'Mmmm. Feel fine, thanks. Any of my favourite apricot croissants left?'

He reached across, pinched the last two from the basket and dumped them on her plate. 'My table's over there.' He cast a careful eye over what she was wearing. In less than an hour now, she'd be a different girl, he knew; he'd promised himself she would be.

'All set for the big day?'

She humped her shoulders up and down, a sort of feminine 'don't care' gesture but he knew different. On the surface, casual, inside, wound up. She'd be fine once they got started, of that he was sure, especially when she'd come to terms with what she had to do, but the more so because of what she would be wearing. How would she react?

Surreptitiously he looked at his watch. Half an hour. How could he get her back to her room? 'Got everything you need? Perhaps that light sweater in case? It may not be too warm, given we're this early - the place doesn't get that warm, it's vast and can be a bit breezy.'

'I'll pop up and grab that sweater then, if you're that concerned,' and she pushed her chair back. 'Won't be a moment.'

'I'll come with you; I think I've left a notebook up there.' *Any excuse . . .*

'Okay.'

Twenty minutes. Could he manage to keep her in her room when they got up there? Oddly, she'd not queried what she would be asked to wear. Perhaps she'd worked up sufficient confidence in the wardrobe department over the last few days; well, her surprise was only minutes away.

She didn't evince any concern when he followed her into her room, but fiddled about in her still unpacked bag.

'Here, girl - haven't you hung your things up? They'll get creased!'

She gave him an old-fashioned look, as if to say 'don't fuss' but did lift out the dress she had and the better skirt and fitted them onto a hanger. Then the knock came on the door, spot on the time.

'Who's that?' she queried but he beat her to it, opened the door, took the proffered parcel, said his thanks, closed the door, to then pass the box onto her.

'What's all this then?' she asked, her voice curious, but then she saw the label and he watched her face go white.

'Largoumans? Karl? What? Why?' then suddenly it dawned on her and the colour came back. 'Donald! You horror! You've sent for my dress! You have, haven't you?' She dropped the box on the bed, tore off the tape and lifted the lid. Her dress, a shimmer of pale gold and ivory, swathed in tissue, beautifully packed, and a hand-written note lying on the top, ribbon fastened to a zip. Sarah's writing. She untied the ribbon, lifted it and read the careful script out loud:

> *'for my father's wonderful girlfriend, so she can shine
> and show him the loveliest girl in Milan. Wear this with
> pride, our darling Paula. With love from Sarah and Karl.'*

He knew she'd cry, not with any emotion other than sheer happiness. The note fluttered through her fingers onto the bed, she reached down and lifted the dress very carefully out of its box, let the tissue fall, held the gorgeous creation up against her, looked at him, eyes shining, he saw the passion in her eyes and hoped, hope against hope, she'd keep the feeling alive under the glare of the lights and into the all-seeing lens of Peter's camera. He wanted her to live the moment, to let it burn an enduring memory into her soul, to hold it as a milestone in her life - and who knows, his as well.

The dress was laid on the bed; she was in his arms, sought his lips, his mouth, kissed as never before, felt his inevitable response, let the tears flow, let him release her to find a handkerchief, to have him dry her cheeks, her eyes, to kiss once more, to bring mind back to the moment and to understand what it was to have someone like Donald care for her, love her . . . *oh, oh, . . . ooohh. . .*

It took another hour before everything was in place at the Gallerie. The morning's early shoppers were carefully marshaled to walk down the one side, keeping clear the planned route for her walk. The lights were there, the reflectors, the camera on its track, the crew in place, Roland in shirt sleeves as was his wont, Peter with his grip guy, Yvette and her clip board, everyone in place, Marco had done his walk through, Annette her pout, Paula had rehearsed her route twice, all set ...the clapper board . . .

'Action!'

She felt absolutely on top of the world. Yesterday's lethargy evaporated, all her nervousness gone, she shone. She knew she shone, the dress flowed around and up, revealing those lovely legs before settling back into the perfection of pleats; the low-cut top with short sleeves above a belt of woven beads accentuating her bust line and the offset highlighting the glimpse of her now not so pale tanned breasts. The overall length at a fraction above ankle level exactly right, a dress that had taken hours of painstaking work from the *atelier*, the accompanying shoes, with the pendant on the gold chain Roland had found for her, she was the star. The walk, the walk across this world-famous floor in this world-famous place of fashion, and she was in a *Largouman* dress. *Too good to be true . . .*

Then it was all over. Roland, cunning old fox, had her do her walk three times, allowing her the privilege of entertaining, nay, impressing, the gathered crowds. After the third 'cut!' a spontaneous roll of applause echoed round before the inevitable drift into anticlimax. Annette had done her close-up with Marco, Roland was satisfied, Donald had seen the play-back on the big monitor and inwardly swelled with pride. *His girl, but Mary's choice.*

She didn't want to take it off; felt two inches taller, her shoulders back, wanted the feeling to last for ever, but time was pressing. Sue, the assistant wardrobe girl, was hovering. 'We need to . . .,' and Donald in his protective mode nodded. They'd borrowed space in the Rizzoli emporium for changing, Annette had already cleared through the room and was waiting for her. 'Paula, my dear girl, that was *fantastic* - you carried it off *beautifully*. You wait; there'll be others after you!'

She frowned. 'It's not really me. I couldn't act like you, or Rosina. I'm too honest with myself.'

'But you managed this absolutely right, spot on. It's what the storyline needed and you gave it its all. The dress is astonishing; I've always loved Largouman creations. Marvelous!'

Donald loved it, adored her too, but practicality had to rise above desire. 'You'd better change back to reality, my love. We need to move on,' and, to borrow the time-honoured expression, added '*the film is in the can*', captured for all time.

The rest was anticlimax. The day went, the last sequences shot, they gathered in the hotel's anteroom prior to the last dinner. Those few lesser mortals who needed to leave had already gone; the project's location team was winding down. Next week, Pinewood, and, as even Roland admitted, it'd be the boring side, collecting the join-ups and backdrop sequences together. Then over to editing which could take *ages* as Annette said in her chat with Paula and Donald before she took the taxi to the airport. 'Such a shame I have to nip back to the States but my agent, you know, he's got another part lined up and this is where I have to be a good girl and do as I'm told. I'll be back in a fortnight, see you all then.'

Going into dinner felt so formal, like a nineteenth century social occasion. The tables had been dressed, white cloths, floral arrangement above the norm, and place cards. Paula found herself alongside Roland, but with Donald on her left. Despite the set-dressing, the atmosphere was subdued, the conversation desultory, rather like a wake. Roland, as expected, 'said a few words' the usual thanks, compliments - including his admiring words about her walk - but she was glad when it came to an end.

After the meal, after another two or three, including Yvette and Jon, had said their farewells to catch overnight flights, Donald eased Paula to one side. 'We'll catch an early morning flight straight back to Gatwick, Paula. Much though I like trains and hate airports, it's quicker and I need a break. You'll come back to the Lakes with me?

'Of course I will. I don't mind flying in this situation either.' She searched his eyes, the warmth and the depth and knew they'd crossed a bridge. He'd found a hand and lightly squeezed; the stress and confusion of the past ten days easing away. The Lakes; oh how she yearned for the soft greys and greens, the feel of the breeze and even the dampening mists, the blurred horizons of distant hills. Vieste and its endless sun, touristy beaches and the blue of bluest Aegean was fine in small doses, but she was a hill-loving girl. 'Yes, *oh yes,* can't wait.'

He took her up to her room; they parted at her door with a lingering kiss. Tomorrow, *tomorrow, they'd* be on their way.

Mary's Legacy 25

She slept during most of the flight back, woke as the aircraft circled, waiting for its slot to land. Donald too, had slept and couldn't recall whether he'd snored or not. Dreamt, yes, and those dreams broke apart into incomprehensible and chaotic snippets of film, place, girl, the journey back to Beckside.

He reached for her, a reassurance. 'Okay?'

She nodded. 'Okay. Not looking forward to the arrivals lounge scrum.'

He chuckled. 'Nor me. At least it's Gatwick, not Heathrow. There'll be a unit car waiting for us, according to Roland. If it's good enough for him, he'd said, it's good enough for you too.' Should he tell her now? Why not, take her mind of the landing. 'He wants to keep you on the list, Paula.'

'What do you mean, keep me on the list?'

'For a start, you'll be moved up the credits and when a suitable opportunity comes up, given an option for a full-blown screen test. In other words, my dear girl, there's an opening there,' and added, without thinking, 'as a present from Mary.'

. . . She was there, in the empty seat alongside, smiling at him, reaching for a hand, mouthing 'well done us' as she'd done so many times. Every time they'd come back from a shoot, the routine, as they'd returned home . . .

'Mary? Oh, Donald . . .' She couldn't say more, the violent grip of emotion silenced her; she stared, not focusing, at the cabin ceiling. Was Donald's past love life always going to influence hers? Was it fair, keeping her memory between them?

The aircraft's engine noise intensified. Imagination or realism? Her mind in turmoil. What he'd said - the future or the past? They'd landed, taxiing towards the terminal, her thoughts subjugated in the necessity to go through barriers, have passports inspected, baggage to collect. The dress, carefully restored to its box, was there, thank heavens. Extra luggage, true, but any expense fully justified. She couldn't be without it, a talisman, a symbol of who she had become.

The car was waiting, the recognisable grey Mercedes, and the pleasant driver whose name, now she knew the system, would be amongst the credits. Odd but comforting to know everyone who played a part was recognised. How would Michaela's name be defined? Alongside Rosina's? Michaela would be arriving next week with her mother. Who'd run the café? A relative, no doubt. Italian families were close knit.

'The studio, sir?'

Donald nodded, 'yes please. No hurry.'

'Of course sir.'

Familiar roads, familiar traffic. 'Not like the Strada 14, Paula. No sea to gaze at. That was a good run.'

Her thoughts spun back. 'Yes. I enjoyed it. Sadly consigned to history, but I'm looking forward to sharing another drive with you, Donald, and you know where!'

'Not in an Alfa.'

'An old Discovery will be fine.'

'Tomorrow, all being well, if Booth will give us time off.'

'That why we're going to Pinewood?'

'He likes a personal de-brief from his chief minions.'

She laughed. 'Chief minions! Bit of a contradiction in terminology. I suppose the others have beaten you to it.'

'Roland will be there. Peter will have gone home, as will Jon.'

'What about that Simon?'

'Back in the States, I expect. He'll creep round Annette though she won't encourage him. Watch that one.'

'Don't worry. Far too suave for my liking.' She changed the subject. 'Where will Michaela stay?'

187

'Studio account hotel, we've two or three on tap. Not large ones, more your exclusive country club style. There's a nice one near Cliveden.'

'How long will she be here?'

'Three, four days I should think. Mind you, if they want to stay on, that's their decision. We'll see.'

The car turned into the entrance drive; they got the welcome wave in from the security guy. 'It doesn't seem like ten days. More like yesterday.' Paula sat up, aware of how life had changed for her. A few short weeks ago she'd been the new girl, naïve, nervous. Now? Passed her informal screen test, given an indication other roles may come her way and she had a wonderful guy alongside.

Up to the entrance doors, handed out of the car. 'I'll see to your bags, sir.'

'Thanks - take especial care of the dress box.'

'Certainly sir,' and he went off with it.

'You want a wash and brush up, girl?'

She pulled a face. 'Do I look that grubby?'

'No, but …'

'Oh, okay. See you in ten.'

He chuckled. 'I love the parlance, Paula. You'd not have said 'see you in ten' two weeks ago.'

She grinned at him, merely slung her handbag over her shoulder and walked off to the ladies.

Donald could do no other than check in with the boss. Booth would expect nothing else. He tapped on the door, went in. The big man put his pen down to lean back in his creaking chair. 'The wanderer returns. Better late than never. How's the trip?'

Two clichés; Booth loved them. Donald dropped into one of the 'visitor' chairs and ignored the 'late' aspect. 'You'll have heard most of it from Roland, but yes, went well. *And* we found our Maria.'

'So I've heard, naturally. She good then?'

He wasn't given to exaggerations, but the description 'marvellous' was the only word to encapsulate how she'd worked. He ran through the way they'd come across her, Booth listened without displaying emotion.

'Then the Paula girl earned her keep by the sound of things. I'm going to look at the video. Want to join me?'

'We've only been in the country a couple of hours,' he tried to excuse them but read Booth's expression and decided he'd have to give in. 'Okay, provided we get away before midnight.' He kept his own face deadpan, rewarded by Booth's grin. This sparring was them, old friends testing boundaries. The knock on the door. Paula.

'Come in; come in, Paula, welcome home!' Booth could be effusive when the nice girls were about. 'We're gonna have a decko at the best bits. Jemma's stayed on 'specially.'

She heaved an inward sigh, having had the idea they'd be back in the flat by supper time and she could switch off; now it'd be delayed. She glanced at Donald. His very slight flick of eyebrows told her 'behave' so she gave in. 'That'll be nice,' she said and stayed standing. The mini-cinema was next door.

Booth heaved himself up; they followed his bulk into the screen room. They slid into the bucket seats, Jemma, his long suffering p.a., did the honours, the rough cut sequences rolled. Ten minutes of Vieste before Michaela's walk in across the sand and Booth sat up. 'Yes!' he said, emphatically, before subsiding again as the café sequences followed. No comment about the Lecce parts, though Donald would know if - what - he'd dislike by a hand-tapping on a knee but he stayed immobile. Then they saw Milan, the Gallerie, broadview shots before the opener of Annette sitting on the bench, Marco haranguing her, the way he casually looked round, the cut-in to Paula's stroll and the reaction - but then the close-up shot of the walk she'd done, the way the dress flared across her legs. She couldn't believe what she saw.

Booth sat up again, bolt upright. 'Gee, gal, that's some sway, and the dress! Where did you get that dress!' He waved at Jemma, the screen went dark. 'Yes, you did good, guys. We'll have a better run through, say a couple of day's time? Let you cool down, eh? Give the boys time to smooth the edits?'

'Monday?' asked Donald, hoping they'd squeeze at least the two days in the Lakes.

Booth eyed him, read his thoughts. 'Okay.' He turned to Paula. 'I ain't wrong. You did well, gal. Speak more later. Now go home.'

No further bidding required. They left Booth shuffling back to his desk; he'd be there for hours yet. Outside, his office door shut, they were alone in a deserted corridor, the place quiet, a strange contrast to the last couple of frenetic weeks. 'Yes?' he asked her as they walked slowly down to the entrance hall.

'Odd,' she replied, 'very odd, seeing me on screen, seeing Michaela like that when I - we - were there, and knowing it was us, what we did and the coincidence that put it all there.' They reached the double doors, Donald pulled one open for her. 'Peter's good with the camera,' she added as they moved into the evening air. 'Were you pleased?'

'Yes. It'll be a fair deal better after the edit department has had a go at it. Booth was pleased.'

'So I came up to expectations?'

'Of course - better than. I loved it. Proud of you.' He looked down the road and yes, there was the usual Mercedes, patiently waiting; having seen them, the driver was bringing it forward. 'We're going home.'

⁓

The flat was if they'd never left it; she couldn't believe what she'd done, where she'd been in the intervening time as she followed him up the stairs.

Perhaps the innate feel for the girl kept everything on a steady plane. By themselves, in the flat, the flat once home to Mary, the remainder of the evening could have moved into a stressed occasion, but the last thing he'd wish. He wanted her to stay warm and cosy in the thought she'd done well, had fitted so neatly into the role he'd carved out for her, and not to extend into any other mode, not tonight.

They had a simple supper, sausages out of the small freezer, she did something splendid with some uncooked potatoes left from before the trip, added grated cheese, opened a bottle of not too grand a red, comfort food as he said, eaten to the background of a favourite Shostakovich piano concerto, to then clear and wash up before they called it a day.

Left alone in the guest bedroom - Sarah's room - Paula could properly relax, all hurdles jumped. Early this morning she'd left a plush Milan hotel to be in a simple north London flat this evening and tomorrow, likely a sleeping bag in a draughty shepherd's hut in the depths of the Lake District. Yesterday, she'd worn a four-figure Largouman dress; tomorrow evening, it'd be twenty pound jeans and a very warm sweater. Such a set of contrasts. Warm, cosy, comforted, and loved. Sleep came easy.

∽ ∽ ∽

Mary's Legacy 26

Easy to slip back into routine; the adrenaline rush of the last few days ebbing away; breakfast, repack a bag, check over its contents again, secure the flat, walk to the road end to catch a cab to Euston. This time they had to buy tickets, ouch, expensive. 'What comes of not being ultra organised, should have had Pat briefed. Not to worry.' Donald scanned the departure board. 'The 10.30 will do. Platform three. Away we go.'

The walk up the platform, happily a choice of seats, risked the possibility of sharing a foursome and sat opposites to bag windows. 'Don't mind travelling backwards?'

'Not really. We can always swop,' and she nestled into her corner. 'If I go drowsy, will it matter?'

He grinned at her. 'Nope. You're allowed. No script notes this trip. Don't you read?'

She shrugged. 'Novels have never been my thing, but I suppose I could.'

'I read all the time; extends my vocabulary, opens new windows. Takes one's mind off the mundane, that sort of idea.'

'Better buy me a book then.'

He glanced at his watch. 'Ten minutes, hmm. Right, keep my seat,' and he shot off; she saw him head off down the platform towards the kiosks. The minutes passed, he didn't return. She heard the guard's whistle and panicked. Where was he? No sign - what should she do? Get off? But decision time was past; the train was on the move, nothing she could do. Alone, with a ticket, fortunately, and the shared bag. Now what? Had he his mobile phone, for she'd got hers? She gave him a couple of minutes before she tried. No reply. Her mind whirled round at all the possibilities, from the simplistic that he'd got trapped in a till queue, to the downright horrible thought there'd been a medical problem. Nothing she could do now as the train gathered speed; next stop goodness knows where, she wasn't familiar with the route - and the idea of climbing off midway didn't appeal either. Three hours or so to Carlisle and she had to accept it. She settled back in her seat and closed her eyes to the problem.

✑

Donald: He'd messed up. It took far longer than he'd thought, the choice, a payment, the fast walk out of the shop area - only to see the barriers lock shut, to hear the whistle and know he'd left her alone, and now on her way north without him. He checked his pocket for his phone, to text her, tell her not to worry. The phone wasn't there. Never before, not in the multiple years of travel up and down, had this happened to him and Mary. But Paula, dear girl, was now left by herself. Rationale, he had to apply rationale. She was a sensible girl. She had her ticket - he'd made sure of that. She knew where they were going. He could follow on; the next train was - looking at the departure board - in an hour's time. Would she wait at Carlisle? Or, if brave, perhaps go on to Aspatria, even take the bus to Bassenthwaite? Where was his phone? Of course, damn, silenced and in his coat pocket, and that coat with the bag - in the train. So even if she'd rung or messaged him, the phone wouldn't have told her of the error. He didn't often swear but gave way to a few of the messier words, not that it helped. What now? The only way forward - catch the next train, see what happened. A sudden twinge of thought that she'd get off at the first stop - Milton Keynes of all places - he dismissed. No, head north on the next train and hope; at least they'd be closer . . . and that's what mattered. For the first time in what, three months, they were apart, a weird thought, one which had not previously crossed his mind. Throughout the whole of Italy, they'd been together; all the days in the office, together. Ever since the very consequential day when she'd come to him in desperation, they'd not ever really been away from each other; been in the same house, the same office, on the same journeys, in the same hotels . . . but now she was moving away, the miles growing as the Virgin train flew north; somehow he felt lost, a gap opening up, a coolness in the world around. Where was Mary?

✑

Paula: The train swept on, northbound. She'd never been alone on a train long distance until after that life-changing hiking weekend. Not as a child, not as an adult, never had the need. The hike weekend, they'd travelled up as a group but she had gone home alone, pining for a relationship.

The carriage wasn't empty, but not full either; different people travelling for different reasons. Anyone on an assignation? Anyone dealing with a relationship? Or in a relationship and going to a family home, or to a holiday let? Or travelling for work, to work, to an arranged meeting? Endless reasons. Where did she fit? Assignation, no, dealing *with* a relationship, no. Travelling to a holiday let, sort of. Not for work, certainly. Away from work, yes. A parallel, being a secretary who'd just seen her boss walk away and disappear . . .but in this instance, she felt her role wasn't a mere secretary, a personal assistant or whatever, but a - a what, confidant, hand-holder, companion, even, lordy, bed warmer? There were aspirations maybe, undefined but very very normal ones between eligible man and needy woman. Was he eligible? A widower with a hole in his life and an oft-quoted bequest from his beloved dead wife to 'look after a needy girl'? Was she the 'needy' girl? Yes, dammit, yeah, she was. She needed him.

She felt dizzy, light headed. Breakfast long gone. Stress building. Head down, girl, don't faint, no, don't faint ….

The train swept on.

Donald: Fifty minutes until the next train. A cup of coffee, a sticky bun, keep the blood sugar up to par. A seat somewhere out of the way but where he could people watch, gain an idle summation of the why's and wherefores of the milling travelers. Why they were there, the destinations, the reasons for the journeys, work, business, domestic, family, relationships being extended - or terminated. A fascinating study, should one have an interest in people. Mary had always had that fascination, how she managed to make friends so well, getting to know what made them tick. What would she have thought about Paula? That she'd have surely loved her was a comforting thought. Sarah had taken to her and, like mum, like sibling. How was his girl coping? That they'd be reunited wasn't a worry, just the time in between, whether anything would happen to her - and this brought other thoughts scything into focus. He cared, a depth of concern not previously explored, unnecessary because she'd always been around. Maybe the odd moments when the pressure of the film had inserted a draughty gap between them; these were errors soon blown away to restore the warmth of togetherness. Even Michaela's arrival, a psychological shock at the time, had helped strengthen his feelings for Paula. She was becoming more of a Mary every day, and Mary his ultimate spiritual guide. Amongst the scurrying travelers and meet and greet people, he could imagine her, her spirit, coming across the concourse, a smile, a takeaway coffee, a swirl of skirt, a drift of careless hair, his Mary - or his Paula? Another half hour.

൧

Paula: A moment, a moment's blackout, she must have banged her head on the table as she went briefly unconscious. At least she hadn't been standing up or in a public place when all hell would have broken out at her collapse. Very carefully she looked around, had anyone seen her faint? To visibly crumple is a very embarrassing scenario as she'd known once, way back when she'd fainted in a school assembly and been unceremoniously carried out of the hall, all legs, arms and dangling hair. She rubbed at her forehead. Would there be a bruise? It might happen again if she wasn't careful, and to be carted off to some hospital or other would really mess things up. What should she do? The scenery flashing by, the train was rattling on, except it didn't rattle. Mr Branson wouldn't be amused if he was told his trains rattled. An inner smile. What would Donald be thinking? It was his fault - or hers for asking - telling - him to buy her a book. What would he have chosen? Whatever, when reunited it'd be a topic of avid conversation and she'd never forget the manner of its acquisition. Sit still, girl, stay calm. I know, and she homed in on a positive thought; I'll stay on the platform at Carlisle. He'd come on a later train, she'd wait for him, they'd be reunited on the platform like something out of one of those romantic films, except there'd be no steam or smoke to provide the backdrop. Wasn't it 'Railway Children,' when the father was reunited with his elder daughter, emerging from a misty cloud of whatever? She wasn't the elder daughter. Would she still be a daughter in his mind, or the legatee, the girl who needed him? She took deep breaths, vowing they'd make something out of this. The train was slowing. Where? Huh, Milton Keynes. She'd never been here, and didn't much fancy the place. Stay on board. Oh, goody, the refreshment trolley. Salvation!

195

Donald: Time to board. Be good to get onto the train, into a hopefully warm carriage. Too much Italian sun has lessened the body's response to colder English climate. A decent seat without a reservation, against a window. Not in the mood for idle conversation, so hope it won't be crowded. Another hope, likely, - that it wouldn't hang about. I can imagine Paula, waiting on the Carlisle platform for me. Chilly. Will she be there? Yes. She'll be there. An assignation, like out of the film 'Brief Encounter', romance smothered in steam and smoke. The real 'encounter' in that sense, was way back, months ago up in the hills. No smoke there. I imagine her, curled up in the corner of the carriage seat, lonely and wondering. Hope she's alright . . . the usual whistle, the hardly perceptible movement . . . three hours.

Donald: No, he wouldn't take lunch, thank you. The thought of eating alone did not appeal, and anyway, Paula would probably need feeding. The steward moved on. He dragged the newly bought book out of its bag and thumbed through it, something to pass the time. An idle choice, stabbing a guess at her inclinations, certainly not crime, emphatically not fantasy, and so it veered into the relationship genre. Not too simple a tale; and he knew enough to steer clear of the cheapy so-called 'chick-lit', the easy-read easy to forget fodder for the less intelligent female. He'd chosen an historically based one - no requirement to understand modern technicalities, either in transport or communications. Nothing quite like old-world romance, without the modern rush for the bedroom door and drop your knickers stuff. She wasn't that sort of a girl.

It trapped him. Carried away into the seventeen-nineties Northumbria, into the simple requirement of putting food on a table and keeping the right side of the Squire, looking after a horse and courting a feisty girl or two - he had to inwardly grin at his earlier thought-train about knickers, when a girl lost her virginity on soft grass under Cheviot skies. No underwear in them-there days. A couple of hours soon went; another half hour or so and they'd be reunited provided she'd done what his telepathy told her to - maybe . . . maybe Mary's guidance too?

196

Paula: Carlisle. She made sure she'd got everything, the bag, yes, her own handbag, his coat. Nothing else. Off the train, within minutes it was away, to head north, destination Glasgow. First job, check the arrivals board for the next one - oh joy, only an hour behind. He'd be on that one, she knew. Telepathy. Stay on the same platform. There was a bench seat - a seat for fifty minutes patience. The packet of chocolate biscuits and an indifferent paper cup of coffee with double sweeteners had sorted out the thin blood syndrome, she felt fine. Maybe it was Cumbrian air. The bench carried a left-behind magazine. Couldn't be better - a 'Marie Claire' and in date too. She flicked through the pages. And sat up, startled, for there, amongst a few other photos, a girl in *her dress*! She read, heart beatingly, the article on Karl - *her* Karl. A report on the Paris fashion show - Sarah had been . . . turn the page, *Yes!* Sarah! It had to be her, lovely girl, wearing another Largouman creation. What a huge coincidence - or was it preordained? *Mary, are you being mischievous?* Perhaps it should have been in 'Vogue'? Never mind, this was a real treat to be given her by an unknown traveller - *thank you so much!*

⤙

Donald: The train was slowing. He checked his watch, yes, on time. Despite all his declared *sang froid*, his normally rational outlook and the disciplined unflappability so essential in his profession the heart beats accelerated, a tensed-up feeling wouldn't be denied. The girl, was she going to be there? A slow arrival, easing alongside the platform as though on purpose to tantalize and tease. With no bag, no coat, nothing to take out other than the book, standing at the carriage exit, unfazed by any other disembarking passengers, he watched, looked, stared across the concourse as the Virgin train edged further in, oh, was it really that measured or his perception edgily slow? Four hours absence. Four interminable hours, this was crazy. How could a rational individual be so het up by another's absence?

There, there - was Mary waiting?

⤙

Paula: Above her the information screen flashed its message. 'On Time', as she stood up, looked down the track, the grey and red sleek nose of the Virgin train appeared. He'd be looking for her. She changed her stance, stood square on, her shoulders back, hair sleeked back. Waited. Was her skirt uncreased, her light sweater unwrinkled? The rumble of the power unit passed, the first class coaches, the buffet car, slow, not slow enough, a squeal of final braking action. A stop. Donald?

In his arms, crushed, kissed. A whispered silly, idiotic *'I've missed you,'* eyes locked to eyes, no more to be said. She led him to the seat, sat him down, his arm came back around her shoulders, hugging her tight. Sense? What sense? Vaguely they heard the train pull away; the passengers dissipated, disappeared, they were left on their empty platform alone, in the vast open echoey space of Carlisle station, alone.

'I'm being silly,' she said. 'So sorry, dear one, I should never have asked you to . . .'

His fingers came up to her lips, a slight shake of his head. 'No matter. I worried.'

'Me too.'

'Daft.'

'Yes.'

'Shall we try and catch the next Aspatria train?'

Paula nodded. 'And together.'

'Together. Paula, I love you.'

'I know. I love you too, so so very much,' but she had to ask, 'will Mary mind?'

He heaved a sigh, *saw his Mary smile through time, through space, saw her blow a kiss and blur away into the spiritual world.* The message came back, clear as clear, *'this is the girl who needs you . . .'* then silence. She'd gone - *into eternal rest,* the phrase.

He picked up the bag with his coat where his phone snuggled uselessly in a pocket, with his other hand he took Paula's, together they walked away. 'No,' he said, looking back at the seat where once his beloved wife had once sat in just such a moment. 'No, Mary won't mind. Not now. You're the girl she's given me. Her gift. Her legacy.'

Mary's Legacy 27

The change in their togetherness wasn't dramatic, wasn't something that remarkable but subtle and sensible. All those little nuances of history and association with a previous love had taken on the softness and warmth of their own, added gold tinges to the tiny new things that happened as their life together began its next chapter.

The train brought them into *their* country, sitting tight together, watching the hills become more distinct. The old Discovery appeared to welcome them; Paula asked and Donald nodded, 'why not?' So she drove, carefully, taking his instructions, learning her way deeper into his life.

He opened the gate. No ghost lay in wait. She did a sterling job of parking the vehicle, absolutely correct, spot on. He told her so, she grinned. She found the key, unlocked the door. No spiritual presence, just warmth.

Supper they managed from a scratch meal with strange things left in the cupboards. 'Shopping tomorrow,' she said firmly. 'We'll have to stock up because you're *not* selling the place. Sarah will agree with me,' the light in her eyes, the way she moved, the lithe quickness a new pleasure to watch. One of the last bottles of red wine, gently brought to *chambre* was opened. Glasses charged, she knew exactly what to say. *'To Mary. To Maria's legacy. To us.'*

They slept peacefully, secure in each other's arms, welcoming the freedom and the future. Unspoken promises firmly placed would stay rock solid. Time would stand still.

The morning brought added brilliance in the clear sunlight, the fresh feel to the early air, the depth of green accentuated in tree, shrub and grass, a verdant lushness. She stood at the door in her unabashed pure naked glory, taking it all in, breathing deep, arms above her head, waiting for the first shiver and the rise of goose pimples to encourage her return to him. How peaceful, how serene her mind, a sense not previously experienced, not even after the way they'd come together in tumultuous joy. Four hours separation, four hours introspective reflection and *she* had approved. '*Mary,*' Paula whispered at the sky, '*thank you. I won't ever let you down,*' that was an unbreakable promise.

'You'll need to speak to Sarah,' she suggested, matter-of-factly after her return to bed had been carefully celebrated in a most acceptable manner; she glowed. 'And congratulate her. Oh, and I forgot, something I need to show you,' to slip out of bed once more to fetch the now rather crumpled copy of '*Marie Claire*' from downstairs. He watched her go, the beauty and the artistry of her, could not adequately express mental appreciation of every part of the girl, what she now meant to him; the spirit within her so familiar, the way she'd taken to their loving, the gift he'd never demean.

She came back, returned to the warmth and showed him the photo. 'Your daughter. Aren't you proud of her?'

Taking the publication from her, he read the article and recognised the dress, *the* dress. 'That'll add value to your scene. The magazine - where did you find it?'

'Left on the seat where I waited for you. Coincidence or what?'

The instinctive thought: *Mary, are you up to your mischievous tricks?* If so, it added another positive dimension to what they'd achieved in such a strange way, in a mere four hour separation. Nothing in Italy had brought them this close, not even the emotional charged moment at Lecce or the earlier adventure back in London when they'd both been, with a wry inner chuckle '*on their best behaviour*'.

'I haven't shown you the book I bought you.'

'I wonder why? Perhaps you were otherwise preoccupied.'

They could joke about it now but at the time, traumatic, though the end result could not be faulted for they were faultlessly together, in mind, spirit and, without hesitation or remorse, body. He stroked her, felt the smooth suppleness of her shape under subtle and sensitive fingers. She shivered; her eyes closed, relaxed into the passive welcoming that allowed the sense of him to carry her once more into the feeling of sublime ecstasy. She purred, no other word for it, but time's passage and circumstances edged her into reality.

'We'd best get up. The day's well under way. And . . .' she unwrapped her long legs to leave him alone once more. 'Back in a mo.'

With arms hand-locked behind his head, he contemplated how, and how well, they'd moved into this wonderful phase in their togetherness. No need to worry about raw sensitivities now, no need to pretend. Time indeed proved to be the true healer; the concerns over the rough edges left unhealed for so long vanished. From now on he could put tremendous energy into getting the film right. Maria - Michaela - would be schooled carefully into her role, the missing bits would not be difficult to complete. It'd be good.

She was back, with a glass of orange juice in each hand as a symbol of a new beginning, an action of hers and hers alone. He told her so.

The brilliant smile offered in response, an uncomplicated honest smile, confirmed the 'thankyou' with a lightly presented kiss. 'I love you,' she said once back alongside, relishing the companionship and the unspoken suggestion they did not need to over-indulge. Time flowed on, moments simply cherished.

'I'm thrilled,' she said. 'Thrilled with what life's thrown at me, thrilled with what we're at, thrilled with where we are. I promise you,' she added, 'I'll try.'

He drained his glass. 'Paula, my love, *we'll* try. Together, we'll learn, we'll build, we'll make sure it'll work and . . .'

She finished the sentence for him; uttering the words gave her the added strength, 'Mary will be proud of you, of us.'

The word 'will' rather than a 'would', putting the potential into the present rather than the past made his heart surge. *This girl is a true gift from the gods, an offering from his late wife's presence in an unbelievable yet believable spirit world . . .* no longer a physical entity but a guiding force. Somehow he'd got to acknowledge her gift, her legacy, within the context of the film. He turned to the new woman in his life, precious Paula, and saluted her once more. 'Time we were up.'

She gave that funny little nod, a trait so very much personally hers, like orange juice in bed, grinned and reminded him she'd said so nearly half an hour ago. 'I'm up,' she said, springing out and offering another glimpse of her totality before stretching across to collect her things from the chair and dressing in three minutes flat. 'I'll go and put the kettle on. See you downstairs in ten,' laughed and left him.

She'd been right, last night, telling him he wasn't to consider selling 'Beckside'. Absolutely right; he reached for his phone, left on the charger by the bedhead. Sarah, beloved daughter, would she be about? Yes, five rings and a pick up.

'Hello dad. You're at Beckside. How's things?'

'Sarah, darling daughter. Yes, we are, how did you guess? And things, as you call them, couldn't be better. I've been told to congratulate you and tell you we're not putting Beckside on the market. Paula won't let me.' He heard her chuckle.

'Dear dad! Hooked, caught and landed? Is dear Paula now in command, then? Bet she looked stunning in Karl's creation, can't wait to see the film. Have you survived? When …'

'Hang on,' he interjected, 'you're rattling on,' and wondered how much to say, how the change in his affairs would affect her. 'You really like Paula? Honestly?'

He sensed her consideration before the reply, so yes she'd be honest. 'Dad, I have an instinctive feel for people, perhaps I got it from Mum, who knows, but yes, I really like her. If you two get on like I think, I guess, you do, then it is fine by me. You deserve to have another lady in your life, my father, and Mum was absolutely on the button when she suggested it,' and the strain in her voice showed emotion so tears wouldn't be very far away. 'I'm coming over. Now, this minute; I need to be with you, with Paula, and Karl will have to agree. I'll let you know when once I've sorted travel. No arguments, dad and I love you . . .' the phone went silent, she'd gone.

Needs to be with us? Here? How long would it take her, for they couldn't stay in the Lakes long, there was a film in the making. Oh lor, Booth, you won't like this, he thought, and looked at his watch. Dare he ring the office? Tell Booth what was happening, ask for some leeway? Would he be there on a Sunday? He had to try.

The phone rang and rang. Later, he'd try later.

The day looked fair, offered no surprises. 'Care for a walk?' he asked her over the second cup of coffee.

'Sure, love to. Take another look at Stu's rock? Where it all began?' her smile, more of a Cheshire cat grin, was infectious.

'Who knows, I might get lucky twice!'

She scowled at him. 'No way, mister, you're mine. To be defended against all comers and that'll include Michaela. When will Sarah arrive, do you think? We can't stay here long, can we?'

He'd relayed his conversation with Sarah and how she'd not been surprised, was even pleased, explained he'd tried to reach Booth but to no avail.

The mobile sat innocuously on the table, he picked it up. 'I'll try him again.' This time an answer on the second ring; Paula heard the cryptic 'Yes' in response.

Donald explained. She heard a mutter, not distinct, watched his expression, saw a flick of eyebrows and a nod before he put the phone down. 'We've got until Thursday morning when there'll be a progress-chase conference. Apparently the second unit ran into problems in Tuscany on the wrap-up scene so they lost a day. In our favour. He understood.'

'I like him,' Paula admitted, 'although he's pretty brusque at times, he's also direct. So we can stay another couple of days?'

'Yep. If Sarah gets her skates on, she'll be here tonight. Flies into Manchester, fast train to Carlisle, she'll ring from there.'

'Can't wait to see her again. And I owe her, organizing the dress and that.'

Breakfast over, they shrugged into coats, stronger shoes, Donald raided the chocolate store for essential energy top-ups and they set out, heading up the estate path, through the gate, across the pasture land beginning to wither in the oncoming winter. The hiker's footpath still showed wear from walking traffic. 'Go right?' he asked.

She nodded. 'Please. A reprise, and I'd like to reflect.'

'Fair enough. We can get to the pub again if you like - we'll make it before they stop serving lunch.'

Walking steadily on, it took less than last time, achieved without conversation, a simple enjoyment of togetherness in harmony. How different from the first meeting, when stress and trauma headed the emotional list; this time she was all contentment and pleasure in country and company. At the last gate before the road and the short stretch to the pub the kiss was natural and lasting. 'I love you,' she breathed in his ear as he held her tight. 'Thank you, dearest Donald. You've made me such a happy, happy girl.'

The distant faint echoes of Mary's voice returned, but only to set a seal. *'Take great care of her'* - did he imagine those words?

∽

His mobile rang at half past eight, just as they were about to sit down to a tinned sausage and bean casserole, a simple if scratch meal from the store cupboard, but then they'd had a decent lunch at the pub before giving in to the necessity of a local shop to lay in some essential supplies.

Sarah: 'On the Aspatria train, dad. There in a quarter of an hour.'

Paula's logical response query was 'have we cooked enough supper' as Donald picked up his coat.

'She may have eaten, but yes, keep it warm. It'll be an hour, maybe hour and a bit at most.' He blew her a kiss from the door, it shut behind him and she was, for the very first time, alone in his cottage as the sound of the Discovery's diesel faded away and left a weird feeling of uncertainty. She put the casserole back into the oven, turned the heat down to lowest. The comforting silence dropped in around her, apart from the old wall clock ticking the seconds away, always wound on arrival.

Mary's armchair took her attention. The cushions left un-plumped, a constant reminder of the departed former lover of the man who'd taken her, Paula, to his heart in lieu of the girl who'd inspired him, lived, loved and won his undying affections, given him a beloved daughter. Who was he, this Donald? A man with restrained ambition, strong morals, easy going yet firm; oddly, not one to seek out the herd and live it up, unlike some she'd come to know in the film world. Respected, even looked up to, one who might well rise to the top of his profession and *she* was his - girlfriend? Partner? Lover, certainly, now. Not a lustful loving, as some might wish, but for her, inexperienced and unaware, notwithstanding her inept fibs, so wonderfully *nice*. Dare she, despite his very early dictat, sit in Mary's chair? She'd taken over almost every aspect of Mary's domestic role. The professional one she couldn't possibly address, other than the minor facet of continuity and props. Courage, girl, take that step.

An extraordinary emotion, one felt as though she'd taken on a new persona, had wriggled beneath the other woman's skin. She'd not be able to explain it, this warmth, an acceptance of where and when, a

204

different view through the window, Mary's vision. The clock ticked away, the remnants of deep gold evening light slanted onto the table; touched her skirt clad legs as she sat in Mary's chair and dozed, dreamt, slipped back in time:

. . . Snippets of the past appeared, unedited clips of cottage life, taming the garden, planting shrubs. The clearance of wild corners, the renewal of decaying bits of the cottage's roof. The re-arrangement of the furniture after they'd bought a new carpet, bringing the Discovery here that first time, time spent putting her books in order on the shelves.

Mary . . . her scent, she's wearing her short tweed skirt . . . she's woken suddenly as the vehicle's lights swing across the window.

With an odd feeling of calm, she stands up, more aware of the past and is proud for the vastness of the future. She won't say, not now, not ever. A death for a life; whatever is demanded, whatever will provide happiness for the man she loves.

As though she's Mary, inside the persona of another girl, she adjusts her skirt, smoothes down the weave, turns to plump up the chair's cushions from where she'd been sitting and goes to greet her step-daughter, her lover and her future in another guise . . .

There's chatter, light-hearted chatter betwixt father and daughter as they enter the cottage. Paula/Mary stands waiting for them . . .

'Paula!' Sarah swooped across the room, held out her arms, took her father's new girl friend in a crushing embrace. 'Oh, how lovely to see you here! Do you like the place - yes, of course you do, dad has told me you said not to sell.' She stepped back a pace, eyed the girl up and down. 'If it wasn't for your beautiful Italian eyes I'd say you're remarkably like some early photos of mum. Why dad fell for you! I like your skirt. Mum had one very much like it. Is the dress safe? Karl can't wait to see the film.'

Donald, initially bemused by his daughter's rush of enthusiasm thus allowing her to prattle on, now felt decidedly hungry, and intervened. 'Supper, Paula? Have you . . . ?'

'Ooops, sorry, no, I dozed,' and opened the oven door. 'Seems okay. How's your appetite, Sarah? Not very cordon bleu I'm afraid. We need to go shopping first thing.' She took the tea towel, held the dish and eased it out and onto the table. Dozed? Dreamt? Reality or . . . the realisation of who she was? *She won't say, not now, not ever. A death for a life . . .*

'I had a snack on the train, but I'll be sociable. I'll set the table.' Sarah chucked her shorty coat at her father and went to the cutlery drawer, back into familiar routine and happy with it.

Conversation over supper followed the progress of the filming in Italy, how they found Michaela, how well the Milanese sequence went and what would happen next. 'Sounds fun, dad,' Sarah rounded it off, 'but you don't normally talk shop at Beckside. You won't sell, will you? I came over specifically to persuade you not to.' She watched her father's eyebrows rise. 'I know I agreed to start with, but now Paula's on the scene and unlikely to disappear from my reading of body language, it's different. Mum will be happy too, won't she?'

He had to nod, add a smile and glance at Paula before giving Sarah her answer. 'We think so, don't we, Paula?'

She drew breath, unsure of what they would think but she had no choice, there was a new inner compulsion. 'I understand a little more of what Mary was like every day, as though I'm absorbing some of her soul and being here . . .' her eyes prickled, she couldn't help it. 'Sorry,' she said and wiped her eyes with the back of her hand.

'Oh, Paula, I didn't mean to make you cry!' With the certainty of her on-going love for the new Mary, the new woman in her mother's place, Sarah got up and put her arms around the girl, hugged her from behind the chair. 'Sorry!'

Donald felt for her, for them both. 'Girls, this is too maudlin, too introspective. I'm not demeaning the situation but don't you think it's time to call it a day?' He got up, began to clear the plates away as something to break the tight mood. 'If I wash?'

Sarah relinquished her hold, straightened up to allow Paula to stand. 'Forgive me?' she asked.

'Nothing to forgive. I'll dry,' she said and found the tea cloth. 'Where do you want to sleep tonight, Sarah? The shepherd's hut will be a trifle damp, won't it?' which query left Sarah in no doubt as to where she'd be.

'I'll use the little room. I won't disturb you. Can we have a conflab in the morning?' and she offered a smile, 'as I'm sure you two have plans?'

Donald looked at Paula, saw an incipient grin. 'Fine. So we'll let you retire!' a nice hint she could leave them on their own.

'Right-oh. Goodnight;' she picked up her small bag dropped when she came in and shut the small room door behind her.

Five minutes later, with everything washed, dried and put away, Donald followed Paula up the stairs. In the darkness of the oncoming night and with no need for lights, the girl's very presence and shape was powerful, an intoxication, skirt short and bare legs in front and above.

In the dark he undressed her with the same care as he had a time or two before, together they lay, together the years rolled away; for him she was his Mary, for her she felt like his Mary. A chosen naturality like no other and a spiritual boon; sleep came too easily and the dawn would bring in the brilliance of a new day, a new certainty.

Mary's Legacy   28

It was to be a day for assessing the estate, for bringing the future into a precise focus as defined by the past.

Donald left the two girls by themselves after an early breakfast to take the winding path up towards the pasture, through the spinney Mary and he had planted those years ago, along the path he'd trod alone barely a week after the funeral to unsuspectingly meet his former wife's legacy, the girl who'd innocently assumed the role, who had applied a natural mastery to the quirks and fancies he'd unconsciously assumed over the years of togetherness with she whose spirit would, he believed, provide a continuous watch over the new affiliation. There would be those who'd ridicule his belief, those who would be uncaring over an indissoluble link between two lives, two human beings with individual abilities who had, maybe extraordinarily, managed to combine unique personalities into one. That belief he'd honour in the continuality of this attachment with Paula. That she'd taken on the *persona* of Mary was truly amazing, the way her little day-to-day actions had adapted and moulded into everyday habits so familiar from years of a previous togetherness. If he had ever philosophised over the eventuality he'd lose Mary's physical being, become deprived of his 'other half' and yet, within days, find another equivalent spiritual partner, he'd probably have heaped scorn upon the concept. Yet she'd happened, his Paula; she had been drawn towards him without encouragement; persistent and practical in her unconscious acceptance of her unperceived destiny. Without regard for society's *mores* they had come together, worked together, dealt with the oddities of people around them and instinctively fitted into that most idealistic attainment of human love, a 'couple', a duo, the Italian's *coppia*. And, happily, Sarah had seen and accepted this attainment without demur, in fact to positively encourage him as he recalled with an effusion of pleasure the night spent with Paula in Sarah's eyrie above the Largouman *atelier*. The dress, Karl's munificent gift, was testimony to that added strength of her determination that she too would not let her mother's spirit wither into insignificance.

As he reached the gate, the physical representation of the turning point, he felt a peace, the mantle of spirituality unwittingly sought but accepted with humble gratitude. Across the pasture the rise of the hills gave a tranquil dimension to the onset of a warmer yet wintry day, wrapping the silence into a magical infinitely wonderful horizon. Mary's spirit would protect them both, guard them and bind them in a loving partnership - he knew she was at one with the girl. He leant on the gate, as he'd done with Paula a short while after their first meeting, unconcerned that she was a half mile down the track, in all probability deeply engaged in a concerning conversation with dearest Sarah.

Down there, in the cottage he'd shared with his first soulmate, were his two girls, the genetically connected daughter and a spiritually connected woman who'd now become his true and fully accepted mate. What had he done, to manage such a phenomenal rearrangement of affairs? That first evening back here after the funeral, in the countryside where he and his life's love had lived, he'd tried to face up to the potential permanent gap in that life and the consequences of being single, agonized that he'd never have the inspiration to manage a successful film production again, that he'd end up as a recluse either here or in London. Then Paula had happened. How had he managed to keep the rapport between them correct? Had it been correct? He hadn't sought to take advantage of her, had he? She hadn't traded on his weakness, had she? Sought to be an odd version of a gold-digger? Was there any sign of a hidden agenda in her mannerisms? He turned round, stared back down the track. If there was any negativity over this situation, surely he would have felt it, Mary's guiding spirit would have alerted him to any probability?

Pure speculation and unwarranted. Yesterday, something had changed. Today, it was a new day, another day. The sun's first rays arrowed across the valley, the brilliance of it dazzling, spearing into the remnants of the mist as though to illustrate the point. Doubts, hesitations, restraints, elements of the mist in his mind, burnt away by the rise of the warmth of the astonishing love from her gift. Her gift, her legacy, the embodiment of all she'd always been. They must honour her, somehow, in a manner befitting. She - dearest Paula - would provide all the support he'd need. Sarah must approve too. What, how, the when's and where's, couldn't be planned. It would just happen, like Michaela happened.

Brilliant girls, all of them. Across the pasture, up on the footpath, a line of early walkers. He couldn't help the wry grin. No disasters today please. He turned, walked steadily down the path, past the shepherd's hut, down to the cottage, down to rejoin his girls.

Paula was sitting in . . . *the abrupt rejigging of thoughts* . . . *the chair he'd always called* . . . *then*; now it would be hers. Paula's.

Sarah was smiling; on the table between them lay the old photo album. He dropped into the vacant seat, caught Paula's coy glance, the query unasked, unrequired. The brief closing of his eyes, the tiny nod, all she needed, his acceptance of her symbolical action.

'What's this then? Reliving the past?' There would be many a quirky moment documented within, literal snapshots of life at Beckside in all its ups and downs. When had this volume last been dragged out of the lower shelf of the bookcase? Ages, absolutely ages. The last photo when Sarah had first gone to University, a posed one in her new costume in front of the door. Then digital had taken over and they'd never bothered to print anything. There'd be the ones taken to record the work done, from raggedy grass to proper lawn, the neat vegetable beds carved out from unyielding soil, the erection of the fence lines, the first saplings. History.

'Don't mind, do you, dad?'

A wry smile: 'Of course not, provided you're not unhappy about Paula seeing you as a babe in arms.' He couldn't, not today, bring himself to gaze at the precious pictures of Mary. Strong sequences of their times here together would only disturb the equilibrium so recently achieved. She'd be uneasy, he knew she would. After the struggle her spirit would have had, working out how Paula fitted into her space and managing to give them both so much love and support, for him to backtrack, to relive those times, would be a retrograde act. The past was the sacred past. Perhaps, after a year . . .

'What shall we have for lunch?' A change in direction, a mundane query, anything to bring matters back to the commonplace.

'I can make some sandwiches; we could go and sit outdoors if it's warm enough. And one of those bottles of cider we bought yesterday?' Paula's decision was a logical one and, for him, a help.

Sarah nodded. 'Maybe the last chance we'll get this year. Dad?'

'True. I'll lend a hand.'

How familiar a scene, easy familiarity and routine, putting such a picnic lunch together. It had been done before, and, his mind relaxed about the recall, might well happen again many times in the future. There were a fair few years ahead of them, here. Yes, here. He - and Sarah and his new lady would never wish to part with Beckside. A rush of pleasure in the thought became perhaps the most amazing delight since . . . since *that* day.

"Let it go, Donald. I'm a happy girl, and Paula, she's the new me." He heard her voice in his head, *Mary's voice*, heard her lovely little chuckle. Looked across the room at his Paula, saw his Mary, saw the realisation, the actuality, of the quoted phrase heard within the village church, one he'd now always remember - *God moves in a mysterious way* - and had to acknowledge there were more ways than the simple to bring love back into life. What was the phrase? A death for a life? Not a birthed new life but a resurrected one. Mary had provided him with the chance to rebuild this girl's world, to give her a new 'life' and that he would do.

'Donald?'

Paula. His name, pronounced in that charming querulous way she had, broke the reverie, managed to pull him back to reality.

'Sorry.' He shook his head to dispel the dream. 'Miles away.'

The lovely little laugh of hers, *of Mary's*, before: 'habit of yours, dearest. How many times do I call you back from dreamland? Come on, sandwiches, before it gets to teatime. Sarah will beat you to it.'

⤺

The peace and serenity of the day would stay with him, always. The light-hearted chatter, the smiles, the chuckles, the cast of the late season's light across the grass, the backdrop purple-green luminosity of their hills, the murmur of the beck and the light playful flick of breeze lifting skirt hems, the wisping of Italianate hair. His soul sang, sang with the knowledge he'd done all she'd asked, her loss diminished in the zest given to another. The hours passed, oncoming twilight crept in, and slowly the glow of the day was changing from pale gold to the richer deeper bronze. Ethereal - and a healing of the wound all but complete; Paula, a precious gift, Mary, a life lived to the full and given.

She stood up, echoed his thoughts. 'I'll always remember this day,' turned and walked slowly across the grass and back to the cottage.

Sarah reached a hand across the white cast-iron table. 'Dad, I'm so, so pleased for you. She's a lovely girl.' As he looked at her, the tears were there. 'Mum will always be mum, but she's given us the best legacy. Look after her, dad,' and she too, got up and followed his beloved Paula into the cottage. He was left alone, but not alone. She'd always be in his heart, in his mind, but never to supplant her gift. He shivered, time to go. Tomorrow, back to London, back to the project.

Mary's Legacy 29

Logistics came to the fore. They went through the routine of shutting the cottage down, told Fiona, the caretaker lady in the village what was happening; her husband would do the last grass cuts, the wood store replenishment from the Forestry would happen, all these essential little things. Fiona's sparse but meaningful words helped, 'ever so glad you's found another gal,' she'd said without any malice or concern. Then the Discovery nosed out of the drive, Sarah hopped out and closed the gate, the drive over to Ted's place was smooth and traffic free, the walk down to the local station silent.

On Carlisle station platform an hour later, he met Paula's look and grinned. No words were needed, but she patted the bench to comment, 'No Marie Claire.'

'Was this where you found it?' Sarah'd had her leg pulled over the photo, though Donald knew she'd suppressed her pride and reckoned it wouldn't be her last photo shoot, not if Karl had his way.

'Yes,' Paula replied, adding, without a hint of supercilious meaning, 'and I'd not object if we agreed your mum conspired to have someone leave it on purpose.' She grinned. 'You wait till you see the film.'

'I know, I'll be jealous. Just make jolly sure I get the invite, dad. I'll never forgive you if I don't get to come to the cast 'n crew showing, let alone the launch.'

'Lot of work before then. Back to the thick of it. Paula won't know if she's coming or going.'

'Huh! Don't you worry, Donald, dear. I'll surprise you.'

'You already have, my love.'

Sarah watched, listened and from the body language she could feel nothing but contentment; her father using 'love', Paula calling him 'dear'. A sturdy relationship was there and happily cemented in the best possible way, that much she knew, hearing Paula's little mew of delight last night. A faint blush, she couldn't help it. She could almost feel jealous, not ever having been physically loved, but her parent's moral strength was within her, so she'd stay content until . . . it'd happen, one day.

The train came. They sat quiet, aware of the significance. At Manchester Sarah hefted her small but extravagant Versace bag down, kissed them both, told Paula 'to look after her dad' and then she'd gone. Her flight was three or four hours away; but she'd be back in Paris before teatime.

The rest of the journey south saw them relax into the quiet satisfaction of a firmed-up triangle of togetherness. Paula's softly spoken admiration of Sarah, her expressed love for her, added to Donald's pleasure at the way their return to Beckside had gone. A few short months ago, he'd never have believed this would be a possibility. The original necessity to tread so carefully around any potential of a deeply satisfying relationship, though considered and acted throughout with every care, had now faded away. He could be himself, build on the restoration of a worthwhile human connection with a beautiful girl, to become all she desired, all she needed. "*A girl who needs you*" ...and the added bonus, had found a new close friend for Sarah.

Returning to the Southgate flat could have been an anticlimax, but it wasn't. It seemed so natural, an ordinary return from a weekend away. The routines, the unpacking of the shared bag, a sharing started from necessity and now a normality that would stay with them for always; a conference over choice of a supper menu, the selection of a bottle of wine, a pleasant time preparing the meal, eating, catching up with the news, looking at the few emails, everything happening as though they'd been together for years. *Yes, Mary would be saying, years.* Tomorrow - well, tomorrow would be another day at the office, or would it not be 'just another day' but a far more meaningful one? As they prepared for bed without any implications other than it was a place to sleep, to rest minds, to gather strength for the next day, the sense of togetherness nearly brought Donald to tears. Too sensitive a mind by far, he told himself, but maybe that's the reason why he could do the job he did, sensing the atmospheres, the emotions, the discernment of moods - and putting it, with Peter's camerawork and Jon's perceptive words, all onto a screen.

Paula, bless her, had those inner sensitivities too; she'd adapted to her new life without any histrionics, quietly accepted his love, his care and returned it threefold. Beckside they'd keep, this flat would be sufficient for now, neither would it become a shrine. The idle phrase quoted when a new monarch took the throne trickled through his head - *the king is dead, long live the king* - stupid really. His wife had died, long live his wife . . . but sleep denied further reflections.

∾

'Ready for this?' he turned and posed the question to her as they entered the office building. Pat was smiling at them, her welcome a genuine 'welcome back' smile.

'Yep,' and grinned. 'Hi Pat.' *Another day but a different day*, Donald had said earlier and she wasn't sure exactly what he'd meant. Was it different? They'd left the office late and only three days ago, so what had changed? Abruptly it came to her; she could feel her cheeks warming and pulled him onward and past Pat's desk before that girl saw her blushing.

In their office - *their office* - in the privacy of their office, she couldn't help herself.

'What brought this on?' the hypothetical query as they finally separated and he wondered if her lipstick was smudgy or kiss-proof.

Her blush was only just ebbing. 'You and me. We left as very close friends, we're back as lovers. That's what you meant? Rotter!' and he got another light kiss. 'How am I going to get through the day without permanently rosy cheeks?'

'Ah,' he said. 'I have an idea.'

'Oh?'

'How about going to see Booth and telling him about our change in status?'

Puzzled, her forehead creased in a small frown. 'Change in status?'

'Mmm. Paula,' and he held onto both hands, looked into her eyes and saw in the incomprehensible depths of honeyed brown the same gaze as he'd known over the past twenty plus years in another, knew her answer before he asked but nevertheless, asked. Not perhaps the

215

exactly right time or situation; he could have designed the place, the set, the lighting, the mood far far better - but this was a necessity. He couldn't have her kept at a disadvantage a moment longer.

'*Marry you!* Marry?'

'Mmmm.'

She thumped him. 'No ring, no down on bended knees, no moonlight, no violins, no champagne? Donald! And you're supposed to be . . .' but couldn't finish, not when he'd wrapped arms round and was giving her a crushing hug with kiss to match.

'So it's a 'yes'?' he asked, and knew it for a rhetorical query.

'*Yeeesssss, ooohhh yeerrssss,*' she breathed in his ear, knowing that the ethereal spirit of a lovely woman who'd given her this man to love was silently applauding . . .

The walk down the corridor, the knock on the door, the moment of moments; Booth looked up. 'Gooodaaay, wanderers returned then. Ready for the fray?'

Donald held her hand. 'Thought we'd let you into a secret. Paula and I . . .'

Booth waved a pudgy hand. 'Yeah, I know, you gonna get hitched. Could see it a million miles away. And,' he flicked the hand in the air, 'don't think it'll be a surprise. Jemma!' he raised his voice towards his p.a.'s office, 'here, girl!'

The smiley redhead put her head round the door then edged in. 'Morning Donald, hi Paula; good weekend?'

Booth's hand waved again in depreciating manner. 'Yeah, they've bin misbehaving. Gotta get spliced,' and his craggy face suddenly creased in a huge open grin. He lifted his bulk out of the chair and came round the desk. 'Go organise some fizz, Jemma. Let's start the day with a happy time. Go girl!'

Jemma's smile changed to a wicked grin. 'I'm frantically jealous! Wish I'd . . .' but sensibly disappeared before revealing her wish.

Booth shook Donald's hand. 'I'm dead pleased for you, man. We don't need to chat about the past neither. You know what you know. This gal,' and he gave her a clumsy cheek kiss, 'getting into your life is the best, for she sure is right for you.' He sounded embarrassed, coughed lightly and escaped back behind the desk. 'Conference room, half an hour. Okay? Now get on with it.'

Outside, in the corridor, the door behind them closed, Paula shook her head. 'What a man!'

'Solid as they come,' Donald added. 'Both in manner and bulk. Are you okay?'

'Mmmm, as you would say. Yes, I'm okay. Surprised, happy, maybe in a slight state of shock. You do know what you've done, don't you?' she asked as they walked back to the Art Director's office.

'I hope so.'

'Caused a flurry of excitement? Made history? Maybe even settled a bet or two? Made a few women my deadly enemies?' Now she was pulling his leg, poking fun at him, and all part of what she was, a mischievous lady.

'Sorry.' They'd reached the office, he opened the door for her, ushered her in.

'Don't be. I'm not. Just incredibly conscious I'm the luckiest girl alive.'

'Maybe you'll regret going for that hike.'

She shook her head as she settled down behind her desk. 'Nope. You might regret offering help.'

'Don't think so, not now. See where it got me.'

'Huh,' then she went solemn as the enormity of it all hit her. 'Engaged. Glory be, engaged. To be married, heaven help me. I'll have to tell my father, and my sisters. Oh dear.'

'Heaven will help you, Paula, or at least one of its residents will. And I'll tell your father - and sisters - if you like. Invite them here, that'll bring 'em in. When?'

'When what, tell them, or get married?'

'Tomorrow?'

'Ha ha,' and she swung round on her chair to face him. 'Don't joke. It's serious.'

'Paula, dearest girl, I'd marry you tomorrow if it was feasible, but it ain't. We've a job to do.'

'Then we'd best get on? What's next for Maria?'

'Detail of the interior scenes, a review of the location work, scheduling the in-filling. We've Michaela here in a few days, remember?'

217

'I hadn't forgotten. I'm quite looking forward to her coming too.' The jocular sparring was over. She'd said 'yes', she was engaged, a factual state of play existed, and the film had to be good, very good.

A knock on the door, Jemma. 'Come on, you two, Booth's waiting.'

'Oh lor, we'd forgotten. Okay, coming.'

They walked, hand in hand, over to the conference room. The last time she'd been in here it was as a nervous newbie, waiting to hear if the film was to be made in the UK, whether she'd have a job, whether she'd manage to re-jig her life. Now, well, life had changed. Jemma opened the doors ahead of them.

Most of the team were there, technicians, admin, Peter and Jon of course, Yvette and her cronies, only the big name stars absent. Booth behind the platform table, a hand up and the chatter ceased.

'Guys,' he said simply, 'I've called you lot together to lay the dust. Our arty guy Donald here has fallen for the gal who pirouetted across Milan's Gallerie floor in the sexiest frock I've seen for ages. Can't say I blame him. So, boys and gals, I'm pleased, nay, proud,' and Paula could have sworn she detected an oddly humbling trace of rare emotion in his voice, 'to announce he's gonna make an honest woman of her. Paula,' he beckoned her forward, 'and Donald too,' so the pair perforce had to walk through to the front, 'we'll all be coming to a wedding once Maria's had her launch. Our congrats and all that.' He reached for a hand from each, held them, before he joined them together. 'These two deserve each other. Now, a quick swig of Prosecco to toast the 'appy couple and then we'll carry on making a film, eh guys?' The applause bounced around, a sure indication of how the majority felt. If there were any sour aspects, they lay hidden. The clink of glasses as Booth proposed a toast echoed around, prefacing a rise in conversation level, a constant round of handshakes, of back slapping, cheek kissing and compliments flying. She coped well, knowing she was alongside the man with whom she'd share the rest of her life.

Then the assemblage was dissipating as people drifted away. Tuesday and it was still a working day. *Engaged . . .*

⤍

The routine settled down. By the end of the week she could see the location sequences in her sleep, run through over and over again, each new edit bringing the story more and more to life. The slots left for

Michaela's close-ups were clearer, more obvious, some of the indoor sequences were being filmed in the studio as the days went by and Marco was summoned. Annette was due back during the middle of next week, a day or two after Michaela was due in. Paula was designated as chaperon, given the logistical task of arranging the flight, the hotel, the studio transport and rose to the task with aplomb. Donald, unspokenly proud of her, decided to treat her to an evening out, maybe for an ulterior motive.

'Where would you like to go?' he asked, suggesting he wanted an opportunity to get her into a proper dress for once.

'A *proper* dress? You don't mean . . .?'

'No, not the Largouman. That one I bought you in Lecce?'

'But it's floral, not an evening dress.'

'Paula, my girl, we'll have a nice Italian meal somewhere, not too heavy, then I can drink my fill of a charming lady who could have been born in Italy and the waiters will fall over each other in the rush to serve you.'

'Okay,' she agreed, accepting his accolades with some light-headed relief she didn't have to be on her best behaviour or wear excessively high heels. The day had been another stressful one; a lighthearted evening in a comfortable and meaningful dress meant she'd be able to let nerves relax.

❦

He must have sought advice - he knew where to go, the taxi dropping them at the door, a smiling waiter there to welcome them in, to guide them to a discreet table, to offer them extravagant menus, offer olives, crusty bread with more olive oil, balsamic vinegar, a wine list with *Chianti* and *Pinot Grigio,* back to the warmth and welcome of her memories of Puglia. Ah, to be in Italy . . .

Settled at the back of the room, an ambiance worthy of the best *ristorante* in Milan, or Lecce, or even Vieste - though perhaps not. She was happy, warm inside, thrilled even. Donald was quietly smart, best shirt, hair well brushed, the worry lines she'd recognised likely to have been brought on by the stress of watching Mary decline and eventually succumb were far less evident. Had she helped? With the full awareness of her role, as companion, confidante, carer, and now, recipient of his

219

capacity for offering the nicest aspects of loving, why, yes, she'd helped.

Donald settled into his chair, watched her relax, absorbed her tranquil beauty, every aspect of her beloved Italianate features, the dark hair, the rounded cheekbones, the dark eyes; the depth of her eyes. And her soul, her spirit; the woman who had taken on the mantle of his former love in a manner he couldn't understand yet had to accept. Mary had dictated the way she would die and had promised him her power of life after the physicality of her persona had been taken away from him. The power of life after death? How many of their acquaintances would scoff at the concept? Dead was dead to them, but he'd disagree. The girl who was sitting across the table, across the white damask tablecloth with the exotic flowers in a crystal vase, the steady flame of a beeswax candle - she was not a mere woman but radiated the infinite power of a spiritual blessing. Mary may have vanished into another realm, but she'd left her thoughts and strength of mind and all that mattered in this world to Paula. A legacy beyond price.

While she studied her menu card so she couldn't see his actions, he carefully fished in his pocket, took out the little dark brown leather covered box, sprung the lid and - there, nestling in the velvet her ring. *Her* ring. Chosen, all those years ago, with bubbling cheeky happiness from a small jewelers in the back streets of Cardiff, an inspirational find on the first true time away together after she'd said 'yes' and he'd had the courage to suggest they escaped the television studio mêlée to have what some would have called a 'dirty weekend'. A total misnomer, for the two nights had been golden bliss and the seal on their future lives commitment. Welsh Clogau red gold with its unique solitary emerald in a diamond chipped circle, sublime and historic, a connection to her roots, once eased away from a cold lifeless finger into the warmth of his hand, to rest as a symbol of a departure yet of a perennial hope. Now, he could swear it was glowing, aware of its potential.

'I'd like '*La Lasagne Vegetariane*' then '*Il Peposo alla Ciantigiana*', if that's okay,' she said very correctly, placing the folder back on the table and adding, rhetorically, 'You'll choose a red wine?'

Having had a quick glance at the menu before the delve into his pocket he'd made up his mind to follow her choice, whatever it was. It'd all be superb, according to Pat, and he trusted her judgment. The waiter, discreetly observing, attentive, took their order, the menu folders went with him, the wine waiter appeared with the chosen bottle, uncorked the *Chianti* with due ceremony; the tasting, the pour, the quiet withdrawal - she lifted her glass, sparkled '*to us*'.

'*To us.*' Glasses clinked, replaced on the table, she adjusted her serviette and her eyes widened as she caught a glimpse of the box . . . 'Donald?'

'I wasn't sure whether I should do the art director's thing and design the appropriate set, Paula, then decided I needed to give you a more tangible form of an engagement promise before anyone else got ideas . . . here, hold out that finger.'

Did her mouth 'drop open'? He couldn't remember, only that when he slipped Mary's engagement ring onto her finger it was a perfect fit. He knew it would be. Into her eyes came Mary's look, except that it was his Paula's look. Her soul, her spirit, her strength, and the promise of an unshakeable permanence to their lives together.

Mary's Legacy 30

The inevitable 'oooh' and 'blimey' and 'oh aren't you a lucky girl' she had to take in her stride. How many times did she have to hold out her hand and have it pawed over - below the chumminess and chat mostly it was awe, amazement, even some angst, only to be expected from those - fortunately few - who'd either thought they'd get their claws into her Donald or might nurse a grudge over her rise to a position, now unassailable, in his life and the film world too.

Ronald caught her alone in the office corridor. 'Paula, my love, not had the chance . . . I'm extremely pleased for you. Well deserved too, for you've really come up trumps. I had my doubts when Donald first brought you here, but he couldn't have found a nicer girl . . .no,' as she started to protest, 'I mean what I say in all sincerity. However he found you, whatever prompted him to take you on, it couldn't have been a better idea. I know how you've risen to the challenges flung at you, but that walk . . . it made that scene, you know that. You wait, girl. Wait till we get 'Maria' screened.' He paused, changed tack. 'Talking of which, Michaela's due in later today, isn't she?'

Paula nodded, grateful of the return to the mundane, except Michaela's arrival wasn't mundane to her. 'I'm taking a studio car to Heathrow at four this afternoon. Then we're going to Taplow.'

Ronald nodded in turn. 'Good hotel, that. Where Billy Connelly did his thing with 'Quartet'. I wish I'd directed that. Still, 'Maria' won't be at all bad, especially with you girls. Annette, Paula, Michaela - and Rosina, of course. Brilliant, all of you. Right, must go - Marco's in Studio 2. Oh, yes, and your ring. You knew it was his Mary's, didn't you?' and he strode off.

She'd guessed. He hadn't said anything, not specifically, supposing, she thought, because he'd expect her to realise the significance. Deep down, an admixture of thoughts, one of emotional stirrings of sorrow, of profound sadness, then on top, a pride that she'd been chosen in an indefinable almost magical way to succeed someone in whose position she'd never ever have dreamt to be placed. She walked slowly back to her desk, sat down, looked at the emerald, at the circle of ancient gold, the Welsh mystery, fashioned with care and years of craft skill into an eternal circle. Round and round. *Wear it with pride; wear it with joy,* the words, the dictat, in her head, in her mind. What joyful moments had it witnessed? How many miles? A conception, a birth, a promise, an utterance of last words in finality, a death. She moved it round on her finger, a twist of fate brought her here, a twist of desire had kept her close, a twist of confidence she'd be true to herself and to him. He wouldn't look at any other woman in the way he looked at her, the way he'd loved her. Not ever; and another twist for a promise to be kept.

She watched the succession of aircraft landing, minutes only between them. Which one was Michaela's? The same taciturn driver with his slow smile; the comforting knowledge he knew where to go and his ability to manoeuvre the big Mercedes through traffic with consummate skill. He'd defend the parking proximity to the exit from the arrivals lounge with equivalent ease; they wouldn't have far to walk once she'd scooped the girl and her mother out of the crowd around the luggage carousel. Time to find them; it wouldn't be difficult; Michaela was a diamond, her mother would be like an armed guard.

Fifteen minutes later, she had them under her wing, slipped through the tangled crowd, the Mercedes with engine running, doors open - and away.

'Good flight?'

'*Buono, si.*' Italian - oh how she wished she'd learnt more when the chance was there. Michaela was at least smiling, and her near-black hair shone. Her mother looked a little frazzled, understandably if she wasn't used to airports and flying. Never mind, staying at the Taplow hotel would calm her, no doubt over that.

'You have found someone to look after the *caffe?*'

'*Si,*' Michaela grinned. 'Yers, *yes,*' and her grin deepened.

Paula could well understand; the girl would be trying hard to perfect her English. 'Then I hope it will be *molto bene* when you return.' She wouldn't ask about a return date; she'd purposely left the ticket open.

They'd headed away from the airport, down the busy section of the M25, onto the M4 towards Maidenhead, onto the A4, through the town, across the Thames, left at the traffic lights, up through the country towards Cliveden.

Paula, sitting alongside the chauffeur, heard Michaela's mother's quick-fire burst of Italian; apart from the initial smile and the halting 'hello', she'd not said much before.

'She has said how green this country is, how many trees there are, and thanks you for meeting us with this lovely car. Are we going far?' Michaela's English was getting better.

'No, not far. You are staying at a charming hotel where another film was once made. Donald and I will join you for dinner tonight, if that is alright?'

'It will be lovely. Grazie!'

Paula got them installed, made sure they were happy and left them to enjoy the peace and quiet - and coolness - of the hotel's English gardens. She'd have liked to stay herself, but duty called. Rob, her studio chauffeur, took her back, opened the car door for her by the office main entrance, gave his slow smile and she heard his *sotto voce* observation before he took the car away - "*good to hear your news, miss, we're ever so pleased for you*" - so nice a man.

She returned to the office in a bright mood; there was the evening to look forward to. Donald looked up from his desk, asked the inevitable question.

'They're fine,' her cheerful reply, 'Michaela's English seems to have improved from what I can remember, her mum's a little out of her depth, I think, but she'll survive. How's the sketch?'

He'd been working on the last few studio sets, scheduled for shooting early next week, mostly the scenes indoors, country house drawing rooms and staircases, nothing dramatic as he'd explained, and chuckled over the 'dramatic' phrase. 'All done.' He stretched, flexed his shoulders, lifted out of the chair. 'Perhaps by this time next week it'll all be over. Voice dubbing, a few bits of static inserts here and there; by the end of the month we should be called to a first cut showing. After that, we wait for Stateside to offer their opinions. Ronald might have to fly over with the discs, just to make sure we don't lose viability - unless we e-mail them; we should hear back within a few days.'

'Then what?'

'We go back to the Lakes and pretend it didn't happen, so if it's abandoned we don't get upset.'

She paled at the thought. 'Has it happened?'

He nodded, and pulled a face. 'Yes, once. A rival bunch shot a very similar storyline to one produced by a unit who I was working for as consultant at the time and beat us to the distribution chain. So it got shelved. It'll still be there, in case. Sometimes an off-beat telly channel will buy up rejects 'cos they're cheap.'

She shook her head, slowly side to side. 'All that effort. All these people, the miles, the stress, the star's fees. I'd be choked, really choked.'

'Don't worry. I've good vibes over this one. The Milanese walk, you know . . . that'll clinch it.'

She looked around for something to chuck at him. Milanese walk indeed . . . 'You wait.'

'Sounds good - time we went home. Booth's gone early, I saw the car go. Roland's out with Marco. So . . .'

He was annoyingly good at these half finished sentences, leaving the cliff-hangers around. He turned back to the desk, shuffled papers back into the folder, shut down the computer screen, picked up his case in one hand and pulled her close with the other. 'You're very good, you know that. Best p.a. I've ever had.'

'The first and only.'

He grinned. 'So come and prove it. We're going home to change. Taplow dinners are legendary.'

&

Indeed, he wasn't wrong. She'd done her best, slipped into the Lecce dress again, assiduously brushed her hair, put on the dreaded high heels and, even though she knew he'd not find fault, being too polite and too in love with her, preened and twirled.

'Love you,' he said and saluted her in the best possible way.

'Love you too,' she replied and let her eyelashes droop in the best 'I'm a starlet' fashion.

He laughed. 'Paula, lass, you're not in Hollywood - yet. Let's go stun 'em.'

And stun them they did. He'd broken out his second best suit, completed the effect with a silk tie and highly polished shoes - and, she learning rapidly how not to be surprised, had a studio car at their disposal. 'After all, it is studio business,' he explained.

Taplow welcomed them. Table settings to die for, rooms exuding comfort and elegance. Michaela and her mother were in the lounge, rising to meet them and Paula drew a big breath. Competition? She was beautiful, wonderfully beautiful as only an Italian girl can be when she puts her mind to the task. Her mother didn't disappoint either. Paula could see Donald was impressed - more than impressed and she surreptiously twirled her engagement ring.

After the greetings, the cheek-on-cheek kisses, the absorption of who was the star of the evening - Michaela - they sat round the low table, politely passed the nibbles round, sipped at the aperitif drinks, selected dishes from the stylish menus and chatted about the way the film was going; what else?

It was an evening reminiscent of the event at Claridges - with one notable difference. Paula had learnt her lesson, kept a careful note of alcohol intake and Donald, she noted, did the same. A truly English style dinner; Michaela took it all in her stride, did a sterling job of interpreter for her mother - who managed very well, considering - and eventually the occasion drew to a close. Nearly midnight, and after the flight up from Italy?

'We should have been a little more thoughtful,' Paula whispered at him as they left the pair waving 'goodnight' at them. 'I'd have been totally bushed had I flown up from Italy this morning. Glad we aren't expecting her to be on set first thing in the morning!'

'Agreed. She's very good though. Precisely what we need. Get her back into that stunning dress tomorrow and Marco will behave exactly as the script suggests.'

So nice to be chauffeured home; as the car took them back through the north London streets, she lent her head on his shoulder, felt his hand move to rest on her knee. Not drunk, but well plied, she felt pliant, willing, happy, 'love me?' she murmured at him, her pulse rate beginning to rise.

The answer came in the way his hand moved, oh glory be . . . home, home quick, please, and . . . her breathing quickened; oh how had she managed all these years without . . .

At home, after a wonderful evening, marvellous. Better and better, uncontainable joy, these feelings magic, sheer magic. There'd be lots of other ways of expressing the things that were happening to her, ways that wouldn't come amiss in other scenes . . . and even in her glow she couldn't stifle a giggle.

'Paula?' He propped himself on an elbow and gazed at the length and fluidity of her, the lithe woman who'd given him back almost everything he'd lost. 'What's funny?'

She stared at the ceiling, raised one elegantly naked limb after another as if in a gym before subsiding back, to bring both arms up with hands clasped and stretched. Her breasts rose. 'If all else fails, I suppose I could do porn,' she said, 'but I don't think you'd approve.'

'Good Lord woman! Certainly not, it's the last resort of the dumb blonde - though that's being uncomplimentary about blondes. Some of 'em are brilliant actors. Actresses.' He rolled over and looked sideways at her. 'I'll take you out to dinner more often, if it has this effect on you. You're sublime, you know that?'

She felt a blush coming on. 'Compliments, compliments. You're not bad yourself either. Sure you weren't thinking about Michaela?'

'Huh. No.' and then as the way some thoughts had a funny habit of coming to the surface, let a moment or two pass in silence before he voiced what those thoughts were. 'Something else, dearest, and please don't scoff, but . . . it's exactly like the first time Mary and I spent together. Does it worry you?'

She thought. This very intense and continuous sensation of taking on the *persona* of the woman who'd been his life for so long had an orgasmic feel beyond description, beyond the ability of adjectival choice. How best to say?

'Maybe . . .' No, how could she be? But he'd loved her and the remaining warm glow encouraged her. '. . . maybe, and don't be cross, I've found something, taken something of her - of her spirit - from here, from Beckside, from the bench on Carlisle station, as if,' and this was weird, 'we're been brought together.' The now vague recall of the

227

episode of first sitting in the armchair at Beckside when she'd felt she'd become, in imagination maybe, Mary, gained clarity.

Silence. She'd stunned him? Now what? She froze, daren't move or even twitch a muscle.

He thought. How logical, or illogical, was this, dependent on your views of life eternal, the life ever after, beyond the grave and all that? Mary's being, or more her spirit, could be dwelling within the beauty, the soul and body, of the girl lying supremely naked alongside him. Frightening? A truly scientific mind, brought up in the world of the laws of physics, mathematics, biology even, would not even begin to accept the slightest aspect of this theory. Was it only theory?

Everything she'd done, since that appearance on the path above Beckside, had something of Mary about it. The way she moved, her mannerisms, her interest in people, even the laugh. Was that why he'd been so attracted to her? Or, because Mary had seen the potential, there had been spiritual encouragement to come back to the cottage, to later phone him that fateful morning and get to come to this flat, to absorb more of her soul? Did it matter? Nothing would change. He loved her, not a modicum of doubt about it, and from every perspective, every single perspective. She was wearing the ring chosen to go on the finger of the woman he'd always loved, never to stray, never to consider any other. Mary, now Paula. In his mind, the last thoughts, the dimming echo of the last words - *find a girl who needs you.* She'd rest in eternal peace now. His life, her life, they'd go forward together.

Simply, 'Paula, we'll always love Mary's memory, but now, let her rest. She's happy, I'm positive she is. And I love you.'

She rolled over, kissed him, and then reached out to switch the bedhead light off. *"Tomorrow was another day",* and in that clichéd thought, found peace and within moments, sleep.

Mary's Legacy   31

She took a lot of pleasure in helping Michaela prepare for the day. Her mother fussed, but allowed Paula space. When Michaela walked into the studio set where she'd be filmed as if in the *caffe* and then at the hotel, both sets carefully reconstructed from innumerable photos, the instant exclamation 'oh, I am back at home!' and the little laugh immediately gained her instant popularity with the crew.

Roland took over; Donald had done his bit with the set design, Peter was behind the camera, Paula stood back and watched it all happen. Take after take after take, the girl took it in her stride even when Marco began to lose his cool. The hours flew by. Finally - 'it's a wrap', and Paula felt the tension ebb. Donald was at her side.

'She's a natural.'

Paula had to agree. Something about the girl had changed since that moment when she'd bobbed up from behind the fridge in her mother's café. 'I've got nice feelings about her too,' knowing her next comment would bring them straight back to last night's deeply thoughtful discussions. 'It's Mary. She helped us, whatever the scoffers would say. So there's something of her in this, I know it,' and after all, Donald had been affected in that oddly disturbing way at the time.

Their eyes linked. He nodded. Nothing needed to be said, they both worked on the same wavelength now, finely tuned and locked into place. Paula moved forward to rescue Michaela from Marco's disappointingly inane comments.

'You've survived,' she said to her, leading her away as Donald stepped in to halt Marco's diatribe. Later on, Paula heard how roundly he'd been told off by Booth and given an ultimatum - behave or else. But now, all she wanted to do was offer support, congratulations and comfort to the girl and return her to her mother who, wisely, had decided to watch the takes from the studio's master control room.

Inside that impressive space, full of screens and control desks, she discovered, not only Michaela's mother but surprisingly, Booth. From what she understood, he didn't normally get involved with the actual production side of things, seemingly content to wait until the first edits had been done and then watch in the comfort of his own little office cinema. He turned round as she and Michaela slipped into the producer's sound-proofed inner office, leaving Michaela's mother with her fifth cup of espresso.

'Well, little girl? What's it feel like to be a Sophia Loren?'

Would Michaela recognise the name? Yes, she did. 'I would never be as good as she was.'

'Ah, but you have given us exactly what we needed, gal, which matters. Miss Loren would have done exactly that. Exactly that. Paula - my thanks.' He brooded, his head sunk into the rolls of fat around his neck. Paula knew better than interrupt his thought train. 'Say,' he said, as he raised his eyes and stared at the young Italian girl who had become the film's mascot, the 'Maria' of the title. 'You wanna become famous, or go back to your ma's café?'

Michaela froze. Paula watched her, afraid she'd cry, or say something silly. She had to stop this, now. 'Can I suggest we give her time? Donald and I will talk to her and her mum. Please?'

Booth didn't move a muscle; his eyes were locked onto Michaela. Then he let out a held breath. 'Okay. Okay. But you did good, gal, damn good,' lifted out of the chair and with no further comment, shambled out of the production suite.

Paula took a deep breath of her own. Was this to be another aspect of the legacy? Or was she fixated on the ever-present concept? Enough; 'come on, let's see what's next.'

⌇

In the end, Michaela and mum were returned to Taplow to have the remainder of the evening on their own, at Michaela's request. Paula understood, Donald concurred. 'We'll pick you up in the morning, about ten-ish, just Paula and I, we'll show you some of the sights? That okay?' So that's how it was left. He and Paula went back to the flat.

She didn't want any more philosophising, last night had been so intense it hurt to even think back. 'Bed,' she said, 'and sleep; and I mean, sleep.'

He chuckled at her. 'Two minds but with a common thought. Good day though. Not far off completion.'

'Pleased?'

'Yep. She was good.'

She nodded. 'Agreed.'

'Not as good as you.'

'Ah, but all I did was walk. She had to express emotion in her face. Which she did, and very well.'

'Your walk expressed emotion too.'

'Don't see how.'

'Love. Love for the dress, for the place . . .'

She stopped him. 'Love for you.'

And that was enough. He scooped her up and carried her through to the bedroom . . . and within a very short while the lights were out, their closeness the catalyst for sleep.

✎

The present from the gods, Donald's comment as the autumnal day turned out not to be cold but with a bright sun, the bronzed leaves of Cliveden's trees reflecting gold as they were driven north. A day just pottering through the Chilterns, a visit to Whipsnade, a walk across the Downs with the almost ethereal views northwards, lunch in the little café there, back past Windsor and its Castle, then another hotel dinner.

They hadn't discussed the film once during the day, but tomorrow, Booth would ask.

'When do you want to return home?' Paula asked, albeit reluctantly for she enjoyed Michaela's company and even her mother's English was beginning to make sense. The answer would be twofold.

'I have decided I wish to return home and to the *caffe*, to support my mother. For the time being. That is the most important, to support my mother. Then we will see.'

'You're sure?' Donald wasn't surprised, but in a way, disappointed.

'I am sure. If it is possible, we would wish to return home within the next day or two. England is very pretty, very green, but not as warm and where is the sea?'

That produced a chuckle from both he and Paula. How right they were - he'd a hankering to return to Puglia himself. 'Right-oh. Paula will organise the flight home; we'll be sorry to lose you, but if we may, we will come and visit you - as soon as the film is properly launched.'

'Oh yes!' Michaela beamed at them. 'That will be *splendido!'* and they all laughed.

✍

They stood hand in hand and watched the plane take off, maybe with unspoken regrets that they weren't on board. Booth had been very disappointed, that much was obvious, but he did let on later he'd expected the answer Michaela had given.

The final days of filming dragged on; some of Annette's - she'd been back for a full two days - shorter sequences taking far more time than seemed relevant, but as Paula expressed her thoughts out loud Donald dismissed her comment. 'It's always the way, dear. Has to be right, we can't shortchange it,' and she sensed the deep professionalism that was so much part of him, his attitude and another reason how - not why - she'd fallen for him.

Eventually all the footage - another antique term retained for nostalgia rather than practicality, as digital filming was more megabytes than inches of celluloid - had been 'recorded' and familiar faces disappeared onto other projects or back to luxurious homes abroad. After a few days, they saw the first complete edit through, the file was sent electronically over to the States, thus saving Ronald a trip. The 'big boys' (including that creep Simon, Paula thought) as the bosses at Hollywood were referred to, having seen the transmitted version okayed it, to the great relief of everyone. Now all that remained was the tidying up before discussions started with the distribution company. All done and dusted.

Roland said his goodbyes, kissed her soundly, told her he'd look forward to the cast 'n crew showing in a month's time and went off to his home in France. Jon would remain at Pinewood to work on a television show; Peter had an antipodean project, a unique nature film somewhere in 'the back of beyond' as he said. Yvette just disappeared,

232

probably, as Donald suggested, in a fit of pique. Annette had given them both big juicy hugs and kisses before she'd flown home; Marco, like Yvette, didn't say 'goodbye'.

She gathered up the files from her desk drawers and laid them into the storage boxes destined for the archives. The room echoed, haunted with anticlimactic snippets of the months gone into history. 'It's sad,' she said, pushing her chair back to the desk on the last afternoon. 'All that buzz and so on and it's all faded away. Nothing left.'

'We've made a film,' Donald asserted in a matter-of-factual voice, 'and a good one. Be proud of what we've done, together.'

Together, yes, that was the bit she'd hang on to. Together, they'd worked, played, filmed, decorated sets, done endless talking, and had endless debates over words, actions - costumes too. Her dress, her *couture* Largouman dress was now safe in the Southgate flat. Nothing else left.

'Coming? We'll say cheerio to Booth.'

The walk down the corridor; would this be the last time? Nothing ever changed in the big man's office; he was Pinewood - his outfit, his facility. Jemma still smiled, she was an integral part of the place. Projects would come and go; he'd hire and fire, watch the byplay and see each film without emotion, what he got paid for.

'Been good,' he said, extending the large paw across the desk. 'Shan't let you alone, gal, if there's another one for you. Donald, you look after her now. Another Mary.'

Another Mary. So true. Past the reception desk, Pat was another fixture. She'd been here for nigh on ten years. 'Keep your passes, guys,' she said, 'you'll be back.'

'Perhaps. Next year, maybe.' Donald shook hands with her, Paula got a kiss on the cheek. How long ago had it been? Four months, five? The doors swung to behind them. The grey Mercedes waited, Rob her favourite chauffeur.

'Couldn't let you two walk home,' he said, with a wide grin. 'Booth's parting gift.'

֍

The Mercedes purred away. Go up the stairs, into the flat, shut the door; chuck the brief case onto the desk . . . 'That's that,' and he took her in his arms. 'Thank you, darling Paula, thank you for everything.' He kissed her. 'For being so forward, so scheming, so, oh, - understanding. For putting up with me and bringing me out of despondency.' They locked eyes, as they did, a transmission of thought, soul to soul.

'So now what?' she asked, bringing practicality to the fore. 'A month to the cast and crew showing?'

He released her. 'I could say, you choose. Stay here, go back to the Lakes, go to Paris, even back to Puglia. A month's a long time.'

'Nearly Christmas.'

'True. So?'

'Beckside,' she said with a sudden certainty. 'I want us to walk, to garden, to have lunches in the pub, to take the Discovery on discovery trips, to get Sarah home and enjoy her company. To make new friends, climb new mountains. Please, Donald? I want us to go home.'

. . . .*Mary's words, exactly Mary's words, her legacy*. . .

Postscript:

The cast and crew film screening of '*Maria's Legacy*', one bright late winter Sunday in the Odeon in Leicester Square, was a huge success. Everyone loved it; the proper opening night would follow. Donald managed to get Paula's two sisters and her father tickets - sent them by courier so they'd not dismiss them, and crossed his fingers. He needed to talk to her father, there was an event of his own to plan.

When it came to the First Night in the early spring of the following year, the traditional red carpet affair, Paula proudly wore her Largouman golden dress as carefully fitted by Sarah, did her beautiful walk as expected, and would have nearly outshone Annette if she'd not shown more leg than normal. 'Who's that lovely girl?' was a query heard more than once. 'She looks pregnant to me,' said one paparazzi guy to another. 'So what, she still looks fab. Bet we'll see more of 'er.'

Michaela came too, but on her own. She'd become far more assertive, more practical, more sure of herself, but would not desert her family and the Vieste *caffe*. Not yet. The part of the legacy she'd inherit in a year or two would stand her in good stead, for if Mary hadn't given Donald the incentive to take Paula under his wing, the film may not have gone to Puglia, and she'd still be clearing fridges. But he had, the film was made, and she'd be seen. Questions would be asked, enquiries made, eventually she'd be persuaded, another Sophia would become the nation's darling.

Within a couple of weeks following the film's commercially successful launch, in the quiet and unassuming church not far from Beckside, and without any of the razzamatazz so beloved of the film world, Donald and Paula were married; the guests just a few friends invited from his world, with Booth, of course; one or two from hers, including a proud father, a younger sister - and even older sister Celina seemed pleased.

Towards the end of that year's summer, Sarah, by now a fashion name in her own right even if she was still under Karl's patronage, would become a designated aunt, for being a much older step-sister to a baby girl wasn't an easy thing to comprehend.

Donald and Paula's daughter was christened in the same little village church near to Beckside . . . *Pauline Mary . . .,* and through the sanctity of the church, an echo, an echo came quietly of a beloved soul's desire.

'Find a girl who needs you . . .'

and she'd made him doubly proud, for this was Mary's true legacy; her bright spirit would live on across a new generation. His faith had kept that aspect going, a definitive belief in the unbelievable.

Tree Garth. May 2016.

Author's Note:

The world of film-making has a unique atmosphere; ethereal one moment, earthy the next, ever changing, ever unreal. A tremendous amount of effort can be expended and there's only a recording (in one medium or another) to show for the hard work and money spent. Nevertheless, it can be both an emotionally charged and rewarding experience to - hopefully - become the desired echo in the subsequent viewer's mind.

In 'Mary's Legacy' I have attempted to explore these depths, to also portray in a readable - and enjoyable manner - how a person can cope with, and survive, the demise of a beloved person if given the right support and opportunity. To any reader who has experienced such loss, I sincerely hope it will be of some comfort.

Spiritus intus alit